THE

PILGRIM

A Novel

HUGH
NISSENSON

sourcebooks landmark

Published by Sourcebooks Landmark, an imprint of Sourcebooks, Inc.
P.O. Box 4410, Naperville, Illinois 60567-4410
(630) 961-3900
Fax: (630) 961-2168
www.sourcebooks.com

Library of Congress Cataloging-in-Publication Data
Nissenson, Hugh.
    The pilgrim : a novel / Hugh Nissenson.
        p. cm.
1. Pilgrims (New Plymouth colony)—Fiction. 2. Puritans—Fiction. 3. Self-
actualization (Psychology)—Fiction. I. Title.
    PS3564.I8P55 2011
    813'.54—dc22

                          2011017815

        Printed and bound in the United States of America.
            SB 10 9 8 7 6 5 4 3

For Marilyn, who makes my life and work possible

PART I

I HEREBY PUBLICLY CONFESS MY sins and declare my regeneration, and I pray that, with the grace of Christ, the Saints of Plymouth Colony's godly congregation will elect me a member in their fellowship of the Gospel. Even though there is no precedent in Scripture, Master Brewster of the Plymouth Colony Church hath graciously given me leave to express myself in writing, so that my story may be read to admonish and enlighten godly generations to come.

I shall write in a plain style and tell the truth as near as I am able. I will confess to being an accessory to the hanging of my beloved friend Zachariah Rigdale at Wessagusset, and I will include an account of my sinful life before and after it.

Last night in a dream, I put off the noose from Rigdale's neck as he was about to be hanged and said, "You are saved!" He said, "Today, then, is my new birthday. Praise God, I have been born again."

I was born eight-and-twenty years ago, on the tenth day of March in the year of Christ 1595, in St. James parish, Winterbourne, Dorset. My beloved father, Piers Wentworth, was the rector of St. James's church in the High Street. Father baptized me Charles, after his father.

My mother, Edith Higgens Wentworth, bled to death the night after she gave me birth. Amongst the gifts my father gave my mother when he courted her was a pair of soft gloves of kidskin. He kept them in the carved, oaken chest with brass hinges and hasps in the parlor. I put them on when I was five or six years of age. I cried out, "Mama! Where are you?" Then I covered the gloves with kisses.

My father hired Mary Puckering, one of his poorest parishioners, as my wet nurse. Her sixth child had just been stillborn. Mary weaned me at two years of age. My father paid her two pounds a year, together with meat and drink, to raise me at his parsonage. It was more money and better victuals than Mary had ever enjoyed. She saved the cash and in time was able to buy a spinning wheel for her eldest daughter.

Mary was only allowed to return to her home on Friday afternoon at three of the clock. When she came back to me at sundown, her eyes were always red from weeping. By the time I was seven years of age, I knew in my heart that she grieved because she lived apart from her family, and I prayed to God to forgive me for being the cause of her grief.

Mary's husband, Mark, was a cowherd for two local farmers. He also collected dung which he sold for fuel. When he had the time, he worked as a weaver for a clothier named Wells in Howard Street. It took Mark five and a half years to save the money with which to buy his own loom. Thereafter, he received two shillings for a finished woolen cloth on which he worked for four days. He also earned a few pence by clearing the gutters of St. James. But he never went to church services because, said he, "I have not clothes fit to wear in company."

My father said to me, "Mark's hard life, filled with much labour, proves that he is a good member of our little commonality. Who knows? Perhaps he is one of God's invisible Saints and will in heaven be clothed in glory."

He gave Mark money to hire a cobbler to make him a new pair of shoes and a tailor to make him a new jerkin, a shirt, breeches, and a Monmouth cap. Mark thereafter went to church every Sabbath till the last month of his life.

Mary taught me to fear death and the Devil. One winter afternoon—I remember this very well—when I was six years of age she sat in her chair by the fire and bade me commit to memory the following to recite before I went to bed: "At night lie down prepared to meet thy death. Thy bed is thy grave." Thereafter, I was terrified to go to bed for months.

Mary kept a wary eye for the Evil One. She once took up a mess of my porridge before I had eaten of it, because she had espied therein a great black spider. She plucked it out, saying, "Beware of black spiders. They are the instruments of the Devil."

My father praised her for her vigilance. He said to me, "Think on vast regiments of cruel and bloody Spanish musketeers, with a ringleader over them, overrunning a pillaged neighborhood, and you will have some idea of the work of the Devil and his minions in this world."

My father's forebears were honest yeomen of the country. His father, Charles, freely held a farm of eighty acres of good pasture called the Hempstead in the manor and parish of Harrow Hill, a slender village three miles south of Winterbourne. He tilled skillfully and kept a shepherd, one servant in husbandry, and half a dozen day labourers during shearing time. He saved his money and, in ten years, bought twenty more acres. In time, he also kept a glover's shop in the market-place.

My uncle Roger, who was my father's elder brother, could neither read nor write. Yet, since he was sixteen, he had managed the one-hundred-acre farm and the glover's shop. My father kept the accounts. Roger, who was disposed to great thrift, paid him only two pounds a year. My father, who dearly loved his brother, never complained.

In the fall of 1588, uncle Roger met Eliza Collinson while she was milking her father's cows on his farm near Shaftesbury. They were married the next spring. Eliza was barren. She sold milk, butter, cheese, chickens, and eggs at the Tuesday and Thursday markets in Winterbourne. Within a few years, said my father, she changed from a slim young girl into a sad, fat, matronly woman.

My father had a natural propensity to be a scholar. At the age of six, he went to Winterbourne's Free Grammar School on Bridgeport Road. At fifteen, he was admitted to Trinity College, Cambridge, where he matriculated as a pensioner, his father paying for his lodging, &c. While at Cambridge, my father became an impassioned advocate of the true faith, which prejudiced men derogatorily call Puritan. He took a B.A. degree in Divinity and was ordained a Minister by Bishop Turner of London in the year of Christ 1585. As a candidate for Holy Orders, my father had to accept the Thirty-Nine Articles of Faith of the Church of England, which he did, asking God to forgive him for betraying his belief in our true religion, which rejects the papist doctrines of the aforesaid Church of England.

Once ordained, my father sought appointment to a benefice, which he received in the following year when he became the Rector of All Saints' Church in Little Totham, some six miles southeast of Witham. His living was fifteen pounds per annum.

One of his church wardens was a glazier, Thomas Higgens. Father fell in love with Higgens's daughter, Edith. They were wed in the year of Christ 1589. After my mother's death, my father would not marry again. He called her "my sweetheart" all the remaining days of his life.

In the year of Christ 1595, when I was born, my father was appointed Minister of St. James by Bishop Tiffin of Bristol. My father was but eight-and-twenty years of age, yet much famed for learning. He was master of Latin, Greek, and Hebrew and devoted to the study of the sacred Scriptures in their original languages.

My father's living was forty pounds a year, which he augmented by lecturing on religion in the church, and about the country, three evenings a week for twenty pounds a year paid by the richer sort in his congregation. He gave one-fortieth of his stipend to the poor. He kept five servants in his parsonage, and a woman who was in charge of malting, brewing, and baking.

My favorite of his servants, beside Mary, was Ben Tucker, a gentle and quiet fellow. The year after my birth, Ben was arrested whilst sleeping in the street for being a vagrant without a pass. Ben was condemned to a whipping and, as it was his second offence, being branded with a red-hot iron thrust through the gristle of his right ear. They said, though, he would be spared punishment if an honest householder worth five pounds in goods retained him in his services for one whole year.

Once satisfied that Ben was not a drunkard, my father retained him. Ben learned to be a gardener, and he became my first friend. He taught me the names of our local flowers, herbs and nuts, viz., the pink and purple columbines, the cowslips, the kingslips and lilies, sweet herbs, ivy leaves, hazel nuts, and green rushes.

Ben's father was a beggar who raised him to be a *kinchin koes*—which means "a male beggar child" in the language beggars devised to speak amongst themselves. His father made corrosives and applied them to the fleshy parts of Ben's body, raising odious sores upon them that moved men to bestow alms upon him. Ben showed me the shiny red scars that remained upon his left breast and stomach. He considered himself fortunate that his father did not burn, break, or disfigure his childish limbs after the fashion of other beggars who made their children pitiful to people. Ben's father was an "Abraham's man," a beggar who feigned madness. In the end he went truly mad and drowned himself in the Thames at Wapping in the Woze.

Ben had no knowledge of Jesus Christ till he became my father's servant. He was converted upon learning that Christ spake of a beggar named Lazarus, who was full of sores and, when he died, was carried by the angels into Abraham's bosom.

On a fair, sunshining Sabbath, just without the church after the morning service, when I was seven years of age, my father asked me, "Have you Christ in your heart? Have you true grace? How do you prepare for saving grace? How will you know you are saved?"

I rejoined, "Sir, I know not how I should come by such knowledge."

He replied in words I will never forget: "My son, you will come by such knowledge by having faith in God's grace. My life's journey is to strengthen my faith. But it comes and goes. The truth is, we all live in doubt."

The day following, Mary said to me, "Such a sad face! Where are your merry eye and sweet smile of yesterday? Why the sad face? You are too young to have such a sad face. What's this? A tear in your right eye? Let me kiss it hence."

"Yes," I said. "Kiss the tear from my right eye."

She kissed my eye and said, "'Tis gone, sweet boy. I drank up your sadness."

And she did! My merry eye and sweet smile were once more mine.

Soon afterwards, Mr. Howard Coppinger's house burned down. All black and deformed by the fire, he ran up Chapelhay Street, followed by some friends who wanted to stay him and dress his wounds. Near the end of the street, Mr. John Parkins, a cutler, thinking Coppinger was a felon on the run, had a pole in his hand with which he brained Mr. Coppinger.

Coppinger was one of my father's parishioners. He had been fined several times for not attending church on the Sabbath. Two weeks before the fire, he had left church before my father's sermon and was arrested by a constable for catching birds with a handnet. He was sentenced to two hours in the stocks.

My father said, "Coppinger's discordant death confirms that he was not one of the Elect. Christ is not the savior of the whole world, but only of His elected and chosen people. My question is this: are you and I amongst the saved?"

I had no doubts that my father was saved, but I could not speak for myself. I sank into the dumps.

Winterbourne is a godly town. When my father was presented with a living at St. James, he told the church Elders, "I prefer the primitive church of antiquity to the popish practices of the modern Church of England." He said that he was averse to wearing a surplice, crossing himself while baptizing, bowing at the mention of Jesus's name, and kneeling whilst receiving the sacrament.

The Elders were pleased, but they greatly feared that my father would be clapped up in prison for incurring ecclesiastical censure by not wearing a surplice, &c. So my father wore a torn and soiled surplice in church in protest against the Church of England's papist fopperies.

He was an inspired preacher who exercised himself with much diligence, teaching his congregation and all the country about. It was his custom, when confounded by an insoluble predicament, to seek the help of the Lord by opening the Bible at random and pointing with his forefinger by chance at a verse.

In my seventh year, I began my studies at the new Free Grammar School on Bridgeport Road. Mary returned to live wholly with her family. We wept and kissed at our parting. She said, "Fare thee well, my dear boy. You have been a son to me, as much as any child I ever bore."

I said, "I have twice lost my Mama," and wept anew.

As my school years passed, I learned from Norwell's *A Catechism, or First Instruction and Learning of Christian Religion* that "all corrupt thoughts, although our consent be not added to them, do proceed of our corrupted nature." And, as my father said, faith alone distinguished the saved; those who were predestined before the foundations of the world were laid to know within their souls the Holy Ghost—the Spirit of Christ. My soul knew only its own corrupted nature, emptied of Christ.

I loathed myself but loved words. I ravenously read William Lily's *Short Introduction of Grammar*. I was snared by Lily's exposition of Latin grammar. A well-wrought

English or Latin sentence gave me ardent pleasure. Grammar was yet another demonstration of God's omnipotence, for He gave unto all nations their own languages and rules of grammar when He scattered them from Babel.

I discovered that the meaning of each Latin sentence comes from the inflection of its words. The order of words means comparatively little. The multitude of endings makes for a multitude of possible meanings. All the meanings that a noun or a verb can have depend on close attention to these various forms. Latin is, above all, a concise language. Brevity is beautiful to me. I devoured on my own small, delectable portions of Cicero, Ovid, Virgil, Plautus, Terence, Horace, and Caesar. I resolved that when I reached man's estate I would be as brave as Caesar, who wrote in his *Gallic Wars* that he wore the only red cloak in the Roman army so that when he went into battle, the Gauls would know who he was and strive to be the first to kill him. Thus, in the spring of 1623, when I fought with Captain Standish against the Indians in Wessagusset, I deliberately exposed myself to the Indians' arrows.

One day, when I was thirteen years of age, my father and I compared our experiences in Grammar School. They were much alike. We lingered awhile over the little things: how when the fire was low in winter and our ink froze, we worked the points of our quills across the surface of the paper to avoid blots and blemishes. We rejoiced together at the beauty of the Latin language. My father could still inflect in every detail any noun or verb.

He said then that I was to go to Emmanuel College, the most godly college at Cambridge, wherein I would take a degree as a Bachelor of Divinity and follow him in his calling as a Minister of Christ. Father said, "With God's grace, you will one day shine your light before men that they may see His good works and glorify our Father, which is in heaven."

I said, "I have no faith in Christ. I have no power to turn unto Him."

Said he, "Have patience. I was naught but a year older than you when I was born anew."

I wept often over my unrequited desire for salvation.

My father said, "Your hearty desire for salvation is surely the first evidence that grace is at work in your soul."

So I sought Christ without faith in His grace. I felt it was hypocritical to study at Emmanuel for a Bachelor of Divinity and become a Minister. My father could not afford to send me as a pensioner, in the amount of some forty-five pounds per annum. Satan tempted me to go as a sizar and earn my rations by waiting upon my fellow students, to continue my studies of Latin not in the service of Christ but for its beauty. I was lewdly disposed to beauteous language and could not renounce my satanical yearning for the pleasure it gave me.

Musing in the midst of my dumps, I felt my lack of faith in God's grace more keenly than before. To tell you true, until I was but recently regenerated, I feared that I loved language more than I loved Christ.

My father had been converted in church, when his Minister preached a sermon, the subject being John 10:30. My father had repeated the verse aloud: "I and my Father are one." He was pierced to the heart by the mystery and miracle of the Incarnation. He said to me, "I became very hot for the Gospel. I love the Gospel. Not because I believe it, but because I feel it—the wealth, peace, liberty that arise from it."

I copied down my father's words in swiftwriting, the cipher which I had learned at his behest from my schoolmaster, James Bolt, who wrote down my father's sermons and lectures in cipher for four shillings a year. (My learning swiftwriting as a boy was a special Providence of God that enabled me to make copious notes and then write this Confession of Faith.) After I finished writing down his words, my father scanned the straight lines and curves on my paper and said, "The divers and sundry things that make up the natural world are ciphers writ by God and we must learn to decipher them, just as we have learned to foretell an early spring by the age of the moon at the beginning of January."

I was restless during my last year of Grammar School. I was convinced that I was not destined by God to serve Christ as His Minister. What was I to do with my life? Whither would I go? I envied the apprentices and idle boys of the town who, in the evenings, met to be merry, quaffed ale in the taverns, and played at cards and dice. After work, they lived for pleasure, with no thought of heaven or hell. On May Day, before dawn, they went into Conant's wood with girls and gathered the dew to drink. Then they all danced around the Maypole on the village green. I fancied joining them in Satan's revels. I confessed that to my father, who basted me with a stick.

I welcomed his punishment, though it did no good. Puberty was upon me. The Devil often tempted me, and I surrendered to lust and oft had traffic with myself. I grieved for my soul and betook myself to God by praying. He did not respond to me.

Soon after I finished Grammar School, my father said to me, "My son, I will reveal my heart to you. I am much afraid of breaking the law of the realm because of the fate of the preacher Daniel Harvey, from Foxton. You would not remember him, but his memory festers in my mind. Some years ago, he was tried in London, tortured, and sentenced to death for having in his possession a sermon he wrote against wearing the surplice. Mind you, he never preached it but only wrote it out. He was racked, needles were pushed under his fingernails, and his private parts were burned with a torch. He was kept in an iron cage called the Little One in which he could not stand upright. The Lord took him during the third night.

"Know your father for what I am—a sinful coward! I call for a reformation of the church but want the courage to set a proper example of a godly shepherd to my flock. A soiled surplice! I wear a soiled surplice. What a piddling protest to the papist Church of England. But I am sore afraid of the rack and the torch."

He then said to me, "Even though I'm a vile wretch who cannot close with Christ because of my cowardice, you must have reverence for me. You are enjoined by Scripture to honor me."

Ere every Sabbath dinner, before the servants, Ben Tucker spake the following, taught him by my father: "O Lord our God, seeing thou hast ordained sundry degrees and states of men in this life, and among them Thou hast appointed me to be a servant, give me the grace to serve in my vocation faithfully."

Then my father always said, "The Lord's Day is the market day of the soul, on which we lay on spiritual food for the following week. It is a day that enriches the Elect."

He fasted on the Sabbath before his morning's sermon. After he and his household returned home to dine, he locked himself in his chamber for about the space of an hour. When I inquired of him what he did therein, he replied, "I pray for forgiveness."

My father gave communion to his congregation about ten times a year. It was the practice of the former Minister of St. James to give communion to servants and other common people at five in the morning, with a cheap claret, whilst masters and dames, their children, rich tradesmen, and their families took communion at nine of the clock with a fine muscatel. Over the objection of my father's church wardens, who wanted to spare the cost and preserve the order of the realm, he gave communion to his whole congregation at five in the morning and served it with the dear muscatel. He said to me, "There is but one division in my congregation— nay, the entire world—and that is between the damned and the saved."

During my last two years at Grammar School, I often visited Mary in her small cottage on Old Parish Lane. My father bade Ben accompany me, carrying his oaken staff, to protect me from the nightwalkers with cudgels and knives who had eluded the watch. I remember in particular trudging through the mud one wet October night. We passed The Sign of the Rose on New Street, outside of which, amongst a crowd, the constable had hold of Squire Wilton, who had stabbed the tapster of the inn to the heart. I looked through the window and espied the tapster's corpse lying upon its back in a puddle of blood upon the floor. The sole of his left shoe had a big hole therein.

Arriving at Mary's cottage, I said to her and Ben, "It was the first corpse I have ever seen."

'Twas Mary who rejoined, "Aye, but not the last, my dearest boy."

Said I, "What makes you say so?"

"I dreamed it," said she.

It began to rain. Mary's cottage had a leaky thatched roof. Her four daughters, aged in years from two to twelve, were huddled together in a dry corner, midst the three spinning wheels and the loom. They kept their sow within-door.

Mark kissed Mary tenderly on the forehead. The sow snorted. Mary divided a big round cheese that she had taken with my father's permission. Mark denied himself a bite. He had passed the day keeping watch over his master's cows as they grazed upon the stubble of his master's harvested corn. Mark smelled of cow dung. Bess, being twelve years of age, had tended her younger sisters while spinning yarn for Wells, the clothier.

Said Mary, "That tapster was a bottle-nosed rogue. He's burning in hell, with a burst stomach and steaming guts."

———•◆•———

Toward the end of December, we had extreme frost and much snow, so that many died of cold upon the highways. The town was filled with wandering beggars, bedlams, and vagabonds. My father examined them all, mixing wholesome instructions with severe reproofs. If they had passes to travel by, he scanned them thoroughly, and when he found them false or counterfeit, he sent for the constable, who made new passes and sent the wanderers to their last place of settlement or birth.

My father was righteous also unto the poor of

Winterbourne. In January, five small thatched houses at the west side of the North gate burnt, casting their twenty-one ragged inhabitants out into the icy street. My father collected seven pounds and ten shillings in our three churches and distributed it amongst them.

All that winter, the smallpox was very thick in Winterbourne. Ten men and women, twelve elder folk, and thirteen children died. The deeply pitted faces and hands of the survivors sickened me. My father, the two other rectors in the town, the barber-surgeon, and our physician, Doctor Troth, tended the stricken. Doctor Troth's fee for his ministrations was two shillings; only five people could afford his service. He believed that having survived the malady in his childhood, he could not catch it again. (I could not look upon his pitted face or hands without being desirous of vomiting.) My father declared special days of prayer, fasting, and humiliation for his congregation so that God might have mercy and remove the pestilence from His sinful people.

I lived in dread of dying from the sickness or, worse, becoming disfigured from it. I suffered the insufficience of faith in my soul. I zealously kept the Sabbath, not daring to eat or dwell upon irreverent things. I devoted myself to listening to my father's sermons, reading Scripture, and praying. It availed me nothing; my soul stayed plunged in the depths. And though I could not know it then, the visitation of smallpox was a dire portent to me from Heaven, being the reason why I have dwelt at length upon it here.

Come March, I worked with Ben in my father's garden. We planted red cabbage, carrots, spearmint, onions, sage, Runcival peas, lavender, sorrel, roses, and parsnips, &c.

I remember Ben, after a rain, hanging his shirt to dry upon a gooseberry bush in the garden. I gazed upon his scars, saying, "I have never heard you trouble yourself about the state of your soul."

Ben answered in his mild voice, "My soul was full of sores that Christ, through your father, hath healed. I'm already in Abraham's bosom. This world be now heaven enough for me."

Mary was near her time. In the beginning of July, a neighbor of Mary's sought me out at home. Mark, haunted for three months by a quivering fever, was taken by the Lord in June. And it seemed Mary was near her time as well. The neighbor said that Mary had, ten days before, been delivered of a boy she had named Mark. Satan, the enemy of mankind, had blinded Mary's judgment. She told her aforementioned neighbor, "Without a father, my babe is better off dead than alive."

I hastened to visit her, with a loaf of white bread, a cheese, some dressed beef, and a pot of ale in my knapsack. Mary's four daughters were with kindly neighbors. She nibbled the beef, took one draught of ale, and said to me, "Look you, my dear boy. Our sow died of the white measles. I sold the loom for money to pay a barber-surgeon to thrice bleed my poor Mark and provide him with medicine. I need money for food. I have not tuppence left to rub together. I will come to ruin and disgrace by reason of poverty."

She wore a filthy shift. She said, "My poor boykin hath the hiccups and puked on me." While suckling her babe, she said thrice, "I must go to work. I must go to work. I must go to work."

The babe fell asleep. She laid him in his basket, lay down upon a bundle of moldy straw, and slept. I swilled the rest of the ale and watched over her for almost four hours. Along about five of the clock in the afternoon, I could not hold my water any longer and went outside to relieve myself. When I returned, I found her hugging the naked little corpse to her breast. The babe's much swelled little tongue stuck out between its tiny purple lips.

Mary said, "My poor boykin—my little heart—puked on me again, and I strangled him. The Devil bade me do it!"

She hugged the little corpse to her breast and sang a song I knew well from street singers in the town.

> O death, rock me asleep,
> Bring me to quiet rest,
> Toll on thou passing bell,
> Let thy sound
> My death tell,
> For I must die,
> There is no remedy,
> For now I die.

God forgive me, I loved her still, even though she was a murderer.

Mary was arrested, imprisoned, and, at the next session of the Assizes, condemned to be hanged. Justice Baron Digby allowed her to speak.

"Pity me!" said Mary. "I was doomed by God ere the creation of the world to harken unto Satan and strangle my babe—my precious boykin!—that just after he lived ten days. I am damned! I will burn in hellfire. So pity me! Damned ere the creation of the world! Wherefore? What did I do ere the creation of the world to warrant this fate? Answer me! Who is this hurtful God that hath condemned me? Damn Him that damned me!"

Justice Baron Digby ordered Mary to be gagged.

My father and I visited her in gaol upon the day before her hanging. Her four daughters were there to bid her farewell. She enjoined my father, "Good master, my poor daughters here now abide in the Hospital, amidst other orphans, wherein they spin and card and make bonelace from before the dawn till the coming of the night. Look in on them from time to time, I beseech thee."

I kissed her calloused palms and wet them with my tears. I said, "You are a murderer and a blasphemer—a damned soul—but I love you. God forgive me, I shall always love you!"

She said, "Thank you, master, for your kind words. I love you, too."

Upon the appointed day, at noon, Mary was taken up Gallows Hill in a cart. John Barker, the hangman, was the executioner in Cranborne gaol. My father gave a sermon on Romans 6:23, "For the wages of sin is death."

When Barker put the noose about Mary's neck, she cried out, "Lord, make this quick!"

My father bade me to go home. As I departed, I watched him and Ben make their way to the foot of the gallows. I could not bring myself to look upon my beloved Mary being hanged. On my way to the parsonage house, I heard the crowd roar on Gallows Hill.

Ben and my father soon returned home. Ben alone came within-door. My father waited in the yard, holding his hat in his hand. I went to him. His hat, the nape of his neck, his shoulders, and his upper back were covered with feces. The stench made me nauseous. I held my nose.

My father put off his reeking clothes, and Ben washed his whole body. Ben burned the stinking hat and clothes, while my father donned his old black suit. We entered the house together, and my father said, "Mary's neck did not break when she was hanged. I could not allow her to slowly strangle, so I pulled on her legs with all my might. I heard her neck bone break. Then her bowels gushed all over me."

Father's parish was charged six shillings and eight pence for Mary's burial. The parishioners protested spending the money on a blaspheming murderer's burial. My father paid the fee.

He kept his promise and visited Mary's four orphaned daughters in the Hospital, wherein he learned that the eldest, Bess, had angered the bonelace teacher by being negligent in her work. The teacher had her flogged at the whipping post. She was given six stripes with a birch rod. My father fetched Ben to carry her home and summoned the barber-surgeon to tend her wounds. She shared the kitchen maid's bed.

Upon the next morning, I looked in on Bess, and she said, "Stay a little, I pray you, and speak with me."

We spake for the better part of an hour. Amongst the things she said, were, "Methinks Mama loved you more than me, but I forgive you. Daddy loved me best," and, "Mama said the Devil hath a shrill voice." Another was this: "If Mama burns amongst the damned, then let it be the same for me. Let me suffer with her forever. Yet if Daddy be saved and in Heaven, I would abide with him in bliss. I loved him best. Well, I leave it to God. I put my trust in Him."

The day after, she fell sore sick with a burning fever. Five days afterwards at eventide, she yielded up the ghost.

In July of the year of Christ 1611, my father made his annual journey to Cambridge for Commencement, wherein he passed a week feasting and reveling, in a riot of meat and wine. Then he passed another week catching fire, as he termed it, from praying, fasting, and meditating with other godly Ministers of like belief who had graduated from the University.

During this time I helped my uncle Roger and his husbandmen make hay upon his farm. He said to me, "Your father has but a week of frolic at Cambridge, but for the rest of the year, he must pray and fast and trudge about the town, this way and that, here to a drab, there to a thief or murderer, like your accursed nurse, that slave of Satan's! What sort of life is that for a man? Live with me and your aunt and work my farm. Hard work in the open air will purge the torments from your soul." He belched. "And when my good wife and I die, all that I have will be yours, even unto my black breeches, black stockings, and red cloak."

I considered my uncle's liberal offer. When my father returned from Cambridge, he taught me to keep the accounts he kept of my uncle's farm and shop. The foregoing year, Roger's profit was thirty-seven pounds and six shillings. I exulted in my thoughts of the money that might some day accrue to me if I managed his farm and glover's shop well. So I thus accepted my uncle's offer.

My father was sorrowful that I had relinquished his design for me to go to Cambridge and become a Minister. He said, "Make not Mammon your god!"

"Father," I said, "your God is my God, and I cry unto Him, 'Lord, save me!'"

Uncle Roger hired an attorney to write his will. I was to inherit his farm, glover's shop, and sundry other things, inclusive of his stockings, breeches, and cloak, upon his and his wife's death, the stipulation being that I was to be a servant in husbandry who would be paid two pounds and eight shillings per annum, together with lodging, meat and drink, and livery for as long as my uncle and aunt lived. The Devil bade me wonder how long that would be.

My aunt Eliza wanted her nephew Tom Foot to inherit the farm. She said to me, "Thou art not a husbandman. You are a scholar. Tom was born to work the land."

Said I, "God and uncle Roger have determined otherwise."

Even though my father was compelled by Ecclesiastical law to read the recent translation into the common language of the Bible in church, he had given me a volume of the old wholesome Geneva translation of Holy Scripture and bade me to read a chapter therein every evening for so long as I remained upon the farm, lest I forget my Creator in the days of my youth. I did so.

One evening, I read in Exodus 39:2, "So he made the ephod of gold, blue silk, and purple and scarlet, and fine twined linen." Now I knew from my father that an ephod was an antique priestly garment without sleeves. The English sentence was not only music to my ears, but it conveyed divers, brightly colored images to my mind's eye. The English language bewitched me, and I fell in love with my mother tongue.

On the twelfth of September in the year of Christ 1611, I began living and labouring upon my uncle Roger's farm. I was a student again—but this time, of husbandry and the divers and sundry things which compose the natural world that my father deemed to be ciphers writ by God.

My first task was to help with the harvest. I have a memory that is surely from the latter part of the month: it is a chilly afternoon. The wind knocks the apples together on the trees, and I gather the fallen fruit to fill my uncle Roger's pies. He enjoyed baking apple pies; they were very delicious in taste. He did everything well.

That selfsame autumn, when some of the threshing was done, uncle Roger taught me how to sow his fields with rye and then wheat. I learned to make cider, prune his apple, pear, and cherry trees, and trim his hedges. He taught me to spit on my hands to prevent them from forming blisters.

Tom Foot, the hired husbandman, was a robust youth of my own age. I was weak-limbed and quickly wearied from the vigorous labour. My arms and back ached. But by November, when the autumn planting was finished, my hands were callused and my muscles had grown hard. I learned to slaughter swine and bullocks, the latter with a poleaxe that, at first, took me three or four blows between their big eyes. Covered with blood, bits of bone, and brains, I fully apprehended that we live fallen in a fallen world, wherein life and death feed upon each other.

Thus, I learned much on the farm, but not to ride a horse. I was scared of being bitten by one. My uncle Roger kept two geldings and a mare. They knew that I was frightened of them and tried to bite me. I always walked the three miles into town. I am glad that there are no horses in New England.

Along with an unmarried shepherd by the name of Peter Patch, my uncle kept two unmarried women servants and two other unmarried male servants in husbandry. They were twins named Jacob and Richard Fletcher. Uncle Roger called them "Jacob" and "Esau" because the latter was much hairier than his brother; the hairs grew thickly upon his broad back, chest, and arms.

Now this Esau, like the Esau in Scripture, was a knave;

he refused to accompany the rest of us to St. James on the Lord's Day but slept until dinner. He was a diligent labourer and so my uncle was loathe to report him to the constable, as Esau could not have paid the two-shilling fine. My niggardly uncle would not spend the cash himself; Esau would have been put in the stocks, and my uncle would have lost the former's day's work, or more.

Then Providence willed that during the second year I was at the farm, Esau was much bruised by the fall of a dead elm tree in a high wind and forced to spend almost a week abed. At length, my uncle said to him, "Up with you and return to your labours! For those who indulge themselves in idleness, the express command of God unto us is that we should let them starve."

My uncle commanded Esau to go to church, saying, "God hath warned you not to slink from Him! The next time, you absent yourself from church upon the Sabbath, you will surely die!" Thereafter, Esau Fletcher kept the Sabbath as well as any Christian soul in St. James parish. At Sunday breakfast, my aunt Eliza gave us servants thinner slices of the white loaf, flavoured with nutmeg, and but one mug each of hot boiled milk. For supper, she oft served herself alone a special diet of cow-calf or wether mutton.

The following July, she brake a tooth upon a cherry

stone, and, God forgive me, I had the satisfaction of reciting to myself from Psalm 3:7, "O Lord, arise; help me, my God: for thou hast smitten all mine enemies upon the cheek bone: thou hast broken the teeth of the wicked." The broken tooth greatly pained her until she had it extracted.

Also on the twelfth of September in the year of Christ 1611, which fell upon a Thursday—I made a note of it—on that evening, after supper, upon which I began reading from the Bible, my uncle Roger asked me to also read aloud to him. And thus it became our custom, evening after evening, for three years, three months, and four-and-twenty days. Sometimes, it is true, my uncle fell asleep, particularly during the harvest, sheep shearing, or other long days of hard labour. And sometimes, being otherwise occupied, he missed the occasion. But more oft than not, he harkened to the sacred text.

He confessed that the meaning of the verses oft perplexed him—as they did me—but that—like me—he was bewitched by their melodious sound. He was charmed by similes, metaphors, and imagery, though he was unacquainted with those poetical terms until I taught them to him.

He committed to memory vivid utterances in common speech that he had heard over the years in the market-place, in the streets, in the taverns, at fairs, &c. I wrote these down: "A press of people standing as close as mutton pies in an oven." "From the sprig of his cap to his spangled shoe strap." "Laughing like a ploughman at a Morris dance." And then there was the verse of a song my uncle had learned at the Woodbury Fair held near Bere Regis about the eighteenth of every September:

> The plough is the Lord's pen.
>
> It writes the land to sow our seed
>
> To feed the poor that stand in need.
>
> Neither the Prince nor peasants read
>
> Without this pen, or earn their bread.
>
> It bringeth increase to the most and least
>
> Such food as serveth man and beast.

My uncle Roger said, "I'm a fool for words." When next I looked upon a plough, I thought, "Thou art God's pen."

Uncle Roger reciprocated for my reading Scripture to him by teaching me to load, prime, aim, discharge, and cleanse his musket. I learned to make char cloth from linen strips that ignited by striking sparks from a flint and steel upon the strip, and from the little fire, lighting the tip of the match cord, blowing on its coal to keep it smouldering, and using that to ignite the fine powder in the musket's pan. The match cord, I discovered, was soaked in saltpeter, yet difficult to keep glowing in a high wind, rain, or snow. Roger also taught me how to mold bullets and goose-shot, with which we went hunting and fowling upon the Downs. He was a good marksman; I was not. As such, it was only by an intervention of Providence that my shot shattered the left elbow of the savage Massachusetts Indian in Wessagusset during the spring of 1623.

The Devil engendered my encounters with Jane Fuller. The daughter of Matthew Fuller, a miller in Winterbourne, she was a maid at The Sign of the Bull in the High East Street, whence I delivered some of my uncle's cider in the spring of my sixteenth year. She was a year older than I and jested with me about my being shy.

I said, "Fetch me a cup of ale."

She pulled at my sleeve and said, "You need not fear me."

I said, "I fear you not."

"Then come," she said. "Come, drink a pot with

me." But I hastened through the door and onto the High East Street.

I returned to The Sign of the Bull upon the following market day. Jane reiterated her previous request, and we drank a pot together. She and her father were parishioners of All Saints in the High Street. She fulminated against their rector, Mr. Lane, who had made a goodly profit selling corn to the Mayor for the poor and had become so proud he no longer spake to common folk in his congregation, like Jane and her father.

I tried to persuade Jane to come to services at St. James, but she said, "I will stay with Mr. Lane. Does not Scripture say that pride goeth before a fall? Is that not Scripture? I want to be there when Mr. Lane stumbles and falls upon his bum. God is just; it will happen one day in church. Perhaps on his way to the pulpit. You wait and see!"

I went to see Jane Fuller at The Sign of the Bull every market day for a month. We drank country brew. One afternoon, she wound the string of my shirt about her forefinger and entreated me to go a-maying with her. I refused to take part in a pagan ritual. But at dawn on May Day, I succumbed to temptation and walked into town. I saw Jane return with other maidens and lads from Conant's wood, wherein they had sipped a drop or two of dew from the tips of their fingers.

I confess that I joined them gathering green branches, Wind Flowers, violets, Early Purples, thyme, and Kingcups. Then we all went singing from door to door. I did not sing those pagan songs. But I listened to the music of the pipes and drums in the streets and watched the heathen Maypole, a goodly pine tree, bare of branches, and some fifty foot in length, covered all over with flowers and herbs, being borne to the market square by two yoke of oxen. Each one had a sweet nosegay of flowers tied on the tip of his horns. On the village green by the Maypole, Jane put off her shoes and bared her breasts to me; I fled back to the farm.

For weeks to come, I lost myself in my labour. I became a gardener sorting seeds, a thresher in the barn trying the strength of his flail, a mower whetting his scythe, a husbandman scouring his plow. I hedged, fenced, sowed, reaped, and gleaned until, by the grace of God, I was tormented no more by the thought of Jane Fuller's naked breasts, with their round, roseate buds.

But Satan was hard at work upon the farm. I have mentioned the shepherd, Peter Patch, who with his dog, Hal, tended my uncle Roger's flock of two hundred and thirty-three sheep. Patch drove the sheep twice each day between the hill pastures and the fields. He fed his flock, gathered the lambs, carried them in his bosom, and gently led those that were with young. He smeared Stockholm tar upon the leg wounds of his sheep; it never failed to heal them.

He knew not his own age. I reckoned that he was about five-and-thirty years old. He suffered from sciatica that made him limp upon his left leg. His father was my grandfather's shepherd; his mother, who had lived idly and wandered about the country, went into London and disappeared when Peter was a child.

In the summer, using sprinkled water and smoke, Patch acquired honey for the household from a hive in the hollow oak on the Ridge. It was there at the end of July that I espied him buggering a ewe. His breeches were down about his ankles. He stood half-naked behind the ewe, between her hind legs, which he held by the hooves close to his hips. The ewe, with her rear end in the air, stood upon her front legs. Then Patch saw me and dropped her hind legs. The ewe ran away.

Patch pulled up his breeches and said, "If you tell what you have seen me do this day, they will surely hang me, master, on Gallows Hill."

Tears trickled down his cheeks. He said, "Do not let them hang me, master. Report me not to the constable. But if you must, and they do hang me, I beg a favor of you, master. Soon as I hang there, give my legs a tug and break my neck. Will you do that for me? Do not let me slowly strangle. Hasten my death! Promise me as a godly Christian!"

Said I, "I cannot promise you."

God forgive me, but I could not bring myself to denounce Peter Patch. It pleased the Lord to forgive my transgression, for it was some months thereafter that Christ brought me into His chambers, wherein I rejoiced in His love.

This happened on my twentieth birthday, at about seven of the clock on Friday evening of the tenth of March in the year of Christ 1615, whilst I read to my uncle Roger from Scripture. I had reached the introduction to chapter V of the Second Book of Esdras from the Apocrypha, viz., "In the latter time, truth shall be hid. Unrighteousness and all wickedness shall reign in the world."

My uncle interrupted me, saying, "Read to me instead of the love of Christ for His Elect and ours for Him in the verses of that most excellent Song which was Solomon's." He belched.

I read aloud, "Let him kiss me with the kisses of his mouth," and was filled with a sense of Christ's love and presence. The God of Israel was with me; I was wholly His. He was my soul's husband, my unspeakable love, my exceeding great reward.

I saw no shape but heard a voice only, saying, "Thou art cleansed from the blood and filth of thy sins."

I laughed and wept. The following day, my uncle set Esau to harrow the New Field and bade me have a rake's head repaired at a blacksmith in Winterbourne, wherein I also bought a pound of nails. I then returned to the farm and chopped wood until night. I rejoiced in being saved by the grace of my soul's Beloved.

By earnest prayer, I sought counsel of God, the giver of all good gifts. My father, whose pious judgment and knowledge I much trusted, said to me, "Your rebirth in Christ hath divinely appointed you to serve Him as His Minister. You must take a Bachelor of Divinity degree at Emmanuel College, Cambridge."

I said, "Sir, I must needs confess to you that, even for Christ's sake, I'm loathe to matriculate as a poor sizar obliged to pay my way by waiting upon my fellow students of good rank and quality. To serve them food and drink like a common servant, to fetch and carry for them. I cannot. Not even for Christ's sake! Such is my pride. Help me conquer my satanical pride!"

We bowed our heads, and he bade me pray from Psalm 36:11, "Let not the foot of pride come against me."

I could not conquer my pride. But God forgave me. My uncle said to me that he would pay my full cost of living at the University, in the amount of about forty-five pounds per annum, so that I could matriculate as a pensioner and live in a manner befitting the nephew of a prosperous yeoman such as he. His pride—or perhaps his love for me—overcame his habitual parsimony.

My aunt Eliza protested his decision, but he was resolute. He likewise gave me a goodly pair of red gloves of kid from his shop, and, for travel apparel, his old black stockings, black breeches, jerkin, and his warm blue cloak. Then he hired a tailor to make me a black suit and doublet with silver buttons to wear at Emmanuel, wherein, according to my father, the students wore neither clerical cap nor gown. My uncle said to me, "I want you to do me proud amongst all them high and mighty gentlemen."

My uncle Roger wrote a new will, leaving his farm and glover's shop to Tom Foot. Foot got drunk to celebrate in The Sign of the Bull.

I was admitted to Cambridge for the following Michaelmas term. My father wrote a letter to his friend and former chamber mate at Christ Church, the Rev. William Barstow, who was the rector of All Angels Church, in Ashford in the Weald of Kent; he was the sole surviving heir of two nearby manors, managed by a steward. The Barstows were one of the most ancient of Kentish families. In the years since college, Barstow and my father had met regularly at the annual Commencement festivities held every July. Barstow's son, Robin, aged fifteen, was in his second year as a pensioner at Emmanuel. He hoped to take a Bachelor of Arts, become a Fellow, and one day teach Latin there. His father prayed he would be converted by Emmanuel's godly tutors and abandon his design. He wanted Robin to take a Bachelor of Divinity and become a Minister. Our fathers arranged for Roger and me to live together in a chamber near the library and share the same tutor, whose name was Charles Morton.

I first saw Robin seated by the window in his study, reading a volume of the *Aeneid*. He gazed upon me over the pages of his book and asked in Latin, with a Kentish accent, "How well do you know your Virgil?"

And I rejoined, likewise in Latin, "Passing fair." ("*Satis certe.*") We Cambridge men spake together only in Latin, Hebrew, or Greek.

Robin said, "Then tell me this: how long did Alcestes live, and how many jars of Sicilian wine did he give to the Trojans?"

"I cannot say."

Said he, "Well, neither can I."

We laughed together. With his blue eyes, his ruddy

complexion, his fair hairs, Robin Barstow was the come-liest youth I have ever known.

He joined with me and a company of six or eight others to pray together every evening and discourse about religion, presided over by our tutor in his chamber.

Robin said, "I have need of continual under-proppings to hold up my soul."

When I told him about my conversion, he answered, "Nothing like that hath ever happened to me. I feel that God is at a great remove from my soul. How I envy thee! My father was converted some twenty years ago in Ashford and said that he trembled from the Divine Majesty and holiness which shone within him. The great weight of uncertainty was lifted from his soul. Like you, he knew he was saved! I live in hope of salvation. Be my soul's companion. Help me reach out to God."

At my suggestion, he and I fasted upon every Sabbath. We prayed together every night before we went to sleep. Sometimes during the day I came upon him praying alone. Tears hung upon his long lashes and trickled down his ruddy, beardless cheeks. He confessed to me that he was much tormented by the sin of Onan. Then he cried out, "Save me, O my God. Save my corrupt soul."

Our fellow chamber mates, both from Sussex, were likewise studying Divinity; they hoped to get a nobleman's chaplaincy or a lectureship in London paid for by a rich merchant or Company. There was much talk amongst them of one of the College Fellows receiving a lectureship at St. Sepulchre, in the amount of thirty pounds a year given by a wealthy chandler.

All of us Cambridge men kept a Commonplace Book. I have mine with me to this day. Toward the end of my first Lenten term, I noted how I spent my days of the week:

Item. Chapel every morning at five of the clock. Private devotions.

Item. Breakfasts are breakstudies. I abjure all but a draught of College beer and a morsel of bread.

Item. The rest of the forenoon, disputations with tutor, lectures by Dons, which I copy out, word for word, in Swiftwriting; divers variants of same used by other students. Monday, Wednesday, Friday, lectures on Dialectics (Aristotle's *On Sophistical Refutations*), Rhetoric (Cicero's *Topics*), music. Tuesday, Thursday, likewise in the forenoon, lectures on Greek grammar (the Greek *Testament*), on Hebrew grammar (the Hebrew *Scriptures*), and on ethics (Aristotle's *Nicomachean Ethics*).

Item. Recreation every afternoon until dinner at five of the clock.

Item. I reserve an hour after evening prayers in my study for translating a few lines of Plato's *Phaedrus* or Homer's *Odyssey*.

Item. Before bedtime, prayers and discourse about religion, supervised by my tutor.

Item. Saturday, in the forenoon, lectures on Divinity (Masculus's *Commonplaces of Christian Religion*), Philosophy (Verro's *Ten Books of Natural Philosophy*), Latin poetry (Virgil's *Aeneid*) with emphasis upon grammar.

Item. The Sabbath. Three divine services, conducted by College Fellows. Emmanuel's Head Master, Laurence Chaderton, did not conform to Hampton Court Conference with King James upon his accession in 1603. Hence, with impunity because of Chaderton's friends at Court, we follow a private course of prayer after our own fashion. Communion twice a month. Fellows never wear surplices, nor do we communicants kneel to receive communion, but are seated instead around the communion table, passing bread and cup from hand to hand.

(If I may be so bold, the latter is a godly example of how communion might be served, when the Plymouth Church acquires a Minister.)

Robin and I passed our afternoons together. It was

the most precious time of the day to me. We walked along the Cam, feeding the swans, wandered the streets of Cambridge, or sat and talked under the walnut tree in the northeast corner of the Emmanuel Quadrangle. He told me about his three elder brothers, his younger sister, and his mother, who regularly sent him a jug of strong, Kentish cider, which he shared with me. We were both much troubled by constipation. My father sent me money to buy suppositories, which I shared with Robin. Our intimacy was much noted by many of our fellow students, who called us "David and Jonathan."

One warm, spring evening after supper, under the walnut tree, Robin said to me, "Dear brother, I await in despair for Christ to regenerate me," and I said, "Dear brother, God is withdrawing His presence from me a little more each day. My own regeneration seems at times like a dream."

My recurring spiritual anguish bound me closer to him.

When I returned home for my summer vacation, I went fowling with my uncle upon the Downs. I aimed the musket, loaded with goose-shot, at a gander in a flock of grey geese flying toward me above a thorn thicket, and pulled the trigger. The musket blew up in my hands. I cannot recall a noise; it seemed to me I was at the center of a great flash of light, and the next I knew, I was laid out upon my back with sundry fragments of the piece scattered about me. The barrel was burst in twain. Thanks be to God, I was unhurt, excepting a slight burn on my right wrist.

I knew that there are no such things as accidents. Was my escape from death a special interposition of Providence? Was it a sign that God was not departing from me as I feared? My ignorance tormented me.

Toward the end of my second Michaelmas term, there were grievous sins in Trinity College; a woman was carried from chamber to chamber in the night. The eight culpable students were caught by the College Head Porter, who brought them before Trinity's High Master the following morning. The youngest student, fifteen years of age, was thrashed; one was fined, and the others were sent down.

Robin said to me, "I too long for women. Would that I longed so for God's grace!"

That night, I dreamed about Jane Fuller's breasts. I related this to my tutor, Charles Morton, who said, "God help us, since the Fall we are defenceless against Satan in our dreams."

As the year progressed, Robin spake so longingly of his hope for grace that I loved him better than before.

Our summer vacation drew nigh; my father wrote me a letter, inviting Robin to spend two weeks with us in Winterbourne. Robin accepted.

Because of my fear of horses, Robin and I traveled in a carrier wagon; he had never been west of London. He gazed at length upon Salisbury Cathedral and said, "Let us build such churches in our hearts."

We journeyed over a week, far spent in drink. It was a slow going we had of it because of the heavy rain. Our roof leaked through numerable rents in the canvas. I wrapped my sodden cloak about Robin and myself, and we clung to each other for hours. He guzzled sack and praised the rich soil, the fertile pasture lands, and the lush fields of divers corn. In Dorset, the other traveler in our wagon remarked that the heath surrounding us was a tedious view of furze, fern, and heather.

Robin said, "Look you closer, sir, and you will distinguish dry heaths, marked by heather, and wet heaths—as over there—no, to the left—marked by—what do you call those yellow flowers, Charles?"

"Bog asphodels."

"Is that so?" He took a swig. "Asphodels: the flowers that bloom in Hades. A wonderful paradox! Asphodels in a paradise. For that is what our England is! This lush island garden of ours, so succulent and luxuriant in growth, is a paradise—rainy, 'tis true, and sometimes stricken by drought. But it is nonetheless an earthly paradise, wherein the air is usually temperate, the ground fertile, the earth abounding with all things needful for man and necessary for beast."

We drank to England—"our lush island paradise, sometimes stricken with drought!" Because of the ungodly Church of England, God did not choose a place within our fecund, tamed, and cultivated English garden as the site of a righteous and godly commonwealth of Saints, but He chose here, in New Plymouth, wherein, on last night, I heard a pack of wolves howling in the darkness to the northwest.

I shall briefly relate but one comment my father made to Robin. The three of us were chatting after supper about Latin and Greek writers, and my father warned Robin of the dangers he faced from reading the atheistical works of Polybius, Livy, Epicurus, and Lucretius. He said, "Do not be seduced by their graceful styles. Beware of the godless doctrines they preach."

Robin said, "I shall, sir, you may be sure of it."

But for months to come, Robin said, "Livy sayeth such and such," and "Polybius sayeth so and so." Finally, one afternoon during the Easter term, when we were about to play tennis, he said, "Epicurus says that the soul perishes with the body. Oh, my dear brother! I believe him!"

Then he said, "I have become an atheist. Polybius, Livy, Epicurus, and Lucretius have banished God from my mind."

My eyes filled with tears. Said I, "You have grieved my heart and wounded my soul. But I love you no matter what vile, diabolical doctrine you espouse. I cannot renounce my love for you. I pray thee, keep your atheism hidden from the world. I shall say nothing about it to anyone. God forgive me, my silence will make me an accomplice to your heinous sin."

He said, "Come, let us play tennis."

Robin continued to receive communion and partake of the discussions about religion in our tutor's chamber. Robin harkened to the discussions. He gazed intently upon each speaker's face in turn. I asked him what went through his mind during such times. "Well," he said, "I try to appear that I am reflecting deeply upon what is being said. That is more difficult than you suppose. I am a coward and a hypocrite and am much ashamed of myself."

God punished me for keeping Robin's atheism a secret. On the sixth of January 1618, I received a letter in the early morning from my father's attorney. It informed me that my father had fallen into a shortness of breath, with extreme soreness of the breast, for which he was thrice purged by Doctor Troth. As my father's shortness of breath continued, his attorney thought it wise that I immediately return home. Robin wanted to accompany me but could not—our tutor was to examine him in the evening by dissertation on the question, "Did Virgil foretell the coming of Christ in the Fourth Ecologue of the *Aeneid*?"

I asked Robin, "What will you say to Morton?"

Robin said, "I'll lie and tell him that I believe that the birth of the babe in the Fourth Ecologue heralds the birth of Christ. But now I shall go carousing and whoring at The Sign of the Rose on Dowdiver's Lane. I will join thee in Winterbourne by the end of the week."

The cold wind and snow impeded my homeward journey. Just beyond Puddletown, our wagon brake its front axle-tree in a deep frozen rut; two days were required to replace it. When I arrived upon the seventeenth of January, I learned that Doctor Troth had been prescribing physics, saffron, and sundry powders and drinks to my father—all to no avail. Making violent efforts to breathe, my father passed his days abed reading Scripture.

Once, gasping for breath, he said to me, "I have bequeathed unto you in my will twenty-six pounds in ready money and sums owed to me, together with most of my effects. Use the money to serve God!"

Upon the Sabbath, Ben Tucker wrapped my father in two warm cloaks and carried him to St. James, wherein the young Reverend Styles of St. Peter's, wearing a new surplice, led a prayer for the sick from the papist Book of Common Prayer.

Ben, my uncle Roger, and I tended to my father's every need. At night, he often missed making water into his chamber pot. Whenever that occurred, I arose early next morning and, after saying my prayers, washed the floor of his bedchamber on my hands and knees. My father said, "Thou art my beloved Son, in whom I am well pleased."

I could not meet his gaze.

Upon the Sabbath, on the twenty-fifth of January, the Reverend Styles preached his evening sermon on the parable of "The Prodigal Son" from Luke. I contemplated 15:24. "For this my son was dead and is alive again; and he was lost, but he is found." I resolved to confess my sins to my father and beg his forgiveness.

The morning following, at five of the clock, Robin arrived on a hired bay nag. He was grievous sick with a burning fever, vomiting, uneasiness, and abiding pain in his head and body, all of which of a sudden had come upon him but a quarter of an hour before. I laid him abed in the guest-chamber and summoned Doctor Troth. He examined Robin at length, called me aside, and said, "Your friend hath the smallpox. From what I understood from his confused speech, the young fool fornicated with a whore who had but slight symptoms of the disease—a moderate fever, tolerable pains in her body and head—but sufficient in my extensive observation to give him the virulent variety that will most likely kill him. Nevertheless, and make a note of this, prohibit him wine and drink, excepting small beer with toast in it. Feed him oatmeal porridge and barley broth. Then we shall see.

"I almost forgot," Dr. Troth said. "Robin bade me stable and have his hired mare fed and watered. If you will pay the cost, I will have Charlton at his stable on Sheep Street tend to it."

"Pray do so," said I. "I will pay the cost."

Robin could not swallow the oatmeal porridge I proffered him, nor rouse himself to use the chamber pot. I changed his filthy bedclothes six times in the four-and-twenty hours after his arrival. He gave off a distinctive, sweet smell. I heard him sobbing in the night.

My uncle Roger paid Troth his two shillings. That

day, and every morning thereafter, for the weeks following, my uncle likewise had firewood, wholesome victuals,
and drink brought to the parsonage. Ben, my father's
housekeeper, and the cook, all of whom lived in the parsonage, remained there with my father, Robin, and me;
the two maid servants slept in the small, thatched barn
at the bottom of the garden. Save Ben, they refused to
tend Robin, nor did my father blame them. Ben and I
undertook the task ourselves.

My father's shortness of breath eased. On the third
evening, I decided to tell him the truth about my acqui-
escence in Robin's blasphemy, &c. Father was seated
upon the edge of his bed with his naked feet on the floor.
I confessed everything to him.

He said, "You aided and abetted Robin's blasphemy
and Patch's buggery. For shame! For shame! Shame
on you!"

His face was sweaty and pale. He stood up, grasped
his left arm above the elbow, and cried out, "You have
killed me!"

He fell face down upon the floor, full upon his nose,
and died. His broken nose bled copiously.

I howled. Ben came into the room, lifted the corpse,
and laid it upon the bed. Then he cleansed the bloody
floor with a wet rag.

The word spread throughout the parish during the night that my father was dead. At five of the clock the following morning, four women arrived to wash and lay out my father's corpse. Ben rose above his station for the first time I could remember and dismissed them. I waxed very angry with him, until he said to me, "Sir, these matters with your father's corpse are best handled by us, for our love of him."

He entreated me to pay the women their customary fee and have them fed their customary plenteous meal by the cook in the kitchen. They took the money, ate the food, drank four pots of ale, and fled the house with relief. Ben put off my father's clothes, then thoroughly and tenderly washed his naked body and cut a long strip from clean linen bedclothes. When I had squeezed my father's gaping jaws closed, Ben tied them shut with the length of linen by wrapping it beneath the corpse's chin and about its head. God struck me dumb; I could not speak a word for an hour. Then I said to Ben, "My heart's broken. I shall never be merry again."

I burned my father's surplice upon the kitchen grate. In the afternoon, a joiner and his apprentice, whom my uncle Roger had hired, carried a coffin and two trestles into the parsonage and placed the coffin upon the trestles in the parlor. I took a better piece of linen bedclothes from the household stock for a shroud. Ben and I wrapped my father's naked corpse therein, carried it from its bedchamber, and laid it out in the coffin.

When I lay abed in the dark, all the bugbears and terrors of the night, the fairybabes of tombs and yawning graves remained before mine eyes. I bitterly inveighed with myself and thought that I should cut my throat to be revenged for my father's death.

Because of the smallpox in the house, few of my father's parishioners were brave enough to come and view his corpse. His face was changing before mine eyes: it seemed to me that his sunken cheeks and eyes belonged to a stranger.

Only my aunt Eliza possessed the courage to come and view him. In her heart she was the brave daughter and wife of English yeomen. As was usual, she cast a covetous eye on the carved oaken chest in the parlor. All of my father's former servants viewed the corpse as well. Among my uncle Roger's farm servants, Esau Fletcher and Peter Patch came to the parsonage house.

Esau said, "I shall always remember your father's last sermon. He said, 'Let all be swallowed up and nothing be seen but Christ.' So it is with me. Christ is all I see—everywhere—even here—in the presence of your dead father."

Peter Patch said, "I am here, sir, for your sake—in gratitude to you."

I said, "Lest you get caught by someone else, take care, Peter Patch. Take care!"

Said he, "I will, sir, that I will."

My father's corpse was removed to his church, where it was laid out on view for two more days. My uncle Roger insisted that I pay half the expenses of my father's funeral. My share came to four shillings and six pence.

Early Wednesday morning, I observed small red spots covering Robin's tongue. I asked him to stick it out. He called for the little cracked looking-glass, which belonged to Joan Goare, my father's old housekeeper. Robin methodically examined the reflection of the inside of his mouth and said, "The spots are everywhere, even unto my gums."

I told him the circumstances of my father's death.

He said, "Forgive me, brother. I have no tears left to shed."

Robin bade me write his father in Kent of his plight: "Beg my good father to attend me very soon, lest it be too late. Secondly, send for a Minister."

"A Minister?" said I.

"A Minister," said he. "Write Morton too, and bid him farewell for me. I will not see Cambridge again."

I wrote Morton and the Rev. Barstow, then fetched the Rev. Styles. He came with me at once, notwithstanding the fear that showed in his eyes. He offered a prayer by Robin's bed, and the three of us said, "Amen."

Robin addressed Styles thus, "I am sure the indiscreet Doctor Troth has told you how I caught this loathsome disease. Well, I am justly served. God hath rightly punished me for my whoring. Our God is a righteous God. Let my fate be an example in your sermons to errant youths. Tell my father that I died repenting my sin."

I was much astonished by his words and, after Styles left, inquired of Robin about them.

Robin said, "I lied for my father's sake."

"I told my father the truth, and it killed him," I said.

The day following, Robin's spots turned into sores that burst open within hours and oozed. At the same time, a rash appeared upon his face. By the following evening, it had spread all over his body, down to the soles of his feet. But his fever suddenly broke, and he regained his appetite, feeding himself two bowls of oatmeal porridge. He inquired after his hired mare, saying to me, "I shall yet ride old Nell back to Cambridge. And you? How fare you?"

I said, "God help me, I long for death."

"Death? Speak not of death, dear friend. Not death.

You have never tasted such apples for cider as we grow in Kent, wherein they are ground and pressed in presses made for the nonce. You drank our cider. Was it not wonderful? Our cider bestows good health and long life upon those who liberally imbibe it. Both my grandfathers, who drank only cider, lived well past eighty years of age. Why, I was raised on Kentish cider! Quickly! Write my father another letter and entreat him to bring me at least four jugs. Make that five! No, speak not to me of death."

'Twas then that I knew that it was God's will that I would catch the smallpox and die. I prayed, "Let me be of good courage, for Thou art just. Thou art justly punishing me for my transgressions against Thee, which are a sign that I am damned."

From then on, I looked upon the progression of the disease in Robin as foretelling my future on this earth. His fever returned. He said to me, "After my death, bring Nell back to Drake's stable on Market Hill in Cambridge, wherein I hired her for sixpence a day. Or better yet, bid my father do so. Entreat him, I pray you, to pay my debts. They do not amount to much. Contrary to your expectations, dear brother, I was careful with my money. And take good care of Nell. She is an honest nag."

I never received an answer from Morton, but Robin's

father wrote him that immediately he recovered from a fever and a congestion of the lungs, he would ride in haste to be with his beloved ailing son.

On the third day, Robin's rash became raised bumps; on the fourth, the bumps had hollows in their centers that resembled a navel. Robin called again for the little cracked looking-glass, gazed upon his disfigured countenance, and said, "In truth, being fair of face gave me much pleasure."

My father's funeral was on the thirtieth of January in the year of Christ 1618. His will provided for mourning gowns to be worn by his family and servants, together with seven bushels of wheat to be made into bread and as much cheese and drink as was needful to be given to the poor. That night, by the light of the full moon, I looked upon his fresh grave.

Robin died the morning following. We exchanged no last words. His father arrived, with an obstinate cough, a day thereafter and took Robin's body home to Maidstone, in Kent. He paid Charlton three shillings for stabling and feeding Nell and agreed to have her returned to her stable in Cambridge. Before the Reverend Barstow departed, the Reverend Styles repeated to him, unknowing, Robin's lies that he was repentant for his sins.

I said to the Rev. Barstow, "My solace is that while Robin was dying he was full of Christ and fit for heaven." I could not abide thinking of him writhing in flames with a burst stomach and steaming guts.

Upon the third of February, I began repeating Robin's symptoms, viz., fever, vomiting, &c. I was laid upon the bed wherein he had died and was joined, within a two days, by Ben, who was laid upon coverlets on the floor. Doctor Troth tended us. We each gave off that sweet smallpox smell. My aunt Eliza nursed us. She fetched me the cracked looking-glass. About the fifth day, my bumps became pustules, sharply raised, round, and firm; each felt like a goose-shot stuck beneath my skin. They oozed a liquid the color of honey. My eyelids swelled so I could not see. I heard Ben say, "Hear me, my God! Let me be dead rather than blind!"

Doctor Troth prescribed fourteen drops of laudanum apiece that we drank between six and seven of the clock in the evening to assuage the agitation that came upon us every night. The laudanum sorely constipated us.

We spake together. Ben told me that his father had burned his childish body with ratsbane, spearwort, and crowfoot. He earned two pounds a year together with livery and an additional amount for meat and drink. He hoped the maid servant named Catherine would tend his garden after his death, and once cried out in his sleep, "Runcible peas!"

Awake, he said, "I am saved!"

And I said, "I am damned."

The long and the short of it is that Ben died and I survived, disfigured. I did not have the courage to gaze upon his face nor to look upon the reflection of mine own in the mirror. I wore a black-and-white enamel mourning ring upon the little finger of my left hand. My grief stole my faith. I wrote a little poem:

> My grief stole my faith
>
> And sneaked away.
>
> I cannot trace the thief.
>
> His track of tears
>
> Hath faded from my pitted cheek.

By the grace of God, my aunt Eliza went unscathed. I gave her the carved, oaken chest she coveted; not from gratitude, but out of apathy. Uncle Roger told me that I owed him two pounds and four shillings for the sufficiency of firewood, victuals, drink, and Doctor Troth's ministrations and medicines during the last weeks. I promised to repay him upon the settlement of my father's estate in the Ecclesiastical Courts, which would be four months hence.

We went through my father's effects—his feather bed, pewter plate, candle sticks, &c., which Roger considered were worth some thirty pounds. Together with ready money and the debts owed to him, I would inherit over fifty pounds. Roger was grateful that I had given my aunt Eliza the oaken chest and offered to remove its estimated value from the money I owed him, but I refused. I did not care about the above. I did not care about anything.

I impassively thought of the multitudes of us predestined damned souls who, since before time began, wait upon God to be born unto this earth, only to live a while, then die and burn in eternal hellfire.

A week thereafter, I bade farewell to my father's former servants and returned with thirteen pounds to Cambridge to complete the Michaelmas term.

I wept when I walked through Cambridge's Trumpington Gate. The Head Porter of Emmanuel lowered his eyes from my pitted face. I wept when I stepped into Robin's bare chamber—his father had preceded me—and again, when I saw the leafless walnut tree in the Quadrangle. I could not walk the streets wherein Robin and I had strolled without weeping. A soldier, bearing a pike upon his shoulder, stared at me upon the corner of the High Wand and Penny Farthing Lane.

In the end, I gathered all my possessions and returned

to the Hempstead. I told my uncle Roger that I had left Cambridge for good, and he said, "Play the man, Charles! Play the man! Resume your studies and become a Minister, as was our design."

"I cannot. If you will have me, I am here to stay until I come into my inheritance."

"You may, but you have much disappointed me. Though, I confess, I am glad to save the forty-five pounds a year you were costing me at Cambridge to make something of yourself. Well, you may live here, as you will, for as long as you like. I will feed you from my own table and give you a feather bed to sleep in. All I ask in return is that you keep my accounts, like your father did. Will you do that for me?"

"I am interested in earning money. And my father taught me well how to reckon your accounts. Pay me three pounds a year—and I will see to them for you."

He said, "I will pay you two. You are after all a novice, and a mistake on your part can cost me much."

"Pay me two pounds, ten shillings."

"Done!" he said. "But I will not pay you in addition as my servant in husbandry. Will you serve me as a common servant of husbandry for no fee?"

"I will not. You will pay me what you pay Jacob and Esau."

"Charles, my lad, we are very alike. We both value words. Words and money. Yes, like me, you are a shrewd yeoman who knows the value of a shilling! You would have made a goodly master of Hempstead! But, alas, it was not to be. Tom Foot is now my heir and my bailiff of husbandry. You will have to obey his commands. He is a forward knave who drinks too much, but your aunt Eliza thinks of him as her son—the one she could never have. She takes all things in good part but being barren. She bears great sorrow in her heart for being barren."

"Uncle, I well nigh forgot: I heard the Head Porter of Emmanuel say, 'He came home like a cuckoo in spring.'"

He said, "A good phrase. Why then you are a cuckoo! Welcome home, cuckoo! 'He came home like a cuckoo in spring.' Good! I will remember it. But that nice phrase cost me dear. Think on it! Forty-five pounds this year alone!"

Here will I spill my soul. I had no power to turn to the Lord. I was nothing but a mass of sin. I was scared of the dark, wherein I was stalked by devils.

I was sorely tempted to run my head against the wall and brain myself.

It was ploughing time. After a day's labour, I accompanied Foot to The Sign of the Bull, wherein we each drank a bottle or two of muscatel and ate a loaf of bread and a cluster of raisins.

On my solitary walks upon the Downs. I tried to decipher the song of the skylark, and the clustered bellflower, buttercups, and clovers in the south meadow, but they did not appear to me as ciphers writ by God. They were merely birdsong and flowers—nothing more; the plough was not His pen.

My aunt Eliza gave me a drink of hollyhocks, violet leaves, and fennel decocted in ale. She said, "This may purge your melancholy. I know of melancholy; it hath come and gone with me since I have known that I am barren. I ate artichokes and prayed for five years to conceive a child, but to no avail. And even when my melancholy goes, I fear it will return. I fear so even now, though it hath been four years since I last suffered from the affliction.

"Drink the decoction," she said. "And here are two shillings. I have bidden Tom to fetch Doctor Troth. Consult him. He hath helped me."

I told Doctor Troth everything—everything!—and cried out, "I have crucified Christ anew! I am damned."

He said, "You are not damned! Remove that thought

from your mind! Yours is the broken and contrite heart which Scripture tells us the Lord will not despise. Yours is the poor spirit on whom the Lord pronounces His blessing. Yours is the affliction whereof the spirit of God is called the comforter.

"Remember, the Devil is likewise a spirit and an effectual worker through corporeal means—in your instance, the humour of melancholy which runs in our blood. The humour of melancholy is an apt instrument for Satan both to weaken our bodies and terrify our minds with fantastical ideas. What will not a possessed man conceive? What strange forms of bugbears, demons, witches, and goblins? Why do witches and old women fascinate and bewitch children? Answer me that! Because of the power of Satan!

"In your spiritual and corporeal battle with him, do not play the milk sop. Be of good courage. Struggle with Satan and love God.

"Because melancholy blood is thick and gross, and therefore flows easily, I shall open your vein—the middle one of your left arm, here—and draw off ten ounces of your blood. The middle vein links together head, liver, and spleen, and as melancholy is seated in the brain, bleeding you from there will do the most good."

This being done, Doctor Troth said to me, "Mistress

Wentworth here knows the diet you must follow and will prepare it for you. Things that are wholesome and meet for melancholic folks. Eat only what she serves you; drink her decoctions and only a little ale with your food, for liquor greatly aggravates melancholy. You must abstain from drinking wine or strong spirits."

"Henceforth, I will."

"Good! Now harken unto me. Over the years, these are what I have found are most effective against melancholy. First, exercise thyself, frequently and heartily, with violent labour, even though Hippocrates forbids it. For I have discovered that in this instance he is wrong.

"Next, and most important: the world, as you know, is composed of opposites—God and the Devil, light and dark, wet and dry, &c. The humour of melancholy, for example, is cold and dry, that of choler, fiery and moist. Taken together, opposites make up the whole of every-thing. Therefore, act the opposite of what you feel. You feel vile, useless, and unworthy, therefore constantly do something that makes you feel good, useful, and worthy in God's eyes."

My aunt Eliza, who was standing by my bed, said to me, "That is why I nursed you and Ben, even though I was terrified of the smallpox. It made me feel good, useful, and worthy in God's eyes, as Doctor Troth said, and doing thus, when I can, keeps my melancholy at bay. The Lord judged me right to do so, for He spared me from catching the disease."

I was always in pain between my breasts—as if a great weight were pressing thereon. I suffered palpitations and, like my late father, shortness of breath. I lived in fear, never free, resolute, or secure, and always anxious without reason. Either I was unable to sleep or slept away the day. My aunt Eliza said that both were caused by the melancholic dryness of my brain. My uncle Roger roused me to work, and I exhausted myself with vigorous labor.

I searched for another occupation on the farm that would make me feel useful and worthy, but found none. One day, I watched Hal, Patch's sheep dog, throw a big black ram that had challenged the dog for supremacy over the ewes. Hal ran along the ram's flank, shoved against his shoulder, and as it turned to butt, threw him down. Hal then led the flock away, returned, and with a pull on the black ram's shoulder wool, set him upon his feet again. I laughed for the first time in months. Patch stood by playing upon his shepherd's pipe. The air was filled with his music.

In June, my uncle hired five shearmen. They, Patch,

Jacob, Esau, Foot, and I washed Roger's flock of two hundred fifty-one sheep in his dammed-up stream with a gravel bed, by the pen. We plucked the foul and loose wool from about their udders, while Patch examined their legs and hooves. It took half a day to drive all the sheep through the washing pool. An old ewe, distressed that I had washed her behind the ears, placed her two front hooves upon my breast and shoved me over backwards into the water. I laughed again.

We spent three days shearing the sheep. We sorted them first, letting the young lambs go. We then sheared the ewes that were still suckling. The rams were done apart. Rooks and magpies picked over the sheep for maggots. Patch carried a small box of Stockholm tar to treat blow-fly, maggots, and broken skin. He smeared on the tar and sang the old song:

> A shepherd on a hill he sat,
> He had his tar box and his hat
> And his name was Jolly-Jolly Watt.

In the late afternoon of the second day, a ewe caught her right foreleg in a hole and broke it. Patch slashed her throat with a pair of shears and wept; his tears ran down the sides of his nose. He walked with me into the midst of some green-winged orchids growing in the west meadow and said, "That ewe whose throat I just cut was very like the darling I buggered near the honey tree. I cannot help myself. Whenever I spy a frisky and comely ewe, with a long, thick, soft, and curly fleece, the Devil stretches my yard.

"Goodwife Barret hath a charm for me, a special something wore upon a string about my neck. I know not what. But it costs ten pence. Can you lend me the money until New Year's Day? Goodwife Barret also tells me I must say, 'The Lord is my shepherd,' thrice, whenever a comely ewe catches my eye. But I must needs have ten pence, sir. Could you find it in your heart to give me ten pence?"

"Here you are, sirrah."

"Why, thank you sir, thank you! I am once more in your debt, sir."

After the shearing, the five hired shearmen, my uncle Roger, and the rest of us at the Hempstead fell to quaffing ale and eating much mutton, bread, and clotted cream. I drank but one pot of ale.

The shorn fleece was given over to five hired maid servants in husbandry, who rolled and sorted them according to quality in the wool-chamber and packed it into one and one-half woolpacks. This labour took the women three days. They finished on a cool evening. A fine mist hovered above the warm woolpacks. Patch piped a mournful tune. As weary as I was, I could not sleep and lay awake till dawn.

My aunt Eliza served me suppers meet for my melancholy. Thrice a week I ate calf, wether mutton, and rabbit stew.

My uncle Roger's flock yielded one and a half standard sacks of good quality fleece, weighing three hundred and sixty-four pounds, which we brought three loads in his wagon to Winterbourne and sold them to John Wells, the young clothier in Howard Street, for twelve pounds. We came to an agreement at The Sign of the Man at Arms over two bottles of sack, of which I drank one cup. Wells had recently inherited his business from his deceased father and was seeking a partner to invest in it.

On our way home, my uncle said to me, "I love you, my lad. It pains me to see you moping about. I will lend you fifty pounds without interest if you invest it in Wells's business. Making a profit always makes me merry. It might do the same for you."

I hired my father's attorney, Mr. Dashwood. He and Wells's attorney prepared the contract. On Friday morning of the following week, I became Wells's partner.

He was a plain, honest Christian. For my investment of fifty pounds, he promised me a return of at least three pounds a year when he had sold his cloth. I bought wool from the local farmers, learned to drive a wagon, and took the wool to our women labourers in their cottages to be carded and spun. I paid them for their work and then brought the spun yarn to be woven into cloth by men in their homes. I delivered the woven cloth to the fulling-mill on the Frome, wherein it was washed, shrunk, and tentered. The finishing of the cloth was done at Wells's. He had the cloth dyed by the town dyers.

I have related the above in detail because I rejoiced in witnessing the honest labor that fed and clothed sixty-nine Christians and their families. I watched Goodwife Stone carding, John Johnson at his loom, Robert Hayman raising the cloth's nap, &c. My work was essential to them and eased my soul. I was no longer stalked by devils.

With the ten pence I lent him, Peter Patch bought a charm from Goodwife Barret that would calm his passion for ewes. The charm was a dried ram's pizzle, which he wore about his neck on a string. It smelled of sorcery to me. Goodwife Barret also bade Patch to recite the first verse from Psalm 23—"The Lord is my shepherd, &c."—whenever he spied a frisky ewe, with long, thick, soft, curly fleece.

It rained every night during the first week of November. When the sky cleared for a few hours, a blazing star appeared in the southeast. About the same time, there were many reports of wars between England, France, and the Low Countries. The Reverend Styles preached in a sermon that the comet foretold that the End of Days was at hand. The battle of Armageddon between Protestants and Papists—Christ and Antichrist—had begun, and it would soon end with the Second Coming. It was reported that there was a great stir in Bohemia about choosing a king, whom we hoped would be a Protestant. That might have helped to make a Protestant Emperor in Germany.

In January, we heard that there was a very great Armada provided and gathered in Spain for England. It was reported to be greater than the one in '88. But God was with us, as you know, and nothing came of it. Yet we all felt in Winterbourne that the Last Days were upon us. The pastors of Winterbourne's three churches called for three days of mortification and fasting. I felt overjoyed at the imminent coming of the Last Judgment. Soon I would know whether I was damned or saved.

Wells sold his cloth in December to a traveling buyer for a London cloth merchant. The price of cloth had risen—I earned four pounds and three shillings. Thereafter, I laboured all the day about the farm. Once, upon a frosty morning, I spied Peter Patch, wrapped in his ragged cloak, driving his flock. Icicles hung from his beard; tufts of fleece stuck to his hair. When it snowed, he and I drove the sheep into the steading next to the barn and packed them tight to keep them warm.

Tom Foot was oft drunk but was able to manage the Hempstead. Patch's sciatica was worse. He hobbled on his left leg and leaned upon his forked staff to help him walk. My uncle Roger's hair and beard had turned grey, while his long mustache remained brown. Aunt Eliza, like myself, was most melancholic during the autumn and winter.

She said, "I hate the long, cold nights, wherein I am exhausted by sadness, but the Devil keeps me awake till dawn."

We mated the sheep in May and June. Then we washed and sheared them and sold their wool to Wells. I returned to work with him in Winterbourne. Lambing would be in October. The little lambs were born in hovels and lambing pens. We reared the lambs in the Hempstead farmhouse for the Christmas market. Patch stopped milking the ewes at Lammas to let them grow strong and ready for the rams in the autumn.

Late on a subsequent August afternoon, after I had returned from working in town, I happened upon Patch gazing lovingly at a ewe. Because I was behind him, he did not see me. He fingered the dried ram's pizzle about his neck and thrice, in a loud voice, quoted from the first verse of the Psalm, "The Lord is my shepherd." Of a sudden, he looked about, saw me and into my eyes, and started away, hobbling upon his forked staff.

Then, on a rainy April day, Esau caught Patch buggering a ewe upon one of the hill pastures and bade him drive the flock down to the farmhouse. There Esau cried out, "To the gallows with you, and after that, hell!"

Then he said to uncle Roger, "Master, bid him kill the unclean beast," but Roger said, "If you buy me another, I will."

Patch said to me, "You warned me, sir, but I paid you no heed. Satan, by his wicked Ministers in the form of ewes—darling ewes!—drew me unto him. There's no hope for me, save an easier death than strangling at the end of a rope. Sir, I charge you once again: break my neck upon the gallows tree. Will you promise me?"

I did not answer him.

He said, "Give me leave to bid farewell to Hal," and called the wet, stinking dog after him into the tool crib. The dog's fur smelled like wet wool. We heard a yelp and ran within. Patch had slashed Hal's throat with a pair of shears. Patch said, "I do not have the courage to kill myself. Hal, you died an easier death than your master will. All for my love of ewes with long, thick, curly fleece. Ah, me! Alas that I was not born a ram."

Patch was indicted, tried for buggery, and condemned to be hanged at the latter part of May. After the trial, at which Esau was a witness, he asked me if I was disposed to breaking Patch's neck, and I rejoined that I was not.

"Good," said he. "Let him strangle slowly."

My uncle hired another shepherd, a youth named John Cuttler. His dog's name was Pru. I imagined Patch, leaning upon his forked staff, hobbling to the cart that would take him to Gallows Hill. I could no longer go for solitary walks about the Downs and the meadows. I avoided the honey tree. The whole of Hempstead troubled my heart. Almost everything there brought Patch—my disgust and my cowardice—to mind: the hovels and lambing pens, the steading next to the barn, the farmhouse itself wherein we had reared the lambs.

I repaired alone to The Sign of the Bull and guzzled sack. The folk there questioned me about Patch. Jane Fuller, averting her eyes from my pitted face, asked me about him. I drunkenly turned away from them all. The Reverend Doctor Styles took as his subject of a sermon,

Leviticus 18:23, but from the new translation of Scripture that smacks of popery. We at New Plymouth know the verse from the Great Bible, which is truly holy writ: "Thou shalt not also lie with any beast to be defiled therewith."

The day appointed for Patch's hanging drew nigh. Throngs from nearby towns and the country round about gathered in Winterbourne. A woman from Dorset was delivered before her time; her babe died. The inns were full. The poor slept on straw pallets in the streets. My aunt Eliza sold cheese, butter, chickens, and eggs to the crowd.

The day before the hanging, I packed my knapsack and two bundles, including my mother's gloves, then bid farewell to my aunt and uncle. They tried hard to dissuade me from leaving, but I was inflexible in my resolve. I knew my conscience would compel me to try to break Patch's neck as he hung on the gibbet. I was terrified that I would bungle the task and prolong his suffering.

I contrived with Wells to continue payments due me on my investment.

He asked, "Whither shall I send you the money?"

I said, "To London. I will write you my place of residence when I am settled there."

I bade farewell to my attorney, Mr. Dashwood, who, by the grace of Providence, was a good friend of Mr. Henry Appletree, a London attorney, whose chambers were hard by The Sign of the Bear and Ragged Staff, at Charing Cross, in the parish of St. Martin in the Fields.

Dashwood said, "Appletree and I studied law together at Gray's Inn. He owes me many a favor. I will write him a letter today commending you for a position as one of his clerks, for which your education—especially your skill in Latin—well qualifies you. If you are diligent at the tasks he assigns you, you may, in time, do more than just copy out legal papers for him. He advises his clients on business matters, family negotiations, wills, and criminal concerns. He is likewise a money lender who negotiates transactions between merchants and goldsmiths."

"What would I earn as his clerk?"

"I should say seven pounds a year, together with bed and board."

"Seven pounds!" said I. "With my three pounds per annum from my investment with Wells, I will live very well indeed."

"You are dressed like a husbandman, in your breeches and jerkin. Do you own a suit?"

"A black one, with silver buttons on the doublet."

"Good! And a cloak? What about a cloak and a hat?"

"I have two worn cloaks, and a black hat with a torn brim."

He said, "You will need a new plain black cloak. Perhaps with a feather. Inquire of Appletree if you can wear a feather in your hat. Spend money on your apparel; 'tis a good business investment. Put yourself in the hands of a goodly London tailor and a haberdasher."

I said, "I'll put myself in the hands of God, a goodly tailor, and a haberdasher, in that order."

He said, "Appletree's twenty-two-year-old daughter, Sarah, had smallpox as a girl of ten. Smallpox! There, you will have something in common—something to talk about! Appletree is seeking a husband for her. Play your cards skillfully, and who knows? Be assured, she will have an ample dowry."

At dawn upon the morning following, at the foot of Gallows Hill, I climbed into the wagon carriage bound for the metropolis.

My uncle Roger said to me, "I have asked Mr. Wells to keep my accounts in your stead."

I said, "I am responsible for my father's death."

"His death was God's will. Blame not yourself. Here is a farewell gift for you. Twenty pounds. Invest it wisely. The goldsmiths in London will give you a return of four or five percent for your money. Look to it! Fare thee well, my dear boy. Send me a simile from London. Oh, I almost forgot. Here's a fine pair of kid gloves from my shop that will keep thy hands warm."

"Thank you. I shall think of you when I wear them."

The wagon pulled away. For an instant, I thought I saw Mary amidst the crowd climbing Gallows Hill.

PART II

ON THE MORNING OF THE eleventh of May in the year of Christ 1618, I alighted from my wagon at the inn named The Sign of the Bear and Ragged Staff in Charing Cross, which is in the City of Westminster, a suburb without the walls of London. The inn was crowded with plump, muddy whores, boy prostitutes, and cutthroats armed with daggers. The press of rowdy maltbugs lugged ale, even as little pigs lug at their dam's teats.

I hastened back into the street and found Appletree's chambers on the right hand.

He said, "I was expecting you. My old friend Dashwood recommends you highly. My business is good, and I have thought for some time past of hiring another clerk. You come at the opportune moment. I favor the fortunate. They bring good luck. Dashwood writes that you studied Divinity at Cambridge but went down because of the death of your father."

"Yes, sir."

"Hence your mourning ring."

"Hence my mourning ring. Yes, sir."

"This gold and coral ring of mine, which cost me five pounds, is inscribed with magic signs that prevail against witchcraft, possession by the Devil, thunder, lightning, storm, and tempest. It hath overcome my enemies and made me famous in my profession. But it prevailed not against the smallpox. My daughter, Sarah, was stricken with the smallpox at the age of eleven. What about you?"

"I was stricken less than a year ago, sir."

"You will enjoy Sarah's company. I had her well educated. 'Twas the least I could do. She sayeth with Virgil, '*Nimium ne crede colori!*'"

"I agree, sir. Trust not too much in your color; that is, your complexion. I took my complexion for granted. I never gave it a thought. God taught me otherwise."

He said, "So my friend Dashwood was correct. You have a command of Latin."

"I do, sir."

"Show me a sample of your handwriting. Copy this out."

I copied out some items of an inventory postmortem of the furnishings of Elizabeth, Lady Berkeley's London house, viz.: "Item, five pieces of tapestry hangings of imagery; Item, a crimson rug, &c &c.," and Appletree said, "You write a fair hand."

Then he said, "I will pay you six pounds per annum, together with room and board, to be my clerk. I have working for me another clerk and seven scriveners. I represent many London merchants who hire out their ships. You will be required to copy out their contracts, as well as others, along with various and sundry deeds, wills, inventories postmortem, and business letters. Some will be in English and some in Latin. Do you accept the position I am now offering you?"

"I will, sir, gladly."

"Do you own a black cloak and hat?"

"I have two worn black cloaks and a torn hat, sir. I need you to recommend to me a good tailor and haberdasher."

He told me where to find them nearby and said, "Buy yourself a simple cloak and hat. We should wear attire everyone to his degree, for it is very hard nowadays to know who is noble, who is worshipful, who is a gentleman, and who is not. You are not a nobleman, a cleric, nor a gentleman, but my clerk. Dress like one."

"I will, sir. May I wear a feather in my hat?"

He said, "That you may. A white feather in a black hat. My daughter, Sarah, wears a white lace veil."

I inquired of him the name and whereabouts of an honest goldsmith with whom I could invest my twenty pounds. He gave me a letter for John Loop by The Sign of the Rook on Goldsmith's Row.

Then he said I was to eat with him, his other clerk, and his family in his chambers in the fair tenement, south of Charing Cross, on the left hand. He bade the other clerk, Michael Hendy, to take me to our chamber on the left hand of The Sign of the Bear and Ragged Staff. We repaired thence, wherein I found a decent bed that we would share, clean bedclothes, a cupboard, a chest, and a table, but only one stool.

Behold an act of Providence! Hendy said to me that a local joiner named Zachariah Rigdale, on Suffolk Street, had recently replaced the rusty iron hinges on the chest. Hendy said, "Rigdale will make us a goodly stool," and we went round to see him.

Thus, for want of a stool, God willed that I meet Zachariah Rigdale, a man of about thirty years of age, who said, "I will make you a joint stool for one pound. Come back for it in a week, as my apprentice and I are presently busy making a table and two chairs."

Then Rigdale said to me, "I see you wear a mourning ring, sir. For whom do you mourn?"

I said, "My father, who is lately dead."

He said, "I mourn my dear wife, Ann, who died two years ago on Mid-Summer Eve. Our babe followed soon thereafter. A cough took her. Her name was Joan. She had the daintiest hands and feet you ever saw!"

Hendy and I later dined in our master's large, well-appointed chambers. Mistress Appletree bore a pretty little spaniel in her bosom. She nourished the dog with meat at the table. The Appletrees used Hendy and me as friends, not servants. They not only allowed us to sit with them, above the salt, but shared the dishes served by their butler. We shared a leg of mutton, a loin of veal, and a chicken.

Appletree said to me, "Shall I be your carver? Will you have this hen's wing?"

"I will, sir, thank you."

"And wine? Some sack? Here, wash your liver with a cup of sack."

"Thank you, sir!"

He bade me greet his daughter, Sarah, who indeed wore a white lace veil. I glimpsed her large dark eyes behind her veil. She gazed at my pitted face. Then she said to me, "Master Michael, here, went to Oxford for two years. Are you an Oxford man, Master Charles?"

"I studied Divinity at Cambridge, Mistress, but did not take a degree."

"How so?"

"My father died, and I did not feel myself fit to be a Minister of God."

She said, "I have wrestled with Him for some years now."

"Indeed!" said I. "You are very young, Mistress, to wrestle with God."

"Our common affliction roused me to it as a child."

"I can well understand that."

She said, "Then, sir, we understand each other."

The morning following, my master said to me, "Well, what do you think of my dear Sarah?"

"I think she is a goodly maiden, sir."

"I am pleased to hear it. You are a big, tall man. She favors big, tall men. Tell me, Wentworth, do you keep the Sabbath?"

"I do, sir."

"All the day?"

"The whole day, yes sir."

"Would you bowl with me in St. James Park this coming Sabbath after church?"

"Oh no, sir. By my faith, I could not."

"By your faith," said he. "And what faith is that? Are you a Puritan?"

"Yes, sir, I am, sir, though I do not like that word. I am not pure, but just one of God's people."

He said, "You are very sure of yourself."

"No, sir, I live in doubt."

He gave me leave, and I went to buy me a black cloak and a black hat, with a French block and a white feather, for five pounds. That left me fourteen pounds to invest with John Loop, goldsmith, by The Sign of the Rook on Goldsmith's Row, the fairest frame of houses and shops that I ever saw within the walls of London. Loop said that I could expect a return of five percent per annum. I put my money with him.

Passing London Bridge, I counted the heads of twelve traitors stuck on spikes on the gatehouse at the south end of the bridge. Five other rotting heads had been blown off their spikes onto the street. One lay hard by my right foot. I looked away.

Upon my return to Charing Cross, I spied a dog carrying a hand between its jaws. I saw the coach of his lordship, the Earl of Warwick. It took up almost the whole width of a narrow cobbled street. The coach's wheels squeaked and clattered upon the stones. I glimpsed the splendors of Whitehall and went into Westminster Abbey, wherein for a penny, I gazed upon the tombs and monuments of the kings and queens of England, covered all over with gilding and carved in a most beautiful manner.

In the crowded streets, I wondered about the people: the porters, the beggars, the gentlemen and ladies, the fish wives, apprentices, merchants, a constable, a vendor of hot oat cakes, the chimney sweeps, the whores, and above all, myself. Who amongst us, if any, was predestined to be saved?

I bought a broadsheet of a ballad called "The Rat Catcher's Song," which I copied out in a letter for my uncle Roger and sent to my attorney, informing the former of my new position and place of residence and of my investment. Then I wrote, "I have not come upon a simile, but here for your enjoyment, dear uncle, is a verse sold on the streets of London town. It is an authentic voice of the City. The line, 'And peepeth into holes' is vivid, is it not?"

I still have the broadsheet; the ballad follows:

> Rats or mice, ha' ye any rats, mice, polecats, or weasels,
> Or ha' ye any old sows sick of the measles?
> I can kill them and I can kill moles
> And I can kill vermins that creepeth up or creepeth down
> And peepeth into holes.

I began my labours early Friday morning, the fifteenth of May. It was tedious. From that day on, I never ceased to contrive how to escape the tediousness of copying out inventories postmortem &c. in English and Latin.

Mr. Appletree, his family, and servants were parishioners of St. Martin in the Fields. The Reverend Doctor Alexander Sommer was our pastor. He wore a gorgeous surplice. The Rev. Sommer was the favorite of the noblemen in the vicinity of Charing Cross. They filled his Sunday services, wearing great ruffs made of cambric, holland, lawn, or the finest other cloth that could be got for money. And their hats! Sometimes they were sharp on the crown, perking up like the shaft of a steeple, standing a quarter of a yard above the crown of their wearers' heads. Others were flat and broad on the crown, like the battlement of a castle. Another sort had round crowns, sometimes with one kind of band, sometimes with another, now black, now white, now russet, now red, now green, now yellow. They held these fantastical plumed monstrosities in their laps during a service, while the Rev. Doctor Sommer took as the subject of his sermon, Mark.14:7 in the new translation of Scripture: "For ye have the poor with you always."

The Rev. Doctor spake four hours. I remember but one thing that he said, "God made some rich and some poor so that two excellent virtues might flourish in the world: charity in the rich and patience in the poor."

After the service, Mistress Sarah said to me, "Why do the streets swarm with beggars? You cannot stand still but ten or twelve of the poor wretches come breathe in your face. Many of them have plague sores! What is the cause that so many pretty little boys and girls wander up and down in the streets, loiter in the churches, and lie under stalls in the cold nights? Can this be God's design? I refuse to believe it!"

Her lace veil stirred with her every breath. I wanted to see her pitted face and yet was repelled by the prospect. I was much moved by her compassion for the poor. Yet I felt nothing towards her as befits a man towards a maid.

I went to an apothecary and asked him for an herb that could encourage me to procreate. He prescribed saffron boiled in sweet wine, saying "Drink but one cup every day, lest more drive you unto a frenzy." I drank one cup every day for two weeks to no avail.

One night, lying side by side abed in our chamber, Hendy asked me, "Are you interested in taking Mistress Sarah to wife? I will confess to you that I have sometimes thought of courting her. 'Tis said her father will provide her with a large dowry. In truth, the prospect of marrying a fortune tempts me, but I cannot help but wonder what lies beneath her veil.

"What of her nose? What is left of it? You cannot tell through her veil. Suppose the flesh between her nostrils has been eaten away? 'Tis possible. One big hole! Pah!"

———✦———

I received an answer to my letter, writ in my attorney's hand, from my uncle Roger.

He thanked me for "The Rat Catcher's Song," writing, "I have already committed it to my prodigious memory—prodigious—that is my new word. I learned it from your attorney." Then he wrote,

> *Peter Patch was hanged after a felon who stole firewood from Sir Francis Fulford. The felon's brother brake his neck. Up to that moment, I was determined to do likewise for Peter Patch but thereafter could not bring myself to suffer that drenching, just as your father, true Christian that he was, had suffered it for Mary Puckering. God forgive me, but I could not do it. Poor Peter paid the price. It took him many minutes to die. I shall spare you the details.*

The evening following, Zachariah Rigdale brought

me my new stool. Hendy was that night at the Bear and Ragged Staff. He reveled there night by night with his wild companions repeating lascivious jests.

Rigdale said, "God help me, I have a great passion to preach the Gospel. I have always had this passion. I was born and raised with my younger brother, John, in London. Poor John! I preached to him on every occasion that was afforded me. My greatest joy as a boy was to harken unto the preachers preaching on a Sabbath afternoon at Paul's Cross. At the age of fourteen, I preached a sermon there on the text of Isaiah 6:7 wherein an angel of the Lord touched the Prophet's mouth with a burning coal saying, 'Thine iniquity shall be taken away, and thy sin shall be purged.'

"I was arrested for preaching without a licence. My master—for I was by then apprenticed to a joiner—paid my fine.

"Look you, I am a master joiner. I make a goodly amount of money. I belong to the Company of Joiners. We keep a garden in Friar Lane wherein I read Scripture on a bench under a pear tree. Sometimes, in the garden, my heart is filled with the spirit of the Lord and I preach to the pear tree. The preaching of the Word is a gift not tied to the person of a Minister!

"But it grows now very late. I want very much to hear

of your life. I warrant that the Lord hath touched you, too. I could tell from the change in your countenance as I spake. Come to my chambers sometime after a Sabbath ends. I live above my shop. There you will speak to me and I will harken unto you, as on this night you have harkened unto me."

One morning, my master bade me accompany Sarah and her maid into London to buy some linen. In the shop, Sarah purchased two ells of cambric to make into lace. On the way home, she asked me when I was stricken with the smallpox and I replied, "Recently."

"Thank God for it! You had a happy youth. I was stricken at the age of eleven. The smallpox killed my two younger sisters. One day, at the age of thirteen, I heard a pretty gentlewoman say to her husband, 'I am sick at heart for that poor girl but cannot wrest my gaze from her pitted cheeks.' I have worn a veil ever since. Why hath God done this to me?"

"Perhaps to bring you closer to Him by your suffering."

"That is what I strive to believe. Have you been born again?"

"Yes, by the grace of God, I have. But my faith in Christ is a feeble thing."

She said, "Alas for us!"

And I said, "Alas for us!"

We walked to the Thames, which was filled with hundreds of boats and hundreds and hundreds of swans, swimming in snowy flocks. We watched a crow drop into the water, catch a dead fish floating atop the waves, and fly away with it.

Sarah said, "I know not if God cares for the sparrow, but 'tis certain that He dotes upon the carrion crow."

My master oft did business in The Bear and Ragged Staff, and I sometimes sat with him and his client, making notes. I learned many words describing the degrees of the drunken, blaspheming vagabonds around us: rufflers (thieving beggars, apprentice uprightmen), uprightmen (leaders of robber bands), hookers or anglers (thieves who steal through open windows with hooks), &c. &c. This was the world of *kinchin koes* wherein Ben had lived.

I yearned for Ben's garden, Dorset's meadows and downs, and the smell of roses and freshly mown hay rather than the noisome stench of horse manure from the mews and offal rotting in the muddy streets. There is a street just north of Charing Cross called Dirty Street, which could be the name of all the streets in London and its suburbs.

One morning, my master said, "Come with me, Wentworth, to Newgate Prison, wherein, at the behest of the prison chaplain, I shall try to save a horse thief named Francis Crocker from a horrible death. He stole a gelding from a stable on Algate Street and sold it for sixteen pounds to a knight before being arrested, arraigned, and imprisoned. The poor fool stood mute and spake not at his arraignment. He would not reveal to the magistrate the whereabouts of his stolen money, which would otherwise be confiscated by the king. As a result, he was sentenced to be pressed to death. Aye, you heard me: pressed to death.

"He'll be pressed to death by huge weights laid upon a board over his breasts, with sharp stones placed under his back. And he'll be pressed slowly. Very slowly. It will take him two or three days to die. In the end, his ribs will break like frozen twigs. Man's sinful desires make him impatient of government and subjection. Untamed spirits require judgment, prisons, even torture and the gallows to keep the world quiet.

"Crocker held his peace to save his goods for his wife and babe. But if Crocker surrenders the sixteen pounds, he will only be hanged at Wapping. He hath hid the money somewhere. His wife knows its hiding place but will not tell without his permission. A dutiful wife, she obeys him in all things. He does not know it, but they will likely put her to the torture. She beseeched the prison chaplain—an idle, drunken lout—who asked me to try to persuade her husband to confess. Not for herself, mind you, but for his sake. She loves him dearly.

"The common people, you know, can love each other dearly. Why, we are told that some of 'em are saved!

"Come with me this morning to Newgate, Wentworth, and I will show you that even though I do not keep the Sabbath as well as you, I am as compassionate a Christian."

"I doubt it not, sir."

"Yes, you do, but durst not say so. Well, I agree with the Reverend Doctor Sommer: God made some rich and some poor for a divine purpose."

Crocker, chained up to a wet stone wall by his wrists, was being fed a loaf of barley bread and given ale to sip from a cup, which was held to his lips by his wife, who had laid their babe on a pile of rotten straw at her feet. Crocker was as pale as a new cheese. He said, "Body of me, wife, pick up the babe! Pick up the babe, or he will be eaten alive by rats. There's a rat in here as big as a cat. I durst not close my eyes to sleep lest he gnaw off my toes. Rats, fleas, and flies! Rats, fleas and flies! Fie! The flies crawl up my nose."

His wife said, "Master Appletree, the attorney, is here to entreat you to reveal where you hid the sixteen pounds."

My master said, "Crocker, I pray you to comfort your good wife by surrendering the money. What say you?"

"I say no! And again no! For if I do, who will care for her and our babe? They will be forced out on the streets to beg and to sleep in the mud beneath the hedges. They will starve or freeze. I cannot inflict that fate on those I so much love. What sort of a husband and father would I be?"

My master said, "You will be the kind of husband that condemns his wife to torture. She will likely be put to the torture unless she tells where the money is hid."

"The torture?"

"The whip and the rack."

"I did not know. I cannot bear it. I will tell."

Appleton said, "Where is the money hid?"

"Do you know Bermondsey? 'Tis a little village on the south side of the river, opposite the Tower. We were born there, my wife and I, and there I thought my money would allow her to buy a cottage, a vegetable garden, some fruit trees, and a cow. I care not for fruit myself. She and the babe could live a goodly life in Bermondsey.

"I worked as a groom in a stable on Algate Street. I stole a milk-white gelding and sold it to a gentleman for sixteen pounds. Sixteen pounds! Body of me, I was a rich man!

"The villainous knave who got me arrested is another groom named William Williams. He wanted eight pounds for himself, but I would not share the money. The Judas betrayed me. God hath marked him with a hare lip. He is a mournful soul who cannot find himself a wife. Tell me, sir. How long does it take to be pressed to death?"

"Two or three days."

"Body of me! As long as that? With God's help, I will endure it for love of my wife and child."

His wife wiped his sweaty brow with a torn rag, kissed his filthy naked feet, and said, "Francis, tell the gentleman where you hid the money."

"I will, my dear Dorothy, I will. Dost think that I would allow you to be whipped and racked?"

He said to my master, "I buried the sack of coins in the churchyard of St. Peter's in Bermondsey, on the right-hand side, beyond the bones by the wall."

"I'll see to it."

"Thank you, sir. Hold our babe up to me, Dorothy, that I may kiss his lips."

My master said to Dorothy, "Here is a pound and sixpence."

"Thank you, master. God save you, sir. You are a true Christian."

"I am of the same mind. But tell that to my clerk here."

Crocker said, "Good wife, call the keeper hither and pay him two shillings. For two shillings he will give me fresh straw, a goodly portion of meat to eat, and cider to drink. I crave a cup or two of cider ere I die. On the other hand, cider is a windy drink. So are all fruits windy in themselves. Call the keeper! We will have us a feast. But no fruit or cider! They make me fart. Dear God, I want to live!"

Then he said to me, "Good master, I thank you for your tears."

"You are most heartily welcome, Sirrah. Would that mine eyes could mint shillings for you."

"Good master, thy tears are worth more to me than shillings, for 'twas your pity for me that minted them. You are a compassionate Christian—a good man!"

"Thank you."

I related what had transpired at Newgate to Mistress Sarah at dinner. She asked me, "'With God's help, I will endure it for love of my wife and child.' Were those Crocker's exact words?"

"They were."

"Dorothy is a fortunate woman. God grant me a husband who loves me as much as Francis Crocker loves his Dorothy!"

I returned to the apothecary for another decoction that would urge me to procreate. He suggested coriander seeds in sweet wine. I drank two cups a day for weeks, once more to no avail.

<hr />

My readers will recall that God's people, like all Englishmen, were subject in the summer of 1618 to a royal decree declaring it lawful to exercise upon the Sabbath after the afternoon service or sermon. Dancing was permitted for either men or women, archery for men, wrestling, leaping, vaulting, May games, Whitsunales, and Morris dances. Yea, even the setting up of Maypoles! On the Sabbath! But not bowling. Bowling was prohibited as a sport of the meaner sort of people.

My master was incensed. "The meaner sort of people! The meaner sort of people! What means His Majesty by the meaner sort of people? Why, the best people bowl. Sir Francis Drake bowled! The richest attorneys in London bowl. My friend, the attorney Christian Martyn bowls! Christian Martyn, who goes in a velvet cloak laid about with russet lace and hath coach-horses and a manor house in Surrey! Christian bowls. We bowled together as youths at Gray's Inn.

"But, of course, His Majesty hath spoken, and he is the arbiter of fashion. If His Majesty sayeth the meaner sort of people bowl, why then I shall never bowl again. I shall miss it, though. I am too old to take up archery or wrestling. Can you see me wrestling? Or vaulting at my age? Ah, me! The world is for the young. You are fortunate, Wentworth, to have your youth! But it shall fly, Wentworth; mark me, it shall fly away, and you will have wasted all your Sunday afternoons by praying. They will reckon in the thousands. How old are you? Three-and-twenty?

"If, by God's grace, you live to be five-and-forty, that will be—I cannot reckon the sum in my head. But think on it, Wentworth! Think on it! Thousands of Sabbath afternoons, free of work, wasted praying! Forget the future. Think on this coming Sabbath, after church. What will you do on the Sabbath that comes in three days? Pray in your close chamber, read Scripture or the *Book of Martyrs*? I'll wager that besides the Bible, that is your favorite book. Am I right? I knew it! It is steeped in Protestant blood. You have the rapt look of a would-be martyr about you.

"Come this Sabbath, you could be out exercising your

strong young body in the fresh air! I bid you, walk again along the Thames with Sarah and Bess. But you hear me not. You might as well have stuffed your ears with shoemaker's wax. All that I spake to you, I committed to the air. You are an incorrigible Puritan, Wentworth. Incorrigible! Well, I am five-and-forty and shall not waste the Sabbath afternoons I have left to me by praying or reading the *Book of Martyrs*! But what shall I do, now that I cannot bowl?"

There was tumult in the realm because the king declared that his decree be promulgated from all the pulpits in the land. The pastors protested so much that the royal declaration stood but need not be read aloud from the pulpit. Even the Reverend Doctor Sommers at St. Martin in the Fields protested—but feebly, for he took as the subject of a sermon, 2 Kings 15: "Elisha said unto him, take bows and arrows, and he took unto him bows and arrows."

The Rev. Doctor said, "His Majesty hath commanded us, and I bid you, obey. Good Englishmen, take up bows and arrows on the Lord's Day and practice with them that we may smite our foes with arrows, as our mighty forebears smote our foes upon the fields of Crécy and Agincourt.

"Also practice with the musket on the Sabbath! Your papist Spanish soldier is an able musketeer."

I knew that God would punish England for violating the Sabbath and went to see Zachariah Rigdale in his chambers above his joiner's shop. He plucked a wood shaving from his beard and said, "On my life, I agree, this is ominous for England. Those who break the Sabbath will suffer curses and wretchedness. Those who observe it shall thrive in the Lord's house and in religion and worldly matters. They shall enjoy true prosperity. God will surely take vengeance upon England!"

We exchanged many bitter words against the form of the established religion. Rigdale fulminated against our churches that hallow water, practice baptism, anoint children by spitting in their mouths, and conduct other lewd ceremonies.

Then he said to me, "Now, Charles, pray tell me about yourself."

"I fear that I am damned."

"Damned? What say you? What makes you think such a thing?"

"I am responsible for my father's death."

"How so?"

I related the circumstances to him, and he said, "His death was God's will. Love God and all things are for the best."

"My uncle said the very same thing."

"God spake through us both."

"I want to believe it, but I am far removed from Him."

"Who is close to Christ all the time? Am I? Surely not. He comes and goes from me like the tide upon the beach I once saw at Dover. At full tide, I am soaked by Him, immersed in His mercy, but then He leaves me high and dry, covered with sandy sea weed. Right now, at this moment, I am high and dry, covered with sea weed, sand, and cockle shells. Yet I have faith that the living waters—His precious blood—will wash over me again."

I said, "We are both of us presently at low tide upon the beach."

"Then let us repent and wait upon the Lord together. Pray with me."

I harkened to him. On the Sabbath following, I attended his church, St. Dunstan in the East, in Tower Street, wherein the Ten Commandments were painted on the wall above the altar, and the pastor wore a torn surplice. He preached a sermon in the morning and the afternoon to a great parish of many rich merchants and other occupiers of divers trades, namely saltars and ironmongers. Why, I could almost have been at Winterbourne again; one day in the week, on the Lord's Day, I felt at home. The young Rector, Joannes Childerly, had taken his degree in Divinity at Peterhouse.

We talked of Cambridge together, and I was back in my chamber there with Robin, reading Scripture. Robin, my Robin! Burning in hell!

———•◦•———

Some months went by. And then, one afternoon at dinner, Mistress Sarah said, "Bess and I go shopping for a loaf of sugar today, Master Charles. Will you bear us company to Fish Street?"

"I will, indeed."

On our way home, Sarah said to me, "Have you found a godly maiden at St. Dunstan in the East?"

"Why, no, Mistress. I have found no maiden there of any kind."

"I am glad to hear it. But if you find one, what should she have to be? Pious, I warrant, and obedient."

"Yes, and have an understanding heart."

"What must her heart comprehend?"

"That all my life I will yearn for Christ more than I yearn for her."

"That's not too much to ask of a Christian maid."

She stopped by a street vendor, sniffed a meat pie, and inquired of me, "Have you not wondered about my face? Nay, that was not fair of me to ask such a thing. I have discomforted you. Forgive me. Chide me!"

I said, "Nay, Mistress. I shall not chide you. I shall never chide you. Why, my sweet, of course I forgive you."

She said to Bess, "Did you hear? Master Charles called me 'sweet'!"

I said, "Pray, Mistress, show me your countenance."

Her entire face and neck were scarred with small lumps of flesh. At the center of each was a little hollow. Her swelled nose looked like a pig's snout.

I said, "Methinks, I am at this moment looking upon a reflection of mine own diseased face. Our complexions seem to me to be decayed. They appear as they will in our graves. Only your beautiful blue eyes look alive."

She said, "As do yours as well."

"Let us gaze awhile into each other's eyes."

Said she, "Yours shine."

Said I, "So do yours."

Said she, "How good God is to light up our eyes in our ruined faces with love."

———✦———

I went to Rigdale's chambers late that very night and said, "My father is among the Saints. I am sure of it. I envy his being saved. My envy of his salvation torments me all the day and in the night season."

He said, "Envy? Who is exempt from envy? I envy

you your education at Cambridge. I envy our rector, the young Reverend Doctor Childerly, that he is licenced to preach to his heart's content. What would I not give for that? The preaching of the Word is a gift not tied to the person of a Minister!

"I'm consumed with envy of Childerly every time he mounts the pulpit. I oft preach the Gospel in my dreams. I'm at Paul's Cross, addressing a throng, or at St. Dunstan in the East, and my text from Scripture is always the same: Isaiah 6:6 and 7: "Then flew one of the Seraphims unto me with a hot coal in his hand, which he had taken from the altar with the tongs. And he touched my mouth, and said, 'Lo, this hath touched thy lips, and thine iniquity shall be taken away, and thy sin shall be purged.' And lo, it comes to pass in my dreams that the iniquities of my congregation are taken away, and its sins purged.

"Speak not to me of envy, Charles. It gnaws on my soul in church every Sabbath while Childerly speaks. The whole of humanity is rotten with envy, Charles. What doth Scripture say? Envy is the rotting of the bones. Verily, Charles, the whole of humanity is rotten in its bones.

"Your envy of your father's salvation is the Devil's work. He so envied God's preference for man over the angels that he tempted us to eat of the forbidden fruit and bring death into the world. How passes the night abroad? Can you tell?"

"Methinks some half hour past midnight."

"Not too late to pray. 'Tis never too late at night to pray. Sit down at this table, the work of mine own hands. Let us pray for strength to resist the temptations of the Evil One, who hath fathered in us the envy that rots our bones."

But I had no power to turn to God. I still see Zachariah, seated at the finely carved oaken table that he had made, with his bright blue eyes closed and his powerful, veined hands clasped together before him.

I thought of Mistress Sarah. To my surprise, I had called her "sweet." It had not been devised with fore-thought; the word had fallen unwittingly from my tongue. I searched my heart and learned that I did not love her; I pitied her. But that, mysteriously, made her very sweet in mine eyes. That, and the prospect of an ample dowry.

I needs must be honest before God: an ample dowry made her sweeter to me still. On a sudden, I knew I did not need decoctions to urge me to procreate. 'Tis myste-rious, I know, very mysterious indeed, but pity for Sarah and the prospect of a goodly sum of money provoked my flesh.

But could a happy marriage come from those things? The morning following, I wrote my uncle Roger for his opinion on this matter. He answered me in part as follows:

The new school master, Nicholas Hopkins, is writing my words down. He is trying to teach me to read and write, but, alas, like at school so long ago, it is for some reason beyond my poor powers. What is wrong with me? Alas, alas, my love for words shall never be fulfilled.

Dearest Charles, my pity for your aunt when she discovered that she was barren hath, in truth, sustained our marriage through all our difficult times together. Is it not written, "In His love and in His mercy, He redeemed them"(Isaiah 63:9)?

You love Sarah not? As the saying is, "Marry first, and love after by leisure." That she is likewise disfigured by the smallpox seems to me all to the good. As the saying is, "Matching with marriage must be with equality."

I reckon that Sarah's dowry will come to one hundred and fifty pounds—perhaps more. A third saying that comes to my mind is, "Love is potent, but money is omnipotent."

Therefore I say unto you, "Marry your Sarah and find happiness."

I asked my master's permission to court his daughter.

He said, "I am well disposed to a match. Sarah is my heart's blood, the only child left to me, and above all else, I want her to be happy. You shall find me very careful for her good. Do you love her, Charles?"

"I find her sweet and gentle and kind—she hath a very kind heart. I cherish her and will strive to make her happy."

"Spoken honestly! I could not ask for more. I did not love my good wife when I married her. I liked her, true, but loved her not. Love came to me in time, as it will come to you. Have you asked Sarah how she feels about you?"

"Not yet, but I believe she's fond of me and will have me for her husband."

Said he, "I believe so, too. You are big and tall, and you are both disfigured. Who else would marry her? Moreover, you have, like her, a kind heart, though it seems to me that you both have an inordinate concern for the poor. She, in particular. Why, you would not believe how charitable she is! She gives alms to half the beggars of Westminster. Well, she can afford to. She hath a rich father.

"But you—you have no resources, apart from what you earn from me and your two meager investments. Money, I warrant, is very important to you. Good! You will come into a goodly amount by marrying Sarah—we shall discuss it anon—and I trust a man who knows the value of a farthing. I trust you to give me an ample return for what I shall settle on you. And what return is that? Why, to make my daughter happy! She hath not had much happiness in her young life. Two beloved sisters dead, a ruined face. With tears in mine eyes, I oft think of her as she was before eleven years of age, with smooth, rosy cheeks and a cheerful disposition. She spake with the prettiest lisp imaginable.

"Yes, I give you my permission to court Sarah. Be good to her, Charles. Make her happy.

"And give me a grandson. Thus I beseech you. But I have learned from life that beseeching you to make my Sarah happy is as good as a shoulder of mutton to a sick horse. Still, I have hope that I'm buying me a suitable son-in-law."

I said, "You may be sure of it, sir. As I love God!"

"God hath many lovers in this world. My daughter hath but you."

<hr>

I said to Mistress Sarah, "Women are creatures without which there is no comfortable living for man. They are a necessary good. It is not meet that man should be without a woman. Therefore, Mistress Sarah, I ask you to become my wife, that we may live together and fulfill all the duties of the covenant of marriage as appointed by God.

"I shall cherish you all the days of my life and, in so far as it is within my power, make you happy, rectifying the unhappiness you have hitherto endured. Marry me, Mistress, I entreat thee. Complete me as I shall complete you, for as you have said, we are opposite reflections of each other. Let us join together and become one. What say you?"

"You once called me 'sweet,'" she said. "Why not again?"

"Marry me, my sweet, I implore you."

"Say 'my sweet' again. Call me 'my sweet Sarah.'"

"My sweet Sarah, marry me."

"Say 'I love you.'"

"I love you."

"You do not."

"Not yet. 'Tis true. I do not yet love you. But as the saying is, 'Marry first, and love after by leisure.'"

"Is that the saying? Ah, Charles! I want to be loved now."

"Will you not wait on me? Most dainty and honey-sweet mistress, marry me. I know I shall come to love you after a time."

"'Most dainty and honey-sweet mistress!' Fie! Your excess of sweetness cloys, Charles. Call me simply 'My Sarah.' My head aches extremely on the sudden, Charles. We shall talk of our marriage anon. Meanwhile, my thanks to you for asking me to be your wife. I am grateful to you. I shall think on your considerate offer, and we'll talk of it again."

She bade me wait upon her reply till the twenty-seventh of December in the year of Christ 1619.

That day she said, "Well, Charles, I accept you to be my husband. I love you, Charles. In truth, I have loved you since first we met at dinner and you said, 'You are very young, Mistress, to wrestle with God.' It seemed to me that you peered through my veil into my soul and witnessed its bitter travail. You perceived my inward self and looked through mine eyes upon the world which was indifferent to my suffering. You immediately understood my perpetual struggle to reconcile myself with God's will. I instantly loved you for your understanding heart, though in truth, I would rather be loved than understood.

"Nonetheless, you are big and tall, Charles. All these attributes of yours commend themselves to me, and I am satisfied—at present. My mother made my father fall in love with her after they were married. She hath taught me how, and I shall work my woman's gentle magic upon you. I shall rouse your love for me by my tenderness. Methinks, no woman hath hitherto been tender to you."

"There was one—my nurse—but, bidden by the Evil One, she strangled her infant and was hanged."

"Poor Charles! My poor Charles!"

"What's this world but a gilt bitter pill that the Devil forces down our throats?"

She said, "I do not believe it. This is the world that God loves and wherein love between man and woman thrives, and likewise love between them and their children. Let us marry, Charles, and pray that God blesses our union with issue. I want a boy and girl, and, by God's grace, the complexion of each shall assuage the pain of our mutual disfigurement. We shall rejoice in their unmarred features that they inherit from each of us: your cleft chin, perhaps, or the slight slant of mine eyes or my full lower lip, as once they were. Our babes shall shape our countenances anew and, in doing so, renew us."

I said, "So be it! Take off your veil. Let me kiss you."

Afterwards, she said, "That was my first kiss."

"Mine, as well."

"You want practice, Charles."

"Then let me give you another."

"No. You shall earn the rest. I want you to court me in the old English manner. Give me five tokens of your love in as many days."

During the next five afternoons, we went walking through St. James Park. Despite the cold wind, Sarah went without her veil. The first token of my love that I gave her was my mother's kid gloves. I told her their history and how I had covered them with kisses when I was a child.

She said, "Then so shall I!"

"Hath my token earned me a kiss?"

"Yes," she said. "Warm my lips."

My second token was a Geneva Bible. My third was a gold ring worth eighteen shillings; my fourth was a girdle and five red ribbons. My last token was an ivory comb that cost me twelve shillings.

On the selfsame day, my Sarah said, "I give you this shilling, my darling Charles, as a sign that I will marry you and be your wedded wife." At that, we kissed again, mingling our warm breaths made visible by the icy air. All in all, in that time, we kissed five times at a total cost to me of one pound, nine shillings.

On the Sabbath following, without her veil, she accompanied me to St. Dunstan in the East, wherein we prayed with Rigdale. He wished us joy in God, many children, and years of happiness together. Then he said, "I count the days until, by God's grace, I am with my beloved Anna and our daughter in heaven. What is death but the entrance to heaven and living out eternity as one of the Elect? God be praised, all this winter, my faith in my election hath returned! I once again relish the taste of the sweetness of the Lord's love, the scent and savour of it.

"I am grateful for each day allotted me upon this earth, that I may praise God in my flesh. Alas, though, not a day passes but He calls me to war with some temptation or other."

I said, "And me."

Sarah said, "Why, then, sirs, I am in good company."

They fell to talking about the poor. Rigdale said, "God prefers the humble poor and gives voice for their precedency. There are some of them who are saved. How horrible to think that they might live without hope of heaven for want of a preacher to open their hearts to their love of Christ. Someday, by God's grace, I shall preach to the poor, without a licence, and gladly pay my fines. All I ask is to reveal from my preaching one elected soul concealed by the sufferings of poverty from its destiny in heaven.

"Meanwhile, let us give the humble poor plenteous alms not only to satisfy the hunger of our brethren but to fulfill and accomplish God's command."

My Sarah said, "Charles and I most heartily agree."

After the service, in frosty Tower Street, we were beset by eight or ten unruly beggars. It cost me two shillings to be rid of them. My Sarah said, "Why, my darling Charles! Except these warm gloves of your mother's, those two shillings are your love tokens that please me most. You are a righteous man."

"Aye," said Rigdale. "And one of the Elect, Mistress, I am confident of it."

"I too am sure of it," said she.

I said, "At this instant, God's love is washing over me again, Zachariah, just as you said it would. My faith in my salvation hath immersed my heart. The world is crystalline! God's love shines through it. My soul hath never before known this sweet peace! I cannot describe the pleasure I feel! No, not pleasure—is there no word that can describe what I feel? Fie! Is there not a word for this?"

Zachariah said, "Be silent, friend! Be silent. Let your silence speak for you."

I said, "Look! Look you into my Sarah's luminous eyes! Therein you can see what I feel."

"Yes," she said. "I too am saved. I am sure of it."

I said, "That makes the three of us. Saved! Saved! By the grace of God, we are all of us saved! Praise Him! Let us thank Christ, who hath given us a moment together of surety and bliss—for want of a word unknown to me."

It began to snow; Sarah caught some flakes on her tongue. She said, "Bliss!"

———◆◆———

Appletree and I had a conference in his chambers, wherein we signed the marriage contract, with free consent on both sides. As a dowry, he presented me with a draft on the goldsmith, John Loop, for two hundred pounds, which I was free to convert to coin or invest with Loop at five percent interest for future use. At his suggestion, I decided to invest it with Loop. He said, "I tried to get you eight percent, but Loop is as mean as a Jew."

I thanked Appletree profusely for his generosity. He said, "If, God forbid, Sarah should die before you, whatever money remains shall, according to our contract, be returned to me in one year. You have a considerable fortune there, Charles. Use it wisely. I propose you rent a house, live therein, and work in the front chamber."

"But at what, sir? At what? What am I capable of doing?"

"Why, being a conscientious scrivener! Hire two or three clerks. I will send you work aplenty and recommend you to my attorney friends. You should make a good living."

"A scrivener!"

"Do you not enjoy your work?"

"I do, sir. Oh, I do."

"I should find it tedious."

We dined at the fashionable Sign of the Bell in Kings Street with Mistress Appletree, her spaniel that licked the matron's greasy lips, and my Sarah, who said, "Thank you, Father, thank you for everything."

"Sarah, do me this service. Henceforth, wear my magical ring. I know you do not believe in its power but wear it to please me."

"I will, Father."

It proved too big for her slim fingers, so she wore it upon her right thumb. I said, "Nay, not there, my sweet. You are a freeborn Englishwoman! As I remember, thumb rings were worn by Roman slaves."

"Then my thumb is the appropriate place for me to wear it, for look you, sir, I am henceforth your humble slave. How now! My nails want paring!"

I poured me another cup of sack and asked, "Are thy nails good and sharp?"

"Like a cat's."

"Then come, puss, and scratch my itchy back."

"*Ubi, domine?*"

"In the middle. No, lower down. There! Ah! Thank you."

"You are welcome."

Her tipsy parents applauded; the spaniel barked. But what I now remember best is the portent from Providence in my Sarah's mention of paring her nails.

She never wore her veil again; I grew a beard.

We were betrothed in St. Martin in the Fields on the fifteenth of April in the year of Christ 1619. When I promised to take her to be my betrothed wife in time convenient, Appletree said, "The time convenient shall be five months hence, on my birthday, which is the fifth of August."

Sarah said to me, "I was going along in the street this morning, coming to church, when on a sudden a voice called, "See here, mistress, fine cobweb lawn, good cambric, or fair bonelace," and I thought of us in the linen shop. I bought two ells of cambric, I remember, and I recall the drooping white feather in your hat. Charles, have you not noticed? Your feather droops like an ass's ear. And the sleeves of your suit are too short. Never mind. I shall find you a goodly tailor, my love, and a haberdasher, too. You also need new shoes."

I said, "And my cloak? What think you of my cloak?"

"You fished fair and caught a frog, as the saying is."

"I am in your hands. Fashion me anew from top to toe."

"I want only to make your heart grow full, like the moon."

I wrote my uncle Roger the good news, and he congratulated me in the return post, "Yes, my dear boy, may your heart grow full, like the moon. A fine simile!"

Sarah accompanied me to buy a new hat, a new suit, and a new pair of shoes. Appletree and I spent two months searching for a house in Westminster. We found one in Axe Yard that was three storeys high. It had seven chambers, including the work chamber on the ground floor. There were two brick fireplaces, a cellar, gables at the front, and a well in the back. The ceilings were plastered. Rigdale, who knew something of carpentry, said it was solidly built with a goodly timber frame. I found two large cracks in the casement windows on the second floor.

The owner asked sixteen pounds a year for rent; we agreed upon twelve. He said he would have the windows repaired at his expense. I agreed to take possession of the house upon the first day of the August following.

I signed a contract with Rigdale to make Sarah and me furniture for a total of twenty-three pounds: a four-poster bed that we would hang with green serge, a dining table, six joint stools, a bench, and two cupboards. We decided to keep her oaken chest at the foot of our bed and cover the wattle walls with painted blue cloths.

I also hired Rigdale to make four desks and six stools for my working chamber, and bought a goodly amount of paper, ink, and pens.

My Sarah said, "When we are married, we shall plumb each other's depths and find such new things therein that rival the discoveries of the New World."

Three weeks following, we went to Rigdale's shop to watch him at work upon our bed. He was making a strong mortise-and-tenon joint, with fish glue and wooden dowels. Thereafter, I said to my Sarah, "We shall soon lie abed, taking pleasure in each other as man and wife, according to the ordinances of God. May our bodily delight be a temporal intimation of our eternal spiritual union with Christ, the husband of our souls.

"And may it bring us children, my beloved. I do so want your children to love."

Providence, though, decreed that my Sarah had less than one month to live.

On the morning of the second of June, while paring the nail of her left forefinger with a pair of scissors, she cut away a piece of flesh around the nail on its right side. Two days thereafter, the little wound was red, hot, swollen, and painful.

Sarah felt feverish and took to her bed. Applegate summoned Dr. Nicholas Bunn. He said the wound was sorely inflamed and prescribed a slender, diluting diet, plentiful bleeding, and repeated purges. The skin around her nail grew very tense and caused her great pain. On the doctor's instructions, I constantly bathed it with a mixture of sweet oil and vinegar and afterwards covered it with a piece of wax plaster.

The morning following, she said to me, "My fever is rising. My finger greatly pains me. My whole body resides there, within each throb. Give me more laudanum, my beloved. Thank you, yes. Ah, thank you! A good thing, laudanum, a most excellent thing. Thank God for laudanum, though it constipates me.

"Such a little thing—a snip of my scissors. I looked away, for an instant, at a stain upon my sleeve, and snip! 'Tis the little things upon which life and death turn. One little snip, and I am done. Yes, I will die, as you shall see. Mine was a short, sad life until I fell in love with you. Tell me the truth. Were you falling in love with me during our last months together?"

"I was."

"God hath apportioned me to spend eternity with

Him among His saints. I am saved. I knew it for sure upon that Sabbath, after church. It began to snow. Some flakes melted upon my tongue. I said, 'Bliss!' Do you remember?"

"I remember."

"I have here your mother's gloves. Keep them in remembrance of me and give them as a token to the woman whom you shall marry. Yes, you will marry, Charles. We shall not be husband and wife in heaven. That vexes me."

Her fever increased during the night, and the tumor on her finger grew larger. She suffered violent pain. I remained awake and tried to promote the tumor to suppurate with a soft poultice. Toward noon, she said, "Tell me again that you were falling in love with me in those few months we had together."

"My sweet Sarah, I love you now."

"Why, look you, my big, tall man weeps! I never saw you weep, Charles. Yes, weep, my beloved, my dearly betrothed. Weep! I shall take your tears with me to my grave as tokens of your love."

All during those four days and nights, at different times, on a sudden, I felt compelled to pray, "O Christ, restore my Sarah's health." The words welled up within me, unbidden, while I wiped my nose or changed her poultice. Once, to my shame, I prayed in the midst of making water; my prayer and my piss streamed together from my vile body, one heavenward and one into the chamber pot.

The doctor came again and said, "See the thinness of skin about the wound? The abscess is ripe for opening." He sliced it with his lancet, to a great profusion of blood and pus. The inflammation became livid. Little bladders oozing green and yellow ichors spread all over the skin. The tumor subsided, and for an hour or so, I hoped for the best. Then her whole forefinger turned black.

My Sarah said, "I bit my tongue," and became insensible. Her pulse quickened, she had the clammy sweats, and at seven in the morning of the ninth of June in the year of Christ 1619, she died at nineteen years of age.

Someone shrieked. I looked about me. It was I. I shrieked again. Then I was benumbed. I neither grieved for Sarah, nor rejoiced in her salvation. I had no pity for her father mourning the death of the last of his three daughters.

In the churchyard, by the open grave, Mistress Appletree clasped her spaniel to her bosom. Sarah's swelled black finger was ever in my mind. I thought of her rotting in her grave and cursed God.

The owner of the house in the Axe Yard agreed to

cancel my lease. I forfeited the one pound I had given him on account. Rigdale showed me the furniture he had made. Even the four-poster bed summoned no emotion in me. Rigdale promised to try to sell everything and return my money; I did not care.

I went to St. Dunstan in the East with Rigdale every Sabbath, and we alternated reading a portion of Scripture aloud in the evenings. He favored the Psalms, saying, "I like to sweeten my mouth with a Psalm before going to sleep."

I said, "I am utterly estranged from God. I will burn in hell."

I returned my dowry to Appletree and continued working as his clerk. I took my breakfasts, dinners, and suppers at The Sign of the Bear and Ragged Staff. I ate only calf, wether mutton, and rabbit stew, according to Doctor Troth's prescription for melancholy. The meat had lost its savour for me. I drank aunt Eliza's decoction of hollyhocks, violet leaves, and fennel, together with a bottle of sack at supper and dinner.

At The Sign of the Bear and Ragged Staff, Hendy and his companions reveled with the plump, muddy whores. One evening, two drunken boy prostitutes, about fifteen years of age, smutted each other with candle grease and soot. I watched them in the smoky room as from afar. I saw myself as at a distance: my drooping feather, filthy cloak, and ragged beard. I felt sundered from myself and the world.

After supper, I wandered round Westminster and the City, visiting again and again those places where Sarah and I had spent time together. Neither the linen shop on Bridge Street, nor a walk under the oaks in St. James Park, brought tears to my eyes.

One rainy afternoon in November, while walking abroad in Candlewick Street, I met by chance one of my former Cambridge chamber mates named Richard Witt, who was from Sussex. We repaired to a tavern. He told me that he had a lectureship in religion at St. Sepulchre's Church, endowed by a rich London linen merchant, that paid thirty pounds a year. Witt was betrothed to the merchant's daughter. He said, "I have had good luck. The Goddess of Fortune hath smiled on me."

"I have no complaints."

"I am glad to hear it. I heard about Robin's death. Is that how you came by the smallpox?"

Said I, "Yes, I caught it from him. He caught it from a strumpet at The Sign of the Rose on Dowdriver's Lane."

Witt said, "Bad luck! He was so comely. *Rota fortunae volvitur.* The wheel of fortune turns. So true! So true!

Share with me another bottle of sack, and we shall drink to the Goddess Fortune, who rules the world."

I said, "Nothing or no one rules the world," and walked out into the cold rain.

Rigdale sold the furniture for twenty-three pounds, which I paid back to Appletree.

On the third of January, Appletree said to me, "Today is Sarah's twentieth birthday. Since she died, I am without the petty anxieties and torturous fears that hitherto vexed me. I pay no heed to the fashion of the king and play bowls. I am no longer frightened of old age, losing my money, sickness, pain, death, or even God's judgment in the hereafter. My soul is calm. My three beloved daughters are dead. Nothing worse in this life or my life to come can happen to me."

Uncle Roger and I wrote each other once a month. At the beginning of February, I asked him if I could return to the Hempstead and resume useful and wholesome work with his sheep. Roger and Wells both entreated me to remain in London; the woolen business was bad because of the rapid decline of the price of cloth. This was the result of the great preparation for war between Protestants and the Papists in most parts of the Continent. The twelve-year truce between Spain and the States of the Low Countries had ended. The German Protestant princes stood ready to defend themselves against the Emperor. Europeans could no longer afford to buy high-quality English cloth. Our merchants had piles of unsold stock on the quays. They bought no more cloth from the clothiers across the country, so the clothiers ceased producing and let their workers go.

Uncle Roger wrote, "The streets of Winterbourne are crowded with idle woolen workers living on charity and poor relief."

I thought of Goodwife Stone carding, John Johnson at his loom, and Robert Hayman raising the cloth's nap, who were now living on charity and poor relief.

Wells wrote that my investment in his business at present earned me only one pound per annum. My income was thereafter diminished to thirteen pounds a year.

Seeking to feel some emotion, I took leave of work on three wintry afternoons and went to Blackfriars Theatre, where I saw three plays by the late William Shakespeare: *The Tragedy of Othello—The Moor of Venice*, *As You Like It*, and *The Tempest*.

Rigdale said, "Mark me! Going to the theatre will lead you to sin. Plays nourish idleness, and idleness doth Minister vice."

For a few hours, on those afternoons, I inhabited the imaginary worlds that the poet had drained of Christ and filled instead with ravishing poetry. Noblemen occupied stools upon the stage. When the play was over, they with small cost purchased the acquaintance of the pretty boy actors and took them away.

Toward the end of *The Tempest*, an actor wearing a false grey beard declaimed, "We are such stuff as dreams are made on and our little life is rounded by a sleep." The beauty lodged in the words of the verse consoled me. The sensation lasted but a moment. And then I re-awakened to my desolate life.

At the end of March, the Devil tempted me to revive my somnolent sensibilities by watching bear baiting on a Thursday afternoon in a ring at Paris Garden in Southwark. Rigdale said, "No godly Christian would see poor beasts rend, tear, and kill others for his bloodthirsty pleasure! And although they be savage animals to us and seek our destruction, yet we are not to abuse them for His sake, who made them and whose creatures they are."

A bear with little pink eyes pursued one of the mas-tiffs, while the other five dogs pursued the bear. One dog clung with his jaws to the bear's left front leg, and the bear bit him through his neck bone and got free. Another dog clung to the bear's belly, just above his private parts. The bear sat up and, with a front paw, struck the dog's left shoulder. He would not relinquish his hold. The bear ripped open the dog's breast with his front claws. I glimpsed the dog's beating heart. The drunken spectators cheered.

Then it was all biting and clawing and yelping and barking and howling and roaring in the ring. The bear tossed the dogs, one after the other. They shrieked and whimpered. When the bear was loose once more, he shook his massive head, spattering his viscous, bloody slaver in the air. The three remaining dogs leaped on him again.

Caring not if the bear lived or died, I took my leave, went to a nearby tavern, and became drunk.

———— ∙⊱⊰∙ ————

I could not abide London while the whole population joyously celebrated St. Bartholomew Fair on the twenty-fourth of August. So, like the two years previous, I saved my money and, with Appletree's permission, returned to the Hempstead in Winterbourne for that selfsame week.

My aunt Eliza's left eye was covered by a cataract. I recited to uncle Roger the metaphor I had gleaned from *The Tempest*.

He said, "I once dreamed that I died, but I remained aware that my swelled body was rotting. My eyes shriveled in their sockets, and my jawbone fell off. My shankbones showed through my putrefied flesh. I thought, one moment more of this, and I'll go mad. Then I was alive again.

"My restored body was drifting in the night sky towards a certain star that I knew was my soul. I heard a voice, resounding throughout the heavens and earth, saying, 'In the end, the soul cometh to meet itself.' Then I awoke. Such is the stuff I'm made on."

Tom Foot, as the bailiff of husbandry, had sold one hundred and fifty of my uncle Roger's sheep. Foot had a surfeit of out-of-work woolen workers who wanted to be hired as day labourers in harvest. With uncle Roger's assent, Foot had lowered the wages of the five men he had hired from sixpence to four pence a day.

There was a local drought for the second consecutive year. Since the previous year, the price of wheat had risen from twenty-five shillings the quarter to forty-five shillings. Uncle Roger said, "With God's help, I will be a rich man."

Herewith, what I learned from my uncle Roger about Winterbourne:

> **Item.** The previous September, a constable, the churchwardens, and overseers of my father's old

parish had been given powers to purchase, erect, or procure a suitable building to be used as a workhouse for setting poor and idle persons on work. The cost of the above was to be paid for through rates assessed and collected in each parish in town.

Item. The said officials had done nothing except appoint a governor who chose another constable to search out and apprehend persons to be punished with fetters and a moderate whipping.

Item. Six people in the town recently died of the plague.

To occupy myself, I reaped, bound the sheaths, and gleaned and winnowed the meager crops with the other day labourers in harvest for a paltry four pence a day.

One evening, after winnowing the south field with Esau, I asked him how he felt abut giving the testimony that had condemned his friend Peter Patch.

He said, "I rejoiced in doing my Christian duty."

At supper, uncle Roger told me, "Patch's whole body shivered, shook, and trembled in the cart beneath the gallows. His teeth chattered. He cried out, 'Kiss me! For Christ's sake, somebody kiss me!' But no one did. The ewe was hanged first, and then it was Patch's turn. It took him a long while to strangle."

Tom Foot said, "Your face is exceeding pale, Master

Charles. You need a dram or two of Aqua Vitae to bring some color back into your cheeks."

We walked to The Sign of the Bull, where we each drank two drams. A young whore smiled at me and sat down at our table. She had a dimple in her left cheek. Her name was Grace Orchard; she was Foot's friend. She also drank two drams of Aqua Vitae and said, "Good sirs, I am hungry. I have not eaten all the day."

I bought her a mutton pie. She smiled at me again; I was beguiled by her dimple.

She said, "My mother and I were wool carders who lived in a cottage in South Street. There was not enough work for both of us, so I left home and became a maidservant to a rich farmer named Long Snooke who freely held a farm of eighty-three acres near Hazelbury Bryan.

"I was begotten of a child by him, and he turned me out of doors, calling me a very lewd girl. I was delivered of dead twins in a ditch and became a vagrant. I wandered from parish to parish. I slept under hedges by the road. Last winter, I was arrested for stealing wood worth ten shillings, but the magistrate freed me when I showed him that I had taken but a few rotten roots and green furzes."

She smiled again, and again I beheld her bewitching dimple. Then she said, "You may have me for a shilling, sir. Tom will tell you that I am well worth it. Tell the gentleman, Tom."

"In faith, she is."

"The chamber upstairs hath a feather bed. You can rent it for us from the tapster for another shilling."

I gave the upstairs door a shove. Grace set her candle on the stool by the bed. I watched her put off all her clothes. She put my shilling in one of her shoes and blew the candle out.

I committed fornication in the dark. For a few minutes, on a fetid feather bed, the Devil fully roused me to life.

———————

Immediately upon returning to London, I confessed my sin to Rigdale.

He said, "I warned you that going to the theatre would lead you to perdition."

"You did. I remember. It hath done so."

"I fear that hell, destruction, and death everlasting will be your fate. Yet ask yourself this: do you still believe in God and accept the principles of Christian worship?"

I said, "Yea and nay; sometimes yes and sometimes no."

I henceforth fasted upon every Sabbath and read Scripture. I was confounded by the text from Isaiah 45:7, "I form the light and create darkness: I make peace and create evil. I the Lord do all these things." I am confounded by it still.

Then the Devil came down in great wrath upon me. For well nigh a year, he came unto me in my chamber almost every evening and drove me into the streets or into inns or brothels to seek out comely, young whores. I often drank myself to sleep. Sometimes, half drunk, I went for a walk with the intention of getting a breath of fresh air. I averted my eyes from the street walkers but always found myself in some inn, looking for a comely, young girl who was for sale. Whenever I saw one, Sarah's veiled face came to my mind, and I ran away.

But I returned like a dog to his vomit. The Devil frequently led me to the brothels in Spital Fields, beyond Bishops Gate, and Whitefriars. Night after night, I sat in their parlors for hours without speaking. Then the bawd in a stew in Shoreditch said to me, "Don't be shy, sir. Choose one of my pretty lasses and enjoy yourself."

I went into a bedchamber with a comely lass and put off all my clothes. A babe wailed from the cradle in a corner. The girl said, "My darling Susan is awake and hungry. I must needs nurse her, or else she will keep crying and spoil your sport. Will you wait, sir? It will not take long."

I put on my clothes and hastened home. With every

subsequent sunset and the coming of the dark, the Devil tempted me, and my resistance to him grew more and more feeble. At length, in February in the year of Christ 1622, I said to Rigdale, "It is only a matter of time before I again surrender to the temptation to fornicate. I have decided that it is a greater evil to live and sin against God than to kill myself. Therefore I will kill myself. But how? Not by hanging. I could not abide that. I will buy a musket and shoot myself in the mouth. I have given the matter much thought. I will prime and load the piece, light the match, stand upon a stool with the butt upon the floor between my bare feet, thrust the muzzle against the back of my throat, and pull the trigger with my big toe."

Rigdale said, "Join me instead in a new life. Come work with me in a plantation that will soon be established in New England. It will be comprised only of men, so you will be free of the temptation to fornicate. I am going there so that I may at last preach the Gospel without a licence and, with God's grace, awaken slumbering regenerate souls to their heavenly destiny."

He told me that a member of his church, a former ironmonger named Thomas Weston, had been the treasurer and guiding spirit of the Company of Merchant Adventurers of London. In 1620, Weston and his

Company had established for profit a settlement of Separatists in New England called the Plymouth Plantation that would trade various and sundry cheap goods with the Indians for beaver skins and hewn timber.

My beloved father, in his heart of hearts, was a Separatist. He believed that the Church of England was no true church because it was a national church governed by the hierarchy of archbishops, and their courts and canons, and thus far removed from the primitive Church of the Gospels. He would have thanked God to see me settled in New England.

Rigdale said that Weston had severed his connection with the Merchant Adventurers, with the idea of establishing a second settlement in New England solely for profit.

He said to me, "A beaver pelt from the Plymouth Plantation sells in London for eleven shillings! Eleven shillings for one pelt! And the timber! A single pine balk fifteen foot in length from New England sells here for one pound, five shillings, and sixpence. We'll be rich!

"This morning, I signed a contract with Mr. Weston to serve as his plantation's joiner for one share of the expected yearly profit together with five pounds, three shillings in money. I am to bring my tool box."

Weston said to me, "Rigdale says you are a scrivener

for attorney Henry Appletree, whose chambers are in Westminster. Appletree represents Edward Williams, the merchant owner of the good ship *Swan* which I recently hired from him for sixty pounds a month, together with a bond of eight hundred pounds."

I said, "Yes, I know. I copied the contracts. The *Swan* is a seaworthy vessel. As I recall, it hath a burden of ninety tons."

Weston said, "I would like to hire you as scrivener for my new enterprise. You will sail on the *Swan* with the other men I hire. You will list the names, occupations, shares, yearly wages, and other particulars of the labourers. Also, of all supplies and their purchase costs that are loaded in London upon the *Swan*. I would pay you the same as Rigdale: one share of the expected profit, together with five pounds, three shillings in ready money."

"How many shares are there in all?"

"Forty-four."

I said, "I will be your scrivener for eight pounds a year in ready money and one share of the expected profits."

"I will pay you seven pounds a year."

"That's what Appletree pays me. You will pay me eight."

"Done! Eight pounds, to be paid you at the end of the first year, together with one share of the expected profits."

I then asked, "What about the Sabbath? Will your labourers keep the Sabbath?"

He said, "Fear not! Religion and money will jump together in my New English plantation. I promised Rigdale that the labourers there will abstain from work on the Sabbath and attend his sermons. Yes, your friend will at last be allowed to preach the Gospel. He must, however, include in every sermon some words in praise of the Christian virtues of discipline and hard work, and some that condemn idleness."

Rigdale said, "And so I will!"

Weston said to me, "Sign here." Then he said, "With God's grace, you will make landfall at the Plymouth Plantation, wherein I have made arrangements with Governor Bradford for all of you to remain until another suitable place for your habitation is discovered in the vicinity. But you will on no account share your supplies with Bradford's people!"

Thus upon my twenty-seventh birthday, on the tenth day of March, in the year of Christ 1622, I signed the contract that set the future course of my life.

———◆———

We parted. I took me to Henry Appletree and told him of my covenant with Weston. He said, "If only I could so easily escape to a new life. Oh, to be young! With God's grace, a long future lies before you. I am five-and-fifty. I would be lucky to count my remaining years on the fingers of one hand. Sarah will gradually fade in your memory. She will linger within you in bits and pieces. Neither of us will forget her oozing black forefinger. Part of me wishes that your life will likewise be cut off. But only part of me. Most of me wishes you well."

We embraced for the first and last time. I recited my little poem over Sarah's grave in the churchyard of St. Martin in the Fields:

> My grief stole my faith
> And sneaked away.
> I cannot trace the thief.
> His track of tears
> Hath faded from my pitted cheek.

On the second day of April, which was a Tuesday, I arrived in Winterbourne to bid farewell to aunt Eliza and uncle Roger. Grace Orchard opened their door. My aunt called out, "Who is it, Grace?"

Grace replied, "A stranger, Mistress."

And I said, "'Tis Charles, aunt Eliza."

"Just in time to dine with us. Come sit you down."

Grace served me turnips and a slice of roast lamb. Tom Foot said, "This is Grace Orchard, Charles. She is an idle carder who lived with her mother on South Street. I hired her to be aunt Eliza's maidservant."

Aunt Eliza said, "Grace is a great comfort to a half-blind old woman like me. Bless the sweet child! I could not live without her."

Grace gave me a dimpled smile. I told my aunt and uncle that I was bound for the New World to work on a plantation for the space of a year. I said, "I go thence to seek my salvation. I hope to learn whether, by the grace of God, I am predestined to be saved. I think that I shall be more free there from temptation."

Aunt Eliza said, "Let us hope so."

Uncle Roger went to his chamber and returned with a jingling purse. He said, "I do not think that we shall meet again in the flesh, Charles. I drink to you, my dear nephew, with all my heart." He drank deep from his mug of ale and belched. "Take these ten pounds. If you return to England within four years, I shall leave you all my worldly possessions. You will be rich. If you remain in New England, I shall leave my fortune to Tom Foot, Eliza's nephew.

"I have ever loved you, Charles. You are a son to me.

When you are a sojourner among savages in the wilderness, remember that the vilest person of earth is the living image of Almighty God."

I embraced aunt Eliza and then uncle Roger, and said, "Since my beloved father's death, you have been my family. I thank you for your care, aunt Eliza, your decoctions, savoury meat stews, and wholesome advice that kept my melancholy at bay. I thank you for your charity, uncle Roger, and the money you have freely given me. I thank you for sharing with me your passion for words. And I thank you both for your love.

"I shall treasure the memory of this moment. In the wilderness across the sea, I shall see in my mind's eye the dying fire, uncle Roger's empty mug of ale, the flickering candle stub on the table. I shall not remember you as you were, when I was a boy, but as you currently appear to me. Your aged faces shall give me joy. Even your cataract, aunt Eliza, is like a pearl to me. Uncle Roger, the skin of your face looks like old parchment upon which the years have inscribed brown blotches and wrinkles at the corners of your eyes. My memory shall preserve your countenances as they are now.

"Look you! The candle hath flickered out. It conspired with my mind to keep therein a few precious moments that have already passed."

Uncle Roger belched again. He said, "Send me some metaphors and similes from the New World."

After dinner, Foot took me aside and said, "If you wish, Grace will come to you in the night. She will cost you nothing. What say you?"

I said, "Bid her come to me at midnight."

He laughed. Awaiting Grace in the dark, I heard a nightingale singing beyond my bedchamber window. God be praised, for it was the earliest in April that I had ever heard one sing. His liquid warble cleansed my soul. I arose from my bed, put on my clothes, grabbed my knapsack, crept out of the house, and walked into Winterbourne.

The departure of the carrier to London was delayed until eight of the clock. I ate breakfast at The Sign of the Bull. The song of the nightingale had sharpened my ears. I went about the town, relishing its familiar sounds: the barking of chained dogs, the clatter of cart makers, the rasping of a wood saw. I listened to children singing in my old grammar school, a blacksmith beating his anvil, a stone mason hammering upon a chisel in Sheep Street.

During the week following in London, I signed on three-and-sixty more men to labour in Weston's plantation. They were brought to him by his brother, Andrew, who was to be our governor. He stank of liquor and tobacco. He and his agents gathered men throughout London—from the streets, the docks, and the stews and taverns. Thomas Weston hired a carpenter named Phineas Pratt for eleven pounds in ready money to be paid at the end of a year's labour. Like Rigdale, Pratt clung to his precious tool box.

Weston turned away a runaway apprentice barber-surgeon named Phillip Bussel because his black pupils were unequally dilated, the right being larger than the left. Bussel was emaciated, with a sallow complexion, and given to profuse sweats.

Weston said, "You are an opium eater. Do not deny it! Get thee hence! You are not wanted here!"

Bussel said, "When I eat opium, my bowels become sorely constipated, but the better portion of my nature becomes divine."

Weston hired one-and-twenty idle husbandmen, an idle needle maker, an idle currier, a former weaver, a former felt maker, and a former haberdasher. They were all to be paid three pounds per annum. He hired six-and-thirty rowdy vagabonds for the same amount each. At least half of them were pitted from small-pox. The one named William Butts was drunk when Andrew brought him into his brother's chamber near the dock. I marked down Butts's name &c. Then he said to me, "Also write: I am alone in this world. I have given over my stinking family duties, for under them lie snapping, snarling, biting covetousness, hypocrisy, envy, and violence."

Andrew said, "Hire him, dear brother. Behold the girth of his arms."

I said, "These rude fellows will be our death."

Butts said, "Look me in the eye! Display no fear! I'm not so tough as I appear."

I reported his extempore rhymed couplet to my uncle Roger in a letter; he replied,

Thank you for your parting gift. The simple couplet, produced naturally without labour from ordinary speech, is much to my liking.

Tom Foot and Grace Orchard are betrothed. I caught you gazing at her dimpled smile across the table. I had the wild fancy that you would remain at the Hempstead and marry her. I would have disinherited Foot.

Why did you flee from here in the night? 'Twas the night I heard an early nightingale in the big oak by the small barn. You must have heard him. I like to think that, however far we will be apart, we will be bound by the beauty of his song.

150

I compiled a list of annual supplies of victuals and drink for Weston's sixty men sailing on the *Swan*.

Item. Victuals and drink. 480 bushels of meal. 120 bushels of pease. 120 bushels of oatmeal. 80 gallons of Aqua Vitae. 60 gallons of oil. 30 gallons of vinegar. Pepper, ginger, nutmegs, cloves, dates, raisins, damask prunes, rice, saffron, salt. 1 barrel of pippin vinegar. 60 barrels of beer. 8 tun of cider.

Item. Arms. 60 long pieces, five foot or five-and-a-half foot in length. 90 pound of powder. 270 pound of shot or lead. 60 bandoleers. 25 melting ladles. 15 bullet molds. 60 forked gun rests.

Item. Tools. 40 broad axes. 40 felling axes. 40 pickaxes. 30 steel hand saws. 30 two-hand saws. 40 hammers. 30 shovels. 30 spades. 30 augers. 30 chisels. 10 grindstones. 400 nails of all sorts. 30 hatchets. 10 pair of pliers.

Item. Household implements. 40 iron pots. 40 kettles. 40 large frying pans. 40 gridirons. 40 skillets. 40 spits. platters. dishes. spoons of wood.

Item. Goods for trading with Indians. 80 hatchets. 40 pounds of glass beads. 30 iron pots. 200 brass bells. 40 broad axes. 40 knives. 30 blankets. 30 hats. 25 ells of red cloth.

Rigdale sold his stock of furniture for fifteen pounds and eight shillings. We both bought four pair of shoes, three pair of Irish stockings, two cloth suits, one suit of canvas, one Monmouth cap, three shirts, one pair of garters, one rug for a bed, one pair of canvas sheets, one coarse rug, and five ells of coarse canvas to be filled with straw, to make a bed at sea. We also purchased one barrel of dried oxen tongues and one barrel of beer for us to consume on shipboard, and two bottles of Aqua Vitae. I took with me my Commonplace Book, and Rigdale and I each carried a Geneva Bible.

PART III

NDREW WESTON, RIGDALE, AND I boarded the *Swan* with Weston's fifty-eight other men at St. Katherine's wharf at five of the clock on Monday morning, the twenty-ninth of April in the year of Christ 1622. The last two passengers to board were a young gentleman armed with a sheathed cutlass sword and a comely maid. We made their acquaintance on the quarterdeck. Their names were Henry and Abigail Winslow. I was relieved to learn that they were brother and sister. Abigail had auburn curls.

The wind being east and north, and the weather being fair, the *Swan*'s crew weighed anchor at about seven of the clock.

Captain Green called out, "Let go forward!" and "Let go aft."

I leaned upon the port rail, just aft of the bow, and said, "Farewell, England."

Andrew Weston said, "Farewell, sack. Farewell, claret and malmsey. Farewell, roasted beef, roasted pork, mutton, woodcocks, and capons."

Rigdale gazed across the Thames and said, "Farewell, Southwark. My beloved Ann is buried in Southwark. Our little daughter, Joan, is buried beside her in St. Olave's churchyard. I hope one day to join them there."

The Tower of London, London Bridge, and St. Paul's slowly receded from my sight as the *Swan* was towed out on the Thames away from the other ships, with their forest of masts, that thronged the river.

Captain Green cried out to his crew, "Cast off tows!"

Henry said, "God be praised! We are free of the Church of England, its bishops, and ecclesiastical courts."

I said, "Its surplices. Its hallowed water. All of its lewd ceremonies."

Rigdale said, "Its profanation of the Sabbath. Its licences to preach the Word of God."

Abigail said, "Its persecution of the Saints."

Andrew Weston said, "Its Book of Common Prayer with St. Chrysostom's prayers. Who is this St. Chrysostom? I warrant St. Chrysostom was a papist."

Henry Winslow said, "Well said, gentlemen. We hold

the same beliefs. My sister and I hope to join our cousin Edward, once of London and Leyden in Holland, who now abides among the Saints in the Plymouth Colony. Are you gentlemen also joining kin who dwell in that godly colony?"

I said, "No, sir. Master Rigdale and I are Master Weston's men. We shall all sojourn in new Plymouth for a little while before we venture into the wilderness and establish a colony of our own. There, with God's help, we shall fell timber for English markets and trade with the Indians for peltry and get rich."

Henry said, "I have read that the Indians of New England delight to torture their prisoners by flaying some with sea shells and cutting off the fingers of others and roasting them to eat."

The Captain cried out, "Man the sheets! Haul and make fast!"

The sailors hauled in the sheets, the wind swelled the mainsail, and the flags atop the mast unfurled. The *Swan* heeled away from the wind to starboard.

Abigail stumbled down the sloping deck into my arms.

She said, "I thank you, sir. You saved me from a grievous fall."

I said, "Would that Eve could have spake thus to Adam."

"You have a keen wit, sir."

"Thank you, Mistress. I honed it in disputations with my tutors at Cambridge."

"So you are a Cambridge man, Master Wentworth. Well, well!" and, for the first time, she looked intently at my pitted face.

Henry said, "Cousin Edward's father and our father were brothers. They were both fervent Separatists. Our mother, of precious memory, was too ill with the consumption for Father to take our family to join cousin Edward and the other Separatists in the Low Countries. Father tended Mother day and night for three years. She died two years ago in the month of September—the same month in which Father, of precious memory, coughed bright red blood into his handkerchief.

"Said he, 'I know the color of this blood. Your mother coughed up bright red blood like this. This is arterial blood. It means my death.'

"The surgeon bled him and gave him infusions, decoctions, and tinctures—all to no avail. I clothed and unclothed him. Abigail made his bed, fetched him water, fed him, and changed and washed his bedclothes for over two years. He died last August 1st, one day after his forty-ninth birthday.

"On his deathbed, he bade us flee England and the dominion of the Anglican church. Said he, 'My children,

I bid you cross the sea and dwell in the Plymouth Plantation with our godly cousin Edward and his brothers and sisters in Christ.'

"I wrote cousin Edward. He answered me thus: 'Come hither, dear cousins, and help build a commonwealth in the wilderness ruled by Christ through His Elect.' I spent twenty pounds of our inheritance to buy our passage in two cabins on this ship, together with six pounds, four pence to dine with the Captain in his cabin."

The *Swan* sailed around a bend in the Thames and passed the Isle of Dogs. We beheld its gibbet, from which a blackened, putrid corpse was hanging in a rusty iron cage.

Rigdale said, "'Tis very like peering into a grave. Oh, Ann, to think that you now look like that."

Henry drew his cutlass from its scabbard and said, "I bought this in London from a soldier. Look you! It hath but one cutting edge. I have pledged myself, by this sharp blade, to become a soldier of the Lord in defense of the Plymouth Plantation. One day, by God's grace, I will cut off a heathen Indian's head."

Abigail said, "My brother is filled with martial ardor in the service of Christ. I am a frail female vessel who thus far is empty of grace. But I have hope that I will discover that I am predestined to be saved. Who knows? Perhaps

God's grace will be bestowed upon me and one day I will dwell as one of the Saints in the Plymouth Plantation."

I said, "I also pray for God's grace. The temptations in England were too great for me, which is why I choose to live chastely in the wilderness among Weston's men."

The wind tossed the auburn curls upon Abigail's forehead and stirred the ends of the white kerchief tied about her long, slender neck.

———◦•◦———

Abigail and Henry lodged aft in two small cabins, each just large enough for a canvas bed stuffed with straw and a cupboard. Andrew Weston lodged with Captain Green in the great cabin. Rigdale and I slept upon our canvas beds stuffed with straw on the crowded gun deck with Weston's other men. For fear of the ship catching fire, the Captain forbade us to light candles or cook our victuals. We dwelt below in perpetual darkness.

On our fifth day out, at about nine in the morning, the wind grew so strong at southwest, and heavy rain withal, that Captain Green ordered the crew to take in the topsail and lower the mainsail. The storm tore the foresail in pieces. I lay upon my bed and listened to the wind howl and the waves break against the hull behind my head. The men about me vomited and groaned.

Then I too took sick. The storm continued all the day and night. I was nauseous the whole time, but only able to vomit a bitter liquid. And after that, I had nothing left within me to disgorge.

The storm slacked off at about five the next morning. I lay there in the dark, too sick to move. At length, I roused myself and made my way up to Abigail's cabin, wherein she said to her brother and me, "There is a common saying that only those who go by sea know what it is to fear God. I learned in the night that the saying is true."

The three of us offered up a prayer of thanksgiving for our deliverance from our first storm at sea, and, with Rigdale, we kept a fast in gratitude to almighty God all the following day.

I soon became accustomed to the stench in the gun deck of the damp, the spoiled victuals, rotting straw, spew, piss, and excrement. At the beginning of our third week at sea, Captain Green told Weston that the filthiness of his men lodged on the gun deck endangered the health of the ship. Weston, who never once went below during our voyage, summoned Rigdale to his cabin and ordered him to appoint men to keep the gun deck clean. Rigdale appointed himself, me, and four other men to keep our room clean for three days; then he appointed six others to succeed us, and so forth.

The next morning, after I had emptied two buckets of excrement over the side, Abigail said to me, "God bless you sir, for cleansing our ship of some of life's filth."

"I am of the opinion that before Adam fell, the whole of the world was always clean."

"Why, that shall henceforth be my opinion, too."

"You are heartily welcome to anything of mine."

"What, then, is your opinion of me?"

"First tell me this: thirteen days ago, when we met here upon the quarterdeck, you gazed intently upon my pitted face. Pray tell me why."

"My father, of precious memory, also had a pitted face. He was stricken with the smallpox at the age of sixteen. Your face brought his beloved face to my mind."

"Perhaps that is why God afflicted me with the smallpox."

"Why is that?"

"Why, to bind you to me at our first meeting."

"And what—if anything—binds you to me?"

"Your curls. My heart is entangled in your curls."

Rigdale led me, the Winslows, and one Phineas Pratt in prayer three times a day. In fair weather, we prayed on the quarterdeck. When the weather was stormy, we gathered in Henry's cabin. Pratt was a master carpenter from Ipswich who had signed a contract with Weston for twelve pounds a year—the most ready money any of us were to receive. He and Rigdale had left their tool boxes in Captain Green's care. One rainy afternoon, in the captain's great cabin, they examined each other's divers tools, viz., augers (both). Various and sundry planes, cabinet scraper, crosscut saw, &c. (Rigdale). Rip saw, framing chisels, gauge, plumb line, hammer, &c (Pratt).

Pratt hammered a nail half way into the wall and then rubbed its head with the tip of his forefinger. He said, "I have the magic touch. You, sir, Master Wentworth, I'll wager you a shilling that you cannot drive this nail up to its head in three blows."

I said, "My religion forbids me to make a wager, sirrah."

He said, "Yes, sir, of course, sir. Never mind the wager. Forget the wager. Far be it for me to tempt you to sin. I bid you to try so that you may behold the effect of my magic touch."

I struck three hard blows, but each time the hammer flew off the head of the nail. Pratt and Rigdale laughed. I laughed, too.

Pratt said, "I played a little carpenter's trick on thee. Forgive me, sir."

"I forgive you, sirrah, if you explain the trick."

"I rubbed ear wax upon the head of the nail."

I laughed. "Henceforth, I will call you, 'Ear-Wax Pratt.'"

He said, "Your servant, sir," and pulled the nail out of the wall.

"Nay, I will not call you 'Ear-Wax Pratt.' I will call you 'Phineas.' Phineas is a noble name. There was once a Phineas who was the pagan king of antique Thrace."

"You mean to say that my father named me for a pagan?"

"So he did, sirrah."

"Father never told me. I'm not surprised. He was a papist. I converted to the true religion when I was a journeyman in London."

"Which religion is that?"

He said, "Why, the Church of England, sir."

Rigdale said, "Would you take me for a member of the Church of England, sirrah?"

Pratt said, "I cannot say. I cannot see into your soul. I know not what you are. Are you a Minister? You lead our little congregation in prayer thrice daily. But why do you not preach a sermon to us on the Sabbath?"

Rigdale said, "I would if I could."

I said, "You do not require a licence to preach aboard the *Swan*."

"God must give me His licence to preach."

On the following Sabbath, the wind slacked about noon, and the cool weather grew very calm. Rigdale's little congregation gathered on the quarterdeck. An immense black whale breached just off the starboard bow. He jumped clear of the sea and dove back beneath the waves. Then he burst to the surface, blew two soaring plumes of water that formed a V from atop his head, and vanished again into the depths.

Rigdale cried out after him, "Leviathan! That was Leviathan! God be praised! We have beheld Leviathan!

"Dear friends, with God's help, I will this day preach a sermon to you on Job 40:20, 'Canst thou draw out leviathan with an hook and with a line which thou shalt cast down into his tongue?'"

He stood awhile in silence and then spake thus: "God help me! I have nothing to say about Job 40:20. I have nothing now to say about anything, save my soul. And I have but one thing to say about that: my soul is a dry land.

"Dear God, licence me to preach a short sermon in the plain style to these godly Christians on the aforesaid words of Job. O, my God, the Jews do not yearn for their Messiah with more devotion than I yearn to preach Thy Word. O Lord, harken unto my prayer."

Another whale breached off the starboard bow and vanished into the sea. Rigdale said, "I took your companion as a sign for me to preach a sermon on Job 40:20. I was wrong."

———————

In fair weather, Henry, Abigail, Weston, Rigdale, and I dined in the great cabin with Captain Green. We had each paid three pounds, tuppence for the entire voyage to eat various and sundry victuals: dried bread and biscuits, salted eggs and salted fish, bacon and cured meats, calf tongues in bran or meal.

We all grew particularly weary of dried bread. One afternoon, at the beginning of June, Weston said, "Last night I dreamed that a warm loaf of freshly baked white bread was set on a table before me. I said to myself in my dream, why can I not smell this delectable loaf of bread?

"Pray tell me, Master Wentworth, can you smell in your dreams?"

"I am thinking on it."

He said, "Whilst you think, I will pour me another cup of Aqua Vitae."

"If it please you, sir, pour me another as well, for I cannot stomach drinking the beer on shipboard. It is either very salty or as thick as pudding."

"Well? What say you, sir? Can you smell divers odors in your dreams?"

"I cannot recall having done so."

"I will tell thee how to do it."

"How?"

"Piss abed whilst you dream you are pissing, and you will smell piss."

I said, "Go piss abed yourself and say that you sweat!"

Henry said, "Gentlemen! I pray you, cease your filthy talk in the presence of my sister."

I said, "I apologize, Mistress. Forgive me. I forgot myself. Swilling Aqua Vitae is a beastly thing. I swear to you that I will never swill the stuff again."

Abigail said, "Thanks be to God, for then we can remain friends."

That night, three of Weston's men forced open a cask of Aqua Vitae in the hold and got drunk. Weston kept them on bread and water and had them clapped in leg irons, with their hands bound behind them, all the next day.

One of the rogues, whose name was Martin Hook, thereafter said to me, "Do you remember me, sir? I remember you. I said to you, 'If I sail not with you on the *Swan*, sir, hang me up from the main-yard.' I said, 'I pray you, sir, show me where to make my mark, that I might earn my four pounds, two shillings, and tuppence for my one year's labor in the wilderness across the sea.'

"I would gladly suffer leg irons again in exchange for another night of tippling Aqua Vitae in the hold. Being drunk is my only time aboard this infernal ship that I do not fear drowning. I was almost mad from fright during the storm.

"I was a lad of twelve, on my father's farm in Sussex, when I carried the corpse of little Elizabeth Fowler out of Laxton Pond. How she come to drown there no one knows. Jane Mayo, whilst washing clothes, spied her under the water and fetched me from the barn. As I cannot swim, I walked into the water up to my chest and held my breath and ducked my head and spied wee Beth lying face up on the sandy bottom, midst the weeds. I remember her long braids floating amongst the weeds. Her eyes were shut. I grasped her right wrist. The flesh was cold and slimy. It was the first time I had ever touched a corpse. I took another breath of air and picked up Bess. She was very light in weight. I carried her out of the pond and laid her upon the bank.

"Bess Fowler was nine years of age when she drowned. Jane Mayo cleansed the vomit from Bess's mouth with her forefinger. I touched Bess's cold, slimy wrist once again. It chilled my heart. I have been terrified of drowning ever since. Sailing across the sea on the *Swan* is the bravest thing I have ever done. I'm doing it for ready money: three pounds, six shillings, and one share of the profits we shall make."

———•◦•———

Abigail and I passed much of our remaining time aboard the *Swan* together. We endured fog, rain, cold, and three more storms, the last of which, on the second of June, split our spritsail in pieces. It was a great mercy of God that it did split, for otherwise it would have endangered the breaking of our bowsprit, and perhaps our topmasts as well. The whole ship kept a fast of thanksgiving.

I must confess that once when Abigail was sick in her cabin, I enjoyed a bowl of Captain Green's Aqua Vitae, after which I asked her forgiveness, which she granted me, with tears shining in her bright blue eyes. I must also confess that those eyes, and her auburn curls, distracted me during our daily prayers. When we prayed in Henry's cabin, I often stared at a big cobweb between the cupboard and the wall. When we prayed on the quarterdeck, I always gazed out to sea, where one afternoon I saw ten porpoises frolicking at starboard. God forgive me, I envied their bestial delight.

Abigail told me something of her life in Boston, Lincolnshire, that is surrounded by fens. Her father was a rich fuller; her mother was a rich fuller's daughter. Their parish church was St. Botolph, which hath a short steeple called "The Boston Stump." Its Minister, George Story, begged his bishop to be released from wearing the surplice and white vestments. The bishop refused him. The Reverend Story then refused to make the sign of the cross over an infant during her baptism. The bishop discharged him. Abigail's father procured a position for him as the chaplain of the godly Sir Francis Fulford.

When Abigail was six years of age, her father hired a godly tutor for her named Thomas White. White taught her to read swiftly and write distinctly. She learned the catechism and, in the years to come, fervently studied the Geneva Bible.

Abigail said, "Beside the Gospels, I favored the Apocrypha. I took Queen Esther's prayer for mine own. Thus I prayed after each of my beloved parents died of the consumption, 'O my Lord, Thou only art our king. Help me, a desolate woman, who hath no helper but Thee.'"

I asked, "And did He answer thee?"

She replied, "I am not now so desolate as I was."

In fair weather, we admired the night sky from the

quarterdeck and thanked God for the new sights in His heavens. The polestar was now lower than in England, and we saw the new moon more than half an hour after sunset. It was much smaller than at any time it shone above England. On the twelfth of June, the full moon illuminated Abigail's upturned face. She returned my gaze, and we looked into each other's eyes.

I said, "Let us henceforth call each other by our Christian names. What say you, my sweet Abigail? From now on, between us, let it be 'Abigail' and 'Charles.'"

"As you wish, Charles."

Then I said,

Charles and Abigail

Set sail.

And Charles loved Abigail.

One night,

By the bluish light

Of the full moon,

He said,

"I love thee, Abigail.

But what doth it avail me?"

Then she said, "What a pretty little rhyme! And extempore, too! You say that you love me and ask, to what avail? To tell you true, Charles, I do not know. I am all in a whirl."

"And my wits are gone a-woolgathering. I do nothing well but think on thee."

The last night aboard ship, Abigail said to me, "I do not deserve your love, Charles. I dutifully tended Father for two years, ten months, and sixteen days. But God forgive me, I wished every day that he would choke to death on his bloody, purulent spittle lest I be stricken with his chest pain, his high fever, and his short, dry cough."

I said, "Why, then we are twins in misfortune. My thoughtless recitation of my sins to my sick father caused his death."

———————

We made land in Plymouth harbor at five of the clock on Thursday morning the eleventh of July, in the year of Christ 1622. We dropped anchor a league from a beach on which there waited a dozen or so men. They discharged their muskets into the air. About half a mile to the starboard, in the south, I beheld two parallel rows of some thirty thatched houses atop a flat hill. They were enclosed by a high wall of sharpened wooden stakes. Just beyond that, to the southwest, atop another hill, there was a platform mounted with four or five cannons aimed toward the sea. Then I beheld a great granite rock protruding from the sand near the foot of the first hill. Half a mile or so to the east, I beheld a dark forest of white pines. Each was at least a hundred foot in height, and some were a hundred foot higher than that. They were the tallest trees I had ever seen.

I cheered with the men on the quarterdeck, and we tossed our greasy caps in the air. Henry waved his cutlass; the sun shone on its blade.

The sun was hotter than in England. A solitary goose flying low and to the northwest above the Bay was much bigger than an English goose.

Rigdale said, "How shall we sing the Lord's song in a strange land?"

Then there came a smell from the shore like the smell of a garden, and two wild pigeons came as well and lighted on the deck beneath the main-yard.

It took the space of four hours for everyone and his baggage to be conveyed ashore in the *Swan's* five boats. I landed on the hot beach with Henry and Abigail. All of us lay about in the shade of some pines and great oaks growing on a strip of land adjacent to the shore. There, within the hour, each of us was given to drink a draught of cool water from earthen jugs carried by a goodly number of men from Plymouth town. A bearded man wearing a steeple-crowned beaver hat gave me mine.

I said, "I thank you, sir. I'll be sworn. This is the sweetest water I have ever drunk."

He said, "This is town water, sir, from the Town brook. When I was an exile in Leyden, I worked for five years as a glover with a Jew named DeCosta who had converted to the Dutch Reformed Church. He knew English well enough to teach me a few Jewish blessings for various and sundry things, which he took upon himself to convert to Christian use. The only one I remember is the one he recited before drinking a draught of water. Whenever I drink our town's cold, sweet water, I think of DeCosta's converted blessing: 'Blessed art Thou, O Lord our God, King of the Universe, at whose word water comes into being, through Jesus Christ our Lord, Amen.'"

Abigail was hailed by a gentleman armed with a cutlass in a black leathern scabbard, who declared himself to be her cousin, Edward Winslow. He said, "God be blessed! Cousin Abigail! Is that really you, sweet coz? Yes. I last saw you as a little girl, but I well remember your eyes. You have your mother's beautiful blue eyes. Were you with her when she died?"

Abigail said, "I was."

Edward Winslow said, "And did she make a good end in Christ?"

Abigail said, "Alas, both my beloved parents, of precious memory, died very hard of the consumption and could not speak a word for the space of several hours before the Lord took each of them away by death."

Edward said, "My beloved first wife, Elizabeth, of precious memory, also sleeps in the Lord. She died of the scurvy last spring at the age of eighteen. Forty-four of our dead lie buried in our graveyard at the foot of Fort Hill. That is almost half our number. We leveled the graves to conceal them from the Indians lest they take advantage of our weak and wretched state.

"I married again within six weeks of Elizabeth's death. 'Tis a common practice amongst us Saints. Widows and widowers cannot survive for long on their own in this wilderness. My new wife is named Susanna. She is twenty years of age. I trust that God will decide who will be my wife in heaven."

Abigail said, "Dear coz, this is my brother, Henry."

Edward said, "I thought as much. You have your father's look about your mouth and chin. Welcome to the Plymouth Plantation, cousin Henry. God grant health to you and your sister. What's this? What's this?

You bear a cutlass! Your cutlass marks you for a soldier, cousin Henry."

Henry said, "I hope to become one."

"Good," said Edward. "Good. We need soldiers here. The Narragansets conspire against us."

"Who are the Narragansets?" said Henry.

"Savage Indians. Our enemies," said Edward. "Captain Standish will explain everything to you. Suffice it now to say that he is our commander. He fought the Spanish papists in the Low Countries and the Narragansets here in defense of our ally, the Indian king, Massasoit, who rules some sixty warriors to the west of us. We estimate that the Narraganset Indians to the north of us can presently muster two hundred warriors. You will serve against them under Captain Standish, like all the men of the Plymouth Colony.

"Now tell me, coz. What gentleman is this?"

Abigail said, "This is our friend, Charles Wentworth, who once studied Divinity at Cambridge."

"Well met, sir," said Edward. "A Cambridge scholar. Well, well. Master Brewster also studied at Cambridge. Methinks 'twas law. I will tell him anon that you have joined us. I warrant that he'll be happy to have an old schoolmate amongst us. I bid you welcome, sir, to a new life among the godly in the Plymouth Plantation."

I said, "Alas, sir, I am a member of Master Andrew Weston's ungodly crew. I have come hither with them to make money trading with the Indians for peltry and timber. And from what I have seen of the straight, tall pine trees that will one day serve as innumerable masts for our stout English ships, we may count ourselves as rich men."

Edward said, "Have you been reborn in Christ, Master Wentworth?"

I said, "No sir, not yet. But I have faith in the Lord."

Edward said, "And you, my dear cousins, have you been reborn in Christ?"

Henry said, "Not yet, dear cousin Edward. But we too have faith in the Lord."

Abigail said, "And you, dear cousin Edward. Have you been reborn in Christ?"

Said he, "I too wait upon the Lord." Then he said, "You and Henry will lodge with me and Susanna and her infant son who was named Peregrine by her late husband, William White. William died of the scurvy about a month before my poor Elizabeth. Peregrine was born during our crossing on the Mayflower. Hence his name."

Abigail said, "I do not understand."

I said, "Peregrine means 'wanderer' or 'traveler' in Latin."

Henry said, "A name that befits us all."

At length, led by two men from Plymouth, the crowd began trudging in the sand to the east. Edward, Henry, and I divided Abigail's baggage between us and, staggering under the load, trudged along with the rest.

Having gone about a mile, we came to the west gate of the Plymouth town stockade. We passed within to face a murmuring throng.

Edward Winslow left me in charge of all of Abigail's baggage and led her under the shade of a nearby oak tree. There he said, "Sister, lie down a little—that always does me good."

Then came here three men: a tall man with a big nose and a man with a grey beard, followed by a very short man in a coat of mail, wearing a pikeman's helmet and carrying a rapier. These were followed by a drummer, a trumpeter, and two musketeers.

The drum rolled, the trumpet sounded, and the crowd fell silent. The tall man stepped forward and spake in a deep voice, saying, "I am William Bradford, the Governor of the Plymouth Plantation. By arrangement with your Master, Thomas Weston, the Treasurer of the Company of Merchant Adventurers in London, I welcome you as our guests. You will remain with us for several months until, with God's grace, you will establish a colony of your own.

"Meanwhile, you will lodge amongst us in our homes without payment of rent. We pay no wages here. We have no use for ready money. We buy and sell nothing but rather exchange our labour for necessaries. All of our assets are equally divided. Our victuals are equally apportioned amongst us from what we call our common house, or general rendezvous, for goods. Some of you will help us weed and hill our Indian corn, of which we have twenty-six acres, as well as six acres of barley and pease. Some of you will help us build our fort atop the hill at the head of the Street. Some of you will draw water and gather firewood for the common use. Others will fish in the Bay for cod and catch crabs, which are, by the grace of God, very abundant hereabouts in the summer season. You shall, like us, gather clams and mussels from the shore or ground nuts and acorns from the forest floor.

"A few of you, who are marksmen, will go a-fowling or a-hunting for deer. The divers game that you take will be equally divided amongst yourselves and the sick members of the colony.

"Once a week, on Saturday, like us, all of you will be recompensed for your labor by our gunsmith and metal worker, William Basset, who is also in charge of our common house. You will receive from him what each of us receive: a peck of Indian corn, some salt, a peck of white pease, and a large bowl of oil of olive, along with gunpowder and whatever shellfish, cod, acorns, and ground nuts that he will apportion you in equal amounts from the common house. Take heed! You must boil the ground nuts and the acorns before you eat them, for they are very bitter to the taste."

Weston's men murmured. One of them called out, "Not as bitter to us as thy words!" Bradford ignored the outcry and said, "Our store of victuals is in perilous short supply. Only God's grace is abundant in these parts. You shall live here, like the rest of us, by the sweat of your brow. We have no oxen, no horses to relieve us from the most oppressive labours."

William Butts yelled, "I did not cross the sea to become a beast of burden!"

Bradford said, "I see, sirrah, that you are clad in filthy rags. You will be provided at no cost with clean and patched apparel from our common house."

One of Weston's men could not stop coughing.

Governor Bradford said, "Good surgeon, Master Fuller, raise thy hand." A bald man in the crowd raised his right hand.

Weston's man coughed and coughed. Governor Bradford said, "Your cough, sirrah, will be treated without a fee by our surgeon, Samuel Fuller. Be so good as to raise thy hand once more, Master Fuller."

Then Governor Bradford said, "We of the Plymouth Plantation have taken what I call this common course out of necessity. We are a poor Christian community, struggling, with God's help, to survive until we achieve greater prosperity and can disseminate an understanding of the Lord among the savage Indians that surround us. For it is by the knowledge of the Lord that they and we are saved.

"We have no Minister here. We are governed instead in spiritual things by Master William Brewster, who was chosen to be our Church Elder in Leyden, whilst we sojourned in the Low Countries for twelve years."

Master Brewster, who was the man with the grey beard, said, "Man is altogether vanity. He passeth away as a shadow. His only true home is Heaven. Strangers and pilgrims are we on the earth. Still the spot on which we stand, this shore, this whole land, is dear to us. We are here in obedience to God's commands.

"We are living our lives as close as we are able to the rules of the early, apostolic church—that sacred time to which the Reformation harkens back—when the Hebrew followers of Jesus became the first Christians. Like them, we celebrate the Sabbath from the setting of the sun to the setting of the sun. And, like them, we are forbidden by Scripture to work or play on the Lord's Day. As you shall see, we spend it praying together and singing Psalms, with love and joy and fear, in praise of the Lord. We keep the Sabbath just as strictly as ever did the Jew.

"We have here neither crosses nor surplices, nor kneeling at the Sacrament, nor the Book of Common Prayer, nor any other behavior but reading the Word, singing of Psalms, and prayer before and after sermons with catechism."

My eyes filled with tears of joy. It was of a sudden all so clear. Providence had brought me across the ocean to the Plymouth Colony, wherein, with God's grace, I shall discover that I was predestined to be one of the elect.

Master Brewster said, "We believe that the equal sharing of our necessaries from the common house will make us happy and flourishing. The strong man here hath no more in division of victuals and clothes than he that is weak. Even I have but one cloak."

Concluding his speech Master Brewster said, "Amen!"

And I repeated the Hebrew word that impregnates our English prayers with sanctity: "Amen!"

Captain Miles Standish was the last of the three men

who addressed us. He was of such short stature that his coat of mail reached almost to his knees.

He said, "I am in command of military affairs in the Plymouth Colony and have accordingly equally divided our eight-and-forty men into four companies. Each company is armed with twelve muskets. Fifteen armed men at a time stand watch over the stockade every night.

"We muster for training every Wednesday afternoon at three of the clock in the glade on the west bank of the Town brook. Our enemies are our next bordering neighbors, the Narraganset Indians, who are over sixty strong and are much incensed and provoked against us. We fear that they have become confederates of the Massachusetts Indians, whose towns lie a few days' march north from here. They are about two hundred strong.

"The Narragansets worship a devil whom they call *Hobbamock*. The Massachusetts call him *Hobbamoqui*. All the savages sacrifice little children to him. He appears in sundry forms unto the savages, as in the shape of a man, a deer, an eagle, &c., but more ordinarily a snake. He appears only to the chiefest and most judicious amongst them—the *powohs* or priests—though all of them strive to attain to that hellish height of honor."

"The *powohs* say that some of them can cause the wind

to blow fiercely. They can raise storms and tempests, which they usually do when they intend the death or destruction of their enemies.

"Thus, in these dark forests of New England, we Englishmen wrestle not only against savages of flesh and blood, but against their dark sovereign princes and their dark powers, against the rulers of the darkness of this world, and against spiritual wickedness in high places."

Edward Winslow, Governor Bradford, Isaac Allerton, the assistant governor, Master Brewster, and Andrew Weston gathered together in the common house, where they spent the rest of the day assigning Weston's sixty men to lodge in each of Plymouth's six-and-twenty households. Of the eight men left over, three were lodged in the beasts' house among the chickens, goats, and swine; three more were lodged in the common house, while two slept in sail-cloth tents. Some of Captain Green's thirty sailors lodged aboard the *Swan*, while the rest slept under sail-cloth tents within the Plymouth stockade's north gate. Abigail and Henry, as they had been promised, lodged with Edward, his wife, Susanna, and their babe, Peregrine.

Edward Winslow told Brewster that I had studied at Emmanuel College in Cambridge, and Brewster therefore invited me, Rigdale, and Martin Hook to lodge with his family. It consisted of Master Brewster, his wife, Mary, and their sons, Wrestling and Love.

Master Brewster said to me, "I understand from Edward Winslow that you are a Separatist."

"That is true, sir."

"And you, Master Rigdale?"

"I am also."

"And you, Master Hook?" Master Brewster said. "To what church do you belong?"

"Wherever I am set down to pray, sir."

Brewster said, "I herewith charge Mister Wentworth to keep watch over thy behavior in our church, particularly during the Sabbath service. We do not use the Book of Common Prayer."

"I do not use it, either, sir," said Hook.

"God give you joy," Master Brewster said.

Hook said, "The truth is, sir, I cannot read anything."

"You have ears, have you not?"

"Aye, sir, by my faith, sir. I have big, hairy ears like an ass, as you can see."

"Then use 'em and listen when the Word of God is read to thee."

Hook said, "Oh, I do, sir, but I have no more understanding of Scripture than a malt-horse. The Word of God is wasted on an animal such as me."

Master Brewster said, "First an ass and then a malt-horse. Nay, sirrah, you are not a beast of burden. You are a man with an immortal soul."

And Hook said, "I have been used as a beast of burden my whole life."

Wrestling, Love, Hook, Rigdale, and I slept that night in our canvas beds stuffed with fresh straw upon the earthen floor of the Brewsters' house. Master and Mrs. Brewster slept in the loft. The whole house smelled of smoke, drying herbs, and full chamber pots.

Before breakfast, Master Brewster bade us to fetch wood from a pile without the south gate and then draw two buckets of water from the Town brook. I carried a charged musket. We startled a milk-white fowl, with a very black head, that fluttered into the air. The sun shining upon its white wings was a fine sight to see. I missed my shot.

At breakfast, I savoured my first taste of Indian corn pudding.

I said to Master Brewster, "I like your victuals."

Then he led us all in prayer. Hook, Rigdale, Wrestling, and I went to work weeding the fields of Indian corn, which was south of the brook to the baywards. Some of the goodly ears of corn were yellow, some red, and some mixed with blue. We crawled on all fours down the rows in the hot sun. I wore my gloves of kid, given me by my uncle Roger, to protect the sharp leaves from slicing my fingers with fine cuts. My knees were rubbed raw. I wrapped them in bloody rags.

I asked Wrestling why each stalk of corn was surrounded about its base by a pile of soil, about a foot in diameter and almost a foot in height.

He said, "Two or three herrings are buried there as manure. An Indian named Squanto taught my father how to grow corn in this barren soil. You will meet him bye and bye."

"Does he worship the devil?"

"He does," said Wrestling.

Hook said to Wrestling, "Tell me, good sir. What kind of Christian name is Wrestling?"

Wrestling replied, "When my father named me, he was thinking of Jacob. He who wrestled with the angel of God."

Hook said, "Pray tell me who is this Jacob the Wrestler?"

Wrestling said, "There was once a godly Hebrew named Jacob who wrestled with an angel of the Lord all through one night. And when the angel saw that he prevailed not against Jacob, he touched the hollow of Jacob's left thigh and put it out of joint. Though Jacob was sorely in pain, he wrestled with the angel until dawn. Finally the angel cried out, 'Let me go, for the day breaketh.' But Jacob said, 'I will not let thee go save thou bless me.' The angel said unto him, 'What is thy name?' And Jacob replied, 'My name is Jacob.' And the angel said, 'Thy name shall not be called Jacob any more. Henceforth thou shall be called Israel. For as a prince thou hast wrestled with God and with men and hast prevailed.' Israel halted painfully on his left leg all the remaining days of his long life."

Hook asked Wrestling, "And you, sir, have you wrestled with the Lord our God?"

Wrestling said, "I would not know how to do so. But I'll tell you this: to be called 'wrestling' by the world these past five-and-twenty years hath made it hard for me. 'Good morrow, Master Wrestling,' people say to me. 'Didst thou prevail against the Lord this morning?'"

Hook asked, "And what do you say to that?"

"I answer, 'God hath not manifested Himself to me in any way. My poor soul is quiescent.'"

Hook said, "What doth 'quiescent' mean?"

Wrestling said, "Something quiet, something motionless, something still."

Hook replied, "Better than poor Annie Watts in Worksop. She tormented herself day and night as to whether she be damned or saved. She could not bear not knowing, so she threw her four-month-old babe, Clyde, down a well, wherein he drowned. Said Annie, "'Tis better to know that I am damned than not to know what God plans for my soul throughout eternity.' They hanged her."

That evening, Master Brewster and I spake together for a while in Latin.

He said, "I was a pensioner at Peterhouse, wherein I dined every day upon a joint of roasted beef, mutton, or veal. In truth, I am weary of dining here upon Indian pudding, mussels, and clams (*placenta indica, mituli, et sponduli*).

We talked about Peterhouse's popish altar.

Brewster said, "Everyone bowed and cringed to it upon entering and leaving the chapel. That repelled me, but being young, I accepted the Romish practices of my elders in the hope of winning their approval.

"I converted to Separatism after I left Cambridge. Pastor John Robinson converted me in the autumn of 1600. At the time, like my father before me, I was the steward and bailiff of Scrooby Manor in Nottingham. I attended services at St. Wilfrid's. The altar, caps, surplices, and crucifixes disgusted me. The tyranny of bishops against godly preachers and people made me look further into things and see the unlawfulness of their callings. But I knew not where to turn.

"Then by the grace of God, Pastor Robinson visited me. I had known him in Cambridge.

"I told him of my plight. He recited to me 2 Corinthians, 6:17, 'Wherefore come out from among them and separate yourselves, sayeth the Lord. And touch none unclean thing, and I will receive you.'

"Pastor Robinson said, 'The Church of England is the unclean thing that blights our land. Separate thyself from it, and Christ will receive you as one of His Saints.'

"So it was, by God's grace, that I became a Separatist and freed my soul from its bondage to bishops, caps, surplices, crucifixes, altars—all the fetters forged by the Church of England that had chained my soul to the earth and deprived it of heaven."

He chewed on one end of his grey mustache and stared into the fire. Then he said, "When James gained the throne, many of us Separatists were clapt into prison. My house was beset and watched day and night. Some of us fled to Holland and left our means of living behind.

"I followed Pastor Robinson to Leyden with my family in the spring of 1607. Most of my fellow Saints, having been farmers, turned to other trades as could be easily learned. They labored twelve hours a day as weavers, wool carders (*lanae pectores*), wool combers (*depectores*), and such like. Children of the best dispositions were so oppressed with labor that their bodies were disfigured.

Then Brewster spake in English, "I taught English and Latin at the University of Leyden. In 1611, I was elected Elder of the Separatist congregation. We have neither Minister nor Teacher in our church. My plentiful life among the godly poor convinced me that when we settled in the New World, there should be no great divide amongst us between the rich and the poor. And so it is. We have no use here for ready money. We share our goods in common. We sow and reap and build our common houses together. We share our victuals to an equal extent, just as Christ shared bread and wine with His disciples.

"Plymouth Plantation is a Christian commonwealth that harkens back to the earliest days of Christ's church."

I said, "Why, then, this is the place for me."

Rigdale said, "And for me."

Hook said, "But not for me. I have come across the sea to earn four pounds, three shillings, and tuppence in ready money."

The next day being Saturday, everyone stopped labouring at five in the afternoon to prepare for the coming of the Sabbath at sundown, which I was pleased to note was the same time that the Children of Israel celebrated the beginning of their Holy Day. We washed our hands and faces and changed our shirts. At sunset, all the inhabitants of Plymouth were assembled by the beat of a drum. Each man who was a member of the Plantation wore a black cloak and carried a musket or firelock. Weston's armed men marched amongst them. Led by a sergeant, everyone placed himself in order, three abreast. Behind the sergeant came Governor Bradford, wearing a long blue robe. Beside him, on the right hand, came Master Brewster, likewise wearing a blue robe. Then there came Captain Standish in his coat of mail, armed with his rapier. He was nigh a head shorter than Master Brewster.

I took my place in the crowd between Abigail and Henry. Everyone marched to the entrance of the common house where four men bore lighted reed torches aloft in the gathering darkness. The flames flared in the wind. Governor Bradford, Master Brewster, and Captain Standish turned about and faced us. At that moment, the waning moon vanished behind a cloud. My left hand brushed against Abigail's right arm. Though I could not clearly see her face in the darkness, I was sure that she was smiling at me. I smiled in return and grasped her right hand.

Brewster said, "We welcome Weston's men and the crew of the *Swan* as our guests and give thanks to Almighty God for their safe arrival at the Plymouth Plantation. Let us walk with our new brethren with tenderness, avoiding jealousies and suspicions, back-bitings, censurings, provokings, and secret rising of spirit against them; but in all offences to follow the rule of our Lord Jesus, and to bear and forbear, give and forgive, as He hath taught us.

"Now, let us all welcome the holy Sabbath, that the Jews call the mystical bride of God, and which we—the new Chosen People—cherish as the holiest day of the week, when the whole universe returns to that state of absolute rest that preceded creation." He preached a sermon on Exodus 20:8, "Remember the Sabbath day to keep it holy."

His words were lost to me, though, for as he spake I again profaned the Sabbath with the fingers of my left hand, with which I caressed the palm of Abigail's right hand, and then her delicate wrist, and then each finger. I could scarcely believe that she allowed me these caresses. But then she slipped her left hand up the cuff of my right sleeve and there she found my pulse with her thumb and pressed it awhile.

She said, "We must fast on the morrow and ask God's forgiveness for our transgressions on the holy Sabbath."

"I was just now thinking the same thing," said I.

———————

And so Abigail and I fasted on our first Sabbath in the Plymouth Plantation. I suffered a headache from hunger all the day. At the morning service, Abigail stood in the row ahead of me between Henry and Edward.

Master Brewster said, "I will now preach a sermon on John 15:17, 'These things I command you, that you love one another.'"

Abigail's head was bowed. God forgive me, I gazed at the auburn curls upon the nape of her neck.

After the service, Abigail and I spake for awhile. Her hands were swelled and red from washing Henry and Edward's clothes.

She said, "Tomorrow, I will cleanse Edward's house. I don't mind the hard work. Were it not for the Indians, this place would be a paradise for me. I could not harken to Master Brewster's sermon. You are to be blamed. I felt your eyes upon me the whole time. God forgive us for desecrating the Sabbath twice in a row."

———————

Governor Bradford came up to me and said, "Did you study Hebrew at Cambridge, Mister Wentworth?"

"I did, sir."

He said, "I studied the holy tongue at the University of Leyden and am at present writing a Hebrew grammar. I should like to show it to you."

"It would be an honor, sir."

A tall man came up to us. The black hair of his head was long behind, but short before. There was none on his face at all. He had the complexion of an English gypsy.

Governor Bradford said, "This is Squanto. He is a Patuxet Indian who was taken to England, where he learned English. After eight years there, he was returned to New England in 1619. He helped us get through the first winter of general sickness. He is our interpreter. He taught us to make our soil fertile with pieces of rotting herring, which we bury with the kernels of corn. He is also our pilot who guides us to unknown places for our profit."

Squanto walked away. Governor Bradford said, "But never forget. Like all the other Indians, he is a benighted, treacherous, heathen savage, who worships the devil.

"How few, weak and raw, were we at our first beginning here and in the midst of barbarous enemies. Yet God wrought our peace for us. We were at the brim of the pit and in danger of being swallowed up. A loving God protected us from our savage enemies."

Abigail said, "Captain Standish told me last night

that almost the entire Virginia colony was massacred in March by the local savages."

"Alas, it's true," said Governor Bradford. "Captain Francis West, being in New England about the latter end of May past, sailed from here to Virginia and returned with the news and a few survivors who thereafter departed for England. The savages dealt a merciless blow to an unsuspecting people. Neither age nor sex was spared, and heinous atrocities were committed upon the living and the dead. The number of those massacred exceeded the whole number of our colonists here by nearly threefold. Up to the hour of the attack, the savages had cunningly borne the aspect of friendliness."

Abigail cried out, "O, my God, help us."

I accompanied Abigail to Edward Winslow's house on the Street.

She said, "So that Squanto is an Indian! I do not like the look of him. Did you notice? He hath not a hair upon his face. Not a one! And his complexion! He hath the complexion of a gypsy."

"That's what I think. An English gypsy."

"We think alike, you and I."

"What are you thinking of now?"

She said, "I cannot take my mind off that massacre in Virginia. And you?"

We had arrived at Edward Winslow's door. I said:

This much I say, and saying bid adieu,
When I wed a maid, it shall be you.

------◆◆◆------

After sunset, I ate savoury Indian pudding at Master Brewster's house. He served me a strong liquor made of pumpions and parsnips and walnut tree chips. He then recalled to me the difficult early days of the colony. He told me about the solitary death of Governor Bradford's first wife, Dorothy.

He said, "Two years ago, she fell from the deck of the *Mayflower* whilst the ship was docked in Cape Cod Bay. Some say she killed herself because she was stricken with melancholy. It is known she left her three-year-old son, John, with her sister in Holland, rather than subject him to the dangers of the ocean voyage. Governor Bradford responded to the news of his beloved wife's death, saying, 'I embrace God's will. He loves me greatly. He greatly chastises those whom He greatly loves.'"

I was much moved. Governor Bradford's faith enabled him to accept his wife's mysterious death, and her possible damnation, as a divine chastisement upon himself—proof that God greatly loved him. Why, this stout man with a big nose was a true Saint. I was sure of it! It was God's will that he had been elected Governor of the Plymouth Plantation, after he had proved to Him that he was worthy of governing His godly people in the New World.

Master Brewster asked Rigdale if he was related to John Rigdale, a haberdasher of London who, with his wife, Alice, came over on the *Mayflower* only to die together without issue during the first winter of the general sickness.

Rigdale said, "I have a brother named John, a widower, living in London. But of this other John Rigdale, I know not."

Brewster said, "In November 1620, when our provisions were scarce and the Plantation was near to starving, Bradford, myself, Captain Standish, John Rigdale, and five or six other men mounted an expedition on Cape Cod. We searched for Indian villages where we could trade a horseman's coat of red cotton and some knives for corn. By the grace of God, Rigdale found a heap of sand, which we digged up, and in it we found a little old basket full of fair Indian corn. We digged further and found a great new basket, full of very fair corn of this year, with some six-and-thirty goodly ears of corn, some yellow, some red, some mixed with blue. It was a very goodly sight. The basket held six or eight bushels. The Indians had apparently buried it for seed corn. After much consultation, we decided to take as much of the corn as we could carry away with us. The rest we buried again for we were so laden with armor that we could carry no more.

"We decided that if we found any savages to whom the corn belonged, we would immediately return it. But Providence willed otherwise, and we brought the corn back home.

"I said to my fellows, 'We have stolen the seed corn the savages require for their next crop. We have committed a heinous crime. We are felons and, according to English law, should be hanged. Let us pray for forgiveness.'

"And so we did. Nevertheless, God punished us with the ravages of disease. On the thirteenth day of March, Winslow's beloved wife, Elizabeth, died of the scurvy, followed in the same month by thirteen others of our members. In all, half of our company died, the greatest part in the depths of the winter for want of houses and other comforts, being likewise infected with the scurvy and other diseases. Of a hundred persons, scarce fifty of us remained. John Rigdale and his wife died within a week of each other of the scurvy. They were stricken with delirium. I remember John saying, 'Let us make a law that whoever falls asleep at the table shall forfeit his head.'"

Abigail said, "Surely there are more than fifty people here."

Master Edward said, "There are eighty-seven of us here, by the grace of God. The good ship *Fortune* brought thirty-seven more of us hither in November 1621. My brother John was amongst them. Alas, many of the others are not truly godly. They must be forced to come to Sabbath services.

"Thomas Weston had sent them hither without enough provisions. He wrote in a letter to Governor Bradford that we would have to stand here on our own two legs. Our Christian duty compels us to feed your men from the *Swan* for as long as we are able. We have weak hopes here of supply and succor. But what of the ample provisions that you brought with you? Let us all enjoy a portion of them."

I said, "I will speak with Andrew Weston about it."

On the day following, Weston said to me, "Some months ago, Bradford agreed with my brother to provide sufficient victuals to us for at least two months—or as long as we are compelled to tarry here. Our scant supplies are for us alone. They must last us at least a year. I set sail next in a week on the *Swan* to search for a suitable place in which we can establish our plantation."

Governor Bradford said to me, "I did not agree with Weston that we are obliged to feed all your men. But since you are here, I shall do my Christian duty and see that you do not starve. You will all continue to weed the cornfield and build the fort in exchange for victuals."

I laboured side by side with Hook, who found the green corn very eatable and pleasant to taste. Late one afternoon, Rigdale and I came upon him and two of his friends stealing the ears of unripe corn in the amount of five bushels. I bade them to desist, saying, "The corn you have robbed belongs to all the inhabitants of the Plymouth Plantation. They will depend upon it for their winter sustenance. Mr. Rigdale and I must report your crime to Governor Bradford."

Hook said to me, "You are a whoreson filthy slave, a dungworm, an excrement! By great, great Caesar's sword, you and your friend will pay with your lives if you betray us."

Rigdale said, "By great Caesar's sword! The knave swears admirably! Like a man who reads the Roman histories."

We reported the three thieves to Governor Bradford. He ordered the magistrates to tie their wrists and ankles together and condemned them to lie that way without meat or drink for twenty-four hours. Master Brewster preached a two-hour sermon to them on the text from Scripture, Exodus 20:15, "Thou shalt not steal."

Their limbs swelled; they were in great pain. They swore to the Governor that they would never steal again. At sunset, I requested him to free them and he did.

Abigail said to me, "You have a kind heart."

I said, "I asked the Governor to release them because Hook threatened to murder Rigdale and me if we betrayed him. I thought if I secured his freedom, he would forswear taking vengeance on us."

"Thank you for being honest with me."

"I could not do otherwise," said I. "I love you."

"I think you were born with 'I love you' in your mouth. You have it as ready as a nightingale hath his song. I love to hear you say it. Say it again."

I said, "I love you."

"And I love you."

"That is the first time that you have said so. What day of the week is it?"

Abigail said, "Wednesday."

"What day of the month?"

"I warrant it's about the fourteenth of July."

"Let us then declare that Wednesday, the fourteenth of July in the year of Christ 1622, is the birthday of our mutual love."

We asked Master Brewster to consult his Almanac. He did so, and then said, "Today is Wednesday, the thirty-first of July."

Abigail and I accordingly changed the birthday of our mutual love.

Abigail said to Hook, "Forswear taking revenge on Master Wentworth and Rigdale. If they come to harm through you, I shall report you both to Governor Bradford and have you hanged."

Hook said, "God forfend such a punishment! I forswear taking revenge on Master Wentworth and Master Rigdale."

On Thursday afternoon, I left off labouring in the cornfields and walked about the Plantation with Abigail. About three of the clock, it thundered. The claps were loud, but short. Then it rained. We waited under a pine tree for the storm to end. Afterwards, the birds in the tree sang most pleasantly.

We walked west up the Street between the two rows of houses and their garden plots.

On the south side, we passed Edward Winslow's house, Francis Cook's house, Isaac Allerton's house, and John Billington's house. With their clapboard walls, thatched roofs, and chimneys made of logs daubed with clay, they all looked alike.

Abigail said, "Cousin Edward told me that they cast lots for the plots, each of them being of the same size. Every man built his own house, but they built the common house together, some making mortar and some gathering thatch."

We continued walking west until we came upon a bush of wild strawberries in a sunny glade. We each picked a handful and ate them while sitting in the shade of a great oak.

Abigail said, "God be blessed. These New English strawberries are heavenly."

I said, "The Plymouth Plantation is heavenly."

Seated in the cool shade, we compiled a list of some of the base and earthly things that the Saints of the Plymouth Plantation had left behind them in England:

Item. Money

Item. Moneylenders

Item. Debtors

Item. The poor

Item. Beggars

Item. The rich

Item. Nobles

Item. Members of the Church of England

Item. Papists

Item. Surplices

Item. Altars

Item. Crucifixes

Item. Heretics

Item. Blasphemers

Item. Murderers

Item. Thieves

Item. Prostitutes

Item. Brothels

Item. Drunkards

Item. Taverns

Item. Stews

Item. Maypoles

Item. Lawyers

Item. Actors

Item. Theatres

Item. Sodomites

Item. Buggers

Item. Cutpurses

Item. Cutthroats

Item. Prisons

Item. Divers and sundry instruments of torture

Item. Gibbets

Item. Heads stuck on pikes

Finally, Abigail said, "Would that I had some fresh English cream with my strawberries. Our heavenly Plantation sorely wants a few earthly cows. And a mill. Why is there no mill here? We must grind our corn in stone mortars like the savage Indians are obliged to do.

"We have Indian corn, boiled pumpion, and boiled turnips in the morning, and boiled turnips, boiled pumpion, and Indian corn pudding at noon, and sometimes Indian corn pudding and boiled parsnips for supper. If it was not for those victuals, and the shellfish and cod, we should be undone.

"I pray God for a quiet and contented mind."

Captain Standish invited Abigail and me to dine upon an eagle that he had shot and dressed. It tasted like mutton.

The Captain said to me, "I know something of you from Master Brewster. You followed your father to study at Cambridge. He was a Minister. My father was the second son of the house of Standwich Hall in Lancashire. My university was war.

"I was bred a soldier in the Low Countries, where as a drummer boy and musketeer I fought for the Dutch Protestants against the Spanish papists for twelve years. Then God called me to join his exiles in Leyden, from whence I sailed with them hither on the *Mayflower*.

"I fought for the space of almost a year at the siege of Ostend under Sir Francis Vere. Look you! This dent in my helmet is from a Spanish musket ball that glanced off it at the Northwest Bulwark. Another ball brake my collar bone. But I will tell you this: I would rather be besieged for a year at Ostend by twenty thousand Spanish papists than sail for eight weeks in that leaking, unwholesome *Mayflower*. We were battered by storms for three weeks. I lived in dread of our God who makes the deep boil like a pot."

Abigail said, "I live in dread of the Indians here on land."

Captain Standish said, "Fear not, Mistress. God is with us. His hand hath already fallen heavily upon the Massachusetts. Five years ago, they were smitten by a plague and died in heaps. The living who were fit ran away without burying their dead. They abandoned thousands of bloated corpses to rot above ground where the wolves, crows, kites, and vermin battened on them. I have seen their bones and skulls scattered among the many places of their empty habitations. By the grace of God, there is now but a small number of Massachusetts left. A plague sent by the Lord hath made the wilderness so much more fit for us Saints of the English nation to inhabit and erect in it Temples to the glory of God."

Abigail said, "God be praised!"

The very next morning, Massasoit, the *sachem* of the Pokanokets, our neighbors to the southeast, arrived at the Plymouth Plantation with ten of his unarmed men. Captain Standish told Abigail and me that Massasoit had made a peace treaty with Governor Bradford at the beginning of the summer. According to the Governor's charge, the savages had left their bows and arrows a mile from the town.

Abigail clung to my arm at the sight of them—tall men, with faces painted black or red from their chins to their foreheads. Massasoit's face was painted dark red. Hanging about his neck was a wide necklace made of white sea shells and a long English knife on a thong. He carried a wildcat's skin over his right arm. He and the others wore deerskins over their right shoulders and leathern leggings, altogether like Irish trousers. Their long black hair reached their shoulders. Some had their hair trussed up with a feather; some had fox tails hanging down behind.

After exchanging salutations, the savages drank liberally of the colony's diminished supply of Aqua Vitae. Then they sang and danced after their manner. They sang in high, girlish voices. Massasoit guzzled two great draughts of Aqua Vitae, but neither sang nor danced. He made semblance unto Governor Bradford of friendship and amity and traded with him. Governor Bradford gave Massasoit a hatchet, a Monmouth cap, and a long length of red cloth, which he tied about his waist. Massasoit gave Governor Bradford four beaver skins and an otter skin.

Squanto was Governor Bradford's translator. Bradford said to Massasoit, "Try to keep yourself from those vices to which Indians are given and which will bring the wrath of God and men upon you, namely drunkenness, falseness, idleness, and thievery."

Massasoit said, "Give me a coat like yours."

Governor Bradford said, "Take mine as a token of our friendship."

He put off his blue coat with brass buttons and gave it to Massasoit. Then Governor Bradford dispatched the Indians from the Plantation.

He said to Abigail and me, "Just before you arrived

here in June, the Narraganset Indians, to the west of Plymouth, made preparations to make war upon us. Reported to be many hundred strong, they made many threats against us. They cast forth many insulting speeches at us, glorying in our weakness. We built a stockade around our town. I made an ally of Massasoit and his Pokanokets. I agreed that if any did unjustly war against him, we would aid him. If any did war against us, he should aid us."

Captain Standish said to me, "I was appointed military commander of the Plymouth Plantation on Friday, the sixteenth of February in the year 1621, a day I will always remember. I divided our strength into four companies of ten men each and chose four men whom I thought most fit to take command. The next morning at a General Muster, I appointed each to his place. I gave each his Company and charged him upon every alarm to obey my orders.

"You and your men, Mr. Wentworth, will face the Indians alone in your new colony. Beware of them! The Indians are cunning and treacherous. Your drunken Master Weston is ill prepared to deal with them. What hath he done about planning for a fort? You must have a carpenter in your company. Is he working on our fort? I warrant not. I am working there and have not heard of him. I suggest that you immediately set him to work on our fort so that he may learn to build one for your company.

"I also suggest that you choose twenty of your most reliable and sober men to join with me and my four Companies next Wednesday at noon upon yonder bank of the Town brook. Each of you bring a musket, five musket balls, two flasks of powder, and a forked gun rest. I will train you to become disciplined musketeers, and you, in your turn, will each train two more companies of twenty men each to defend your plantation."

The next day, I put forth the two proposals to Weston, who was drunk at eleven of the clock in the morning.

He said, "Why, those are fine ideas. Tell the carpenter—what's his name?—to start work on the fort on the morrow. As for the other matter, I leave it in your hands. What was the other matter? Ah, yes, the training of musketeers. Doest thou know the song called 'The Old Musketeer'?"

He sang,

His head as white as milk,
All flaxen was his hair.
But now he is dead,
And laid in his bed,

And never will come again.

So shed a tear

For the old Musketeer.

Then he said, "Mark me, I will not die old." He sang again, "So shed a tear…"

He stopped and said, "My throat squeaks this morning for want of liquoring," and took a swig of Aqua Vitae.

I spake with Phineas Pratt in the evening. He said, "But I am working on the fort. I took it upon myself to do so, in order to learn how to build one for us."

I said, "God be at your labour."

"I have not had the honor of meeting Captain Standish."

I said, "I shall arrange it."

And so I did. Thereafter, Pratt worked with Captain Standish at building the fort.

Pratt said to me, "Before the Governor's house in the center of the town we are building a square stockade upon which four patereros will be mounted. They are small, breech-loaded swivel guns, which will enfilade the streets. Upon the hill, we are building a forty-eight-foot square house, eighteen foot in height, with a flat roof, built of sawn planks stayed with oak beams. Upon the top of that, they will mount six cannon which shoot iron balls of four and five pounds that will command the surrounding country. The lower part of the fort, ten foot in height, will be used for a church."

On Saturday morning, Master Brewster preached a sermon on Genesis 17:8, "And I will give thee, and thy seed after thee, the land wherein thou art a stranger, even all the land of Canaan, for an everlasting possession; and I will be their God."

"Let us pray daily for the conversion of the heathen Indians. We must consider whether there be other means for us to take to convert them. It seems to me that we must endeavor to use other means to convert them. But these means cannot be used unless we go to them, or they come to us. They cannot come to us because our land is full. We may go to them for their land is empty.

"This then is a sufficient and lawful reason to go thither unto them. Their land is spacious and a void, the haunt of foxes and wild beasts. The Indians are not industrious, neither do they have art, science, or skill to use the land. Everything spoils there and rots for want of manuring and cultivation.

"As the ancient patriarchs removed from empty places into more roomy spaces, where the land lay idle and waste, even though there dwelt inhabitants therein, as Genesis 13:6, 11, 12 and 34:21 tells us, so it lawful for us now to take a land which none useth and make use of it.

"Let us then by friendly usage, love, peace, and honest and good counsel live together in peace with the Indians on that land. May they subject themselves to our earthly prince and be persuaded at length to embrace the Prince of Peace, Christ Jesus, and rest in peace with him forever. Amen."

———————

Next morning, at dawn, the *Swan* set sail to search for the place wherein Weston's company would establish a colony. The wind was full east and cool. Abigail and I lingered on the beach until the ship disappeared over the horizon to the northeast.

She said, "Let us make the most of the time we have left to spend together."

We agreed to meet every afternoon when we finished our appointed work.

On the day following, I went to weed in the cornfield. Just before noon, as I pulled a handful of weeds from the crumbling earth, my eye caught the yellowish tassel protruding atop a red ear of corn from its sheath of pointed leaves. I peeled the leaves back an inch or two. An ant was crawling on one of the red kernels. I gazed at my gloved right hand, holding the weeds with their roots covered with soil, and the shallow hole left in the earth around the stalk. Then I digged beneath the stalk's roots. There I saw the backbone of a herring that had rotted away.

Then my soul flowed joyfully into those elements of fecundity, ordained by God to bring forth the fruit of the earth for man. I was one with the sunlight, the soil, the rain in its season, and those herring bones. We were nurturing that red ear of Indian corn together. I sang, "Hey down, a-down, down-derry. Among the leaves so green, o!"

Then my joy dissipated. I was once more sundered from the primal unity of things.

Abigail and I met late that afternoon without the common house. I told her what had happened to me in the cornfield.

She said, "Take care, sweetheart! It may have been the Devil that deluded thee."

"Wherefore?"

"Why, to puff you up with pride."

I said, "In truth, I am proud of what happened to me in the cornfield."

We prayed that God chasten my pride. The sun began to set.

Abigail said, "When I was a child of nine or ten, I

was sore afraid of the dark. Night after night, when my candle went out, I cried out to my darling brother the old childish rhyme:

> Brother, dear brother, fetch me a light!
> Satan's come hither to give me a fright.

And darling Henry came to me with a freshly lit candle and stood at the head of my bed until I fell asleep.

"Now I lie abed by the feeble light of a stinking fish-oil lamp. I cannot sleep for my terror of the Indians. I cannot forget Massasoit's men singing and dancing on the Street. Their high whining voices were demonical. I fear the savages will massacre us in the night, like those savages who massacred our countrymen in Virginia. When that stinking oil lamp flickers out, I cry,

> Brother, dear brother, fetch me a light!
> Satan's come hither to give me a fright.

And darling Henry arises from his bed by the chimney with his cutlass and a burning reed torch and remains by my bed until I fall asleep."

I said, "When we are married, I will watch over you every night."

She said, "And I shall be subject to you in all things. My father taught me that the proper attitude of a wife to her husband should be a reverent subjection. My womanly nature shall ensure my sweet submission to you."

———◆———

I chose twenty of Weston's men who wanted to learn how to shoot. Each armed himself with a match-lock musket, ten pounds of powder, five pounds of shot, and a forked gun rest. At noon on Wednesday, the twenty-one of us lined up on the west bank of the Town brook with Captain Standish's forty musketeers. I spied Henry Winslow, wearing a bandolier and armed with his cutlass, a musket, and a dagger in a green leathern scabbard.

Little Captain Standish looked every inch the soldier in his pikeman's helmet and chain-mail coat, with his rapier on his hip. He spake in a loud voice: "You new men will learn to do everything at my command. I will call out, 'Forward march!' and placing your left foot first, you will march in step together, carrying your muskets, with lit matches, upon your left shoulders.

"At my next command, which will be 'Halt!' you will do just that and remain in a straight line. Then, upon my command 'Rest!' you will rest your musket's barrel upon your forked gun rest."

Next, he taught us the commands to charge our muskets, prime our pans, blow on the ends of our burning matches, take aim, and shoot. He said, "Your target will be that oak, some forty yards to the east, on the far side of the brook. Hold your breath, exhale a bit, and slowly squeeze the trigger."

After three weeks practice, we learned to accomplish the aforesaid orders. I delighted in each roar of our muskets firing together in clouds of sulphurous smoke. From whence comes such indecent joy?

Late one afternoon, Master Brewster said to me, "Squanto espied two great whales in the Bay yesterday, the best kind for oil and bone. They each gave a snuff of water and swam out to sea. We must learn to hunt them."

He and I talked again in Latin about Cambridge. He said, "I practiced archery at Peterhouse. I am as proficient with the bow as Squanto." We discussed the prose of Hermogenes and the orations of Cicero.

After sunset, we walked west with Abigail and Master Brewster upon the highway to the Town brook. I lighted our way with a smoky reed torch dipped in pitch drawn from pine. The wind was full east and cool. Ripening cornstalks rustled in the nearby fields. Crickets chirped in the long grass. The shrill song of the cicadas rose and fell in the bushes and trees.

Brewster said, "God clothes the world in the summer season with a pleasant dress, delightful to the senses and profitable for use. Praise God for the summer season!"

For more than a week, in the evenings, I watched Rigdale make a pine Bible box for Master Brewster. Rigdale carved beautiful embellishments; he taught me their names: rosettes, lunettes, vertical flutes. He gave the box to Brewster on a Tuesday evening, whilst Abigail was visiting us.

Master Brewster said, "I thank you, Mr. Rigdale. You have made me an Ark that is worthy of the Holy Bible that will repose within. What are these fanciful birds that you have carved on top?"

Rigdale said, "They are nightingales, sir, or rather what I imagine nightingales look like. I have never seen one, but I once heard its liquid song in the Southwark graveyard."

I said, "Are there any nightingales in New England, Master Brewster?"

"Alas, we have none. Instead of their liquid song, as Mr. Rigdale so precisely describes it, we have the grievous cry of noisome beasts like the fox and the bear and the wolf."

Abigail said. "And the demonical singing of savages."

Brewster said, "Squanto is teaching me the language of the Pokanokets. We must be more perfectly acquainted with their language, and they with ours, that we may trade with them and press upon them spiritual things. The Pokanoket word for God is *Manitu.* We must council them in the worship of the true God."

Abigail said, "Foxes, bears, wolves, and savages. This is a wild place that God hath given us for our refuge. Wild and strange."

Abigail, Rigdale, Master Brewster, and I left Brewster's house and walked into the bright moonlight.

Master Brewster said, "I was a stranger in Holland for twelve years. My youngest son, Reborn, died of the measles in Leyden. He was but five years of age. We lived in the *Stink-steeg*, which means Stench Lane. Its rancid odors were to me the smell of exile. I feared that my five surviving sons would grow up as Dutchman and lose the true religion and their language—our precious English tongue. Many children of my fellow exiles profaned the Sabbath. Some became soldiers, others sailors; others took to worse courses, to their parents' grief, their souls' danger, and the dishonor of God."

The moon went behind a cloud. I could not see Abigail's face. She cried out, "Son of God, shine on me in the dark. Save my soul!"

Brewster said, "Fear not, woman! Have faith, and God's bowels will yearn toward you in your distress, and His grace will encompass you as one of His Saints."

She said, "How shall I know that I am saved?"

He said, "You will feel separated from your present life, which is a pageant of foolish delight, a theatre of vanity, a labyrinth of error, and a gulf of grief."

Rigdale said, "My life is a gulf of grief for my dead wife and daughter."

Henry decided to build himself and Abigail a house. He said to Abigail, "It will belong to you when you are married."

He cast lots and won a plot on the south side of the Street. Pratt, Rigdale, Captain Standish, Edward Stanton, and I helped with the work. Before we began, Rigdale recited the words from Psalm 127:1, "Except the Lord build the house, they labour in vain that build it."

I had never built a house before. We started in the northern woods, where the inhabitants of Plymouth procure their timber. Stanton handed me a felling ax and said, "Use an up-and-down stroke. Try to keep the blade from turning to the side. Take care that it does not glance off the wood and cut you in the leg. Such a wound will most likely mortify, and you will surely die of it. Above all, cut only one side of the tree so it will fall in the opposite direction."

Though I wore my gloves of kid, the ax handle raised bloody blisters on my sweaty hands. We felled four pine trees, sixty to eighty foot in length, and a tall oak. My education in the wilderness proceeded apace. Standish taught us how to make clapboards on the site from a balk of wood four foot in length. I learned to use a frow and beetle. We dragged the timber down the Street, where we set the large oaken posts into sills that rested upon level stones and tied them together by horizontal oaken beams that marked the space under the rafters.

I learned that the rafters rested on a pair of horizontal beams which were called plates; the floor of the space under the rafters was called the loft; each pair of vertical posts, spaced sixteen foot apart, made what is called a bay. Abigail and Henry's house consisted of two bays— the hall and the parlor. The chimney was in the center.

One evening, I said to Abigail, "When you and I are married, we shall sleep together by the fire in this hall."

She said, "I long for your embrace and long to embrace you."

We dined well. Captain Standish went fowling at dawn every morning and returned with fat ducks and geese. Abigail dressed them and fetched us beer.

One morning, as I was cutting notches in the studs,

I looked east on the Street at the crowd of men and women going about their daily business. I recognized Richard More with his servant, Edward Story, William Mullins, Peter Brown, John Goodman, and Master Brewster. I was sure that each of them was a Saint; each had been regenerated, born again into a new life, which they shared. Edward Story was carrying a bundle of faggots for his master, who clasped Brewster's hand as they spake. How I envied them!

Rigdale made two pine bedsteads, three oaken stools, and a table for Abigail and Henry. Rigdale, Pratt, Henry, Standish, Stanton, and I finished building the house on the twenty-first of August, the day that everyone began harvesting the pot herbs, the salad herbs, and the physic herbs in his garden.

That selfsame day, Abigail and Henry lodged in their house. She said to her brother, "I shall keep house for you until one of us is married. I shall bake your bread, dress your meat, brew your beer, and mend your shirts and breeches. I shall wash your bedclothes and sweep the floors, for you are my only brother and protector, whom I have ever loved."

God forgive me! I was jealous of Henry.

He and Abigail served dinner for eight people: themselves, Stanton, Rigdale and Pratt, Master Brewster,

Captain Standish, and me. We ate three fat geese that Captain Standish had shot.

Stanton said to me, "I was once a printer. I have a library in my house of some two dozen books that I printed in London and Leyden. I was like a soldier who sees no fair weapon, but wishes for it. I could not see a good or rare book, but did covet to print it. Have you read *Pelly's Pilgrimage*?"

"No," I said.

"But you must! It is a revelation! I have a copy in my library. Come borrow it tonight. Its full title is *Pelly, His Pilgrimage, or the Histories of Man, Relating the Wonders of His Regeneration, Vanities in His Degeneration, Necessity of His Regeneration*."

I borrowed it that night and read some twenty pages. I could not stomach its rhetorical style.

About this time, I made the acquaintance of Will Winslow, Edward's brother, who was one of the five-and-thirty settlers who had arrived at Plymouth on the *Fortune* in November 1621.

Said he, "We are called 'the Strangers' by the members of the Plantation who came here on the *Mayflower*. Only five-and-twenty of us are Separatists. The rest are members of the Church of England.

"We were all gathered together in London by Thomas

Weston. Our first glimpse of New England was Cape Cod, which is but a naked and barren place. When we were landed in Plymouth, there was not so much as biscuit-cake or any other victuals for us. Neither had we any bedding, nor pot, nor pan to dress any meat in, nor many clothes.

"We put up our huts made of clapboard and thatched roofs. The Mayflowers, as we call them, cut their daily provisions in half to feed us. But there is a division still between us. We are all lusty young men. Not many of us are married. The Mayflower husbands are jealous of us for befriending their wives. Worse than that, as I said, some of our men belong to the Church of England, and they are not allowed to pray or keep the Sabbath according to their papist customs. They wanted to send to London for a Church of England Minister to tend to their spiritual needs. But of course, Governor Bradford refused them permission. Methinks it will be a long while, if ever, that the two distinct communities inhabiting this place become as one."

Thereafter, I tried to perceive whether a lusty young man I passed on the street was a Stranger or a Mayflower. They all looked the same to me.

By the tenth of September, the victuals in the common house were almost spent. The sky was empty of fowl.

The bay and creeks near us were full of bass and other fish, yet for want of strong netting, we could not catch them. And though the sea swarmed with cod, we had neither tackling nor hawsers for the Plantation's six shallops. (These small sailboats made Captain Standish violently sick, but he often sailed in them.) God in His mercy provided us with divers shellfish that could be taken by hand on the beach. Like the Indians, we ate them roasted and raw.

Late one afternoon, at low tide, I gathered two bushels of mussels, oysters, and clams. I shared them with Abigail and Henry.

She said, "Sea shells! Henry once said that the Indians flay their prisoners alive with sea shells like these. How long do you suppose it would take a flayed man to die?"

"Too long," said I.

At that time, a messenger from the Narraganset *sachem*, Conanacus, arrived in Plymouth with a bundle of new arrows wrapped in a rattlesnake's skin, which he gave to Governor Bradford. Squanto told the Governor that it was an Indian message that imported enmity. Squanto then translated a long insulting speech that the messenger cast forth at Bradford, glorying in the weakness of the Englishmen of Plymouth and saying how easy it would be to slaughter all of us.

The Governor stuffed the skin with powder and shot and returned it to the messenger, saying, "My answer speaks for itself."

Now also Massasoit, the *sachem* of the Pokanokets, frowned on us and did not come to Plymouth as before. We feared that our supposed friend would join with our enemy Conanacus in a confederation against the colony.

Governor Bradford put all of us men to work on the fort, hoping that when it was finished and a continual guard kept there, it would discourage the savages from rising against us. But this drew us away from weeding the Indian corn, and the crop suffered.

———◆———

The *Swan* returned to Plymouth on Wednesday, the eleventh of September. Andrew Weston reported that he had enjoyed a favorable tide and a fair wind. He turned the point of the harbor called the Gurnet, then sailed ten leagues north around the north end of Nantasket. Then he turned west into the Bay of Massachusetts and south to a landing.

Weston told us he had exchanged presents with Wittuwamat, the *sachem* of the local Massachusetts who had survived the pestilence. Weston chose for our settlement a site known by the Indians as Wessagusset, meaning "the place wherein the North River flows," which was near the mouth of a little stream, called the Monatiquot, that empties into the Bay. He chose the place because it lies south of all the principal streams that separate the surviving Massachusetts from the Plymouth territory, thus making intercourse between the settlements comparatively easy.

One day, Abigail said to me, "I'm always hungry."

I borrowed Captain Standish's fowling piece and shot down two wild pigeons, which I gave to Abigail.

She said, "Thank you, Charles."

"I would do anything for you."

"Would you kill an Indian to protect me?"

I said, "Gladly."

"God forgive me, that delights me."

On the night before I left Plymouth on the *Swan*, Abigail, Henry, and I supped with the Winslows in their little clapboard house on the south side of the Street. After supper, Susanna Winslow nursed her babe on the bench beside me.

She said, "Come, my sweet Peregrine. Take my breast and taste that the Lord is good."

Abigail said to me, "Oh, Charles, we shall be parted for a year. A whole year! I shall miss your little rhymes and your pitted face. With God's grace, we shall one day have a son of our own like little Peregrine. May we name him Thomas Arthur for my father?"

I said, "Thomas Arthur, it will be."

When we were alone, she asked, "Will our love endure our separation?"

I sang,

> Hey down a-down, down-derry,
> Among the leaves so green, o!
> In love we are, in love we'll stay,
> Among the leaves so green, o!

The *Swan* set sail from the Plymouth Plantation at dawn on Monday, the twenty-third of September in the year of Christ 1622. I bade Abigail farewell on the beach. She gave me her white kerchief to wear about my neck.

Then she said, "It was so late ere I fell asleep last night that I can scarce open my eyes. Nay, sweetheart, do not look at them. They are red and swelled from weeping."

I next took my leave of Governor Bradford, Master Brewster, Henry and Edward Winslow, and Captain Standish.

Governor Bradford said, "I'm sorry that you did not

have the chance to read my book, *Exercises in Hebrew Grammar*. I should particularly like your opinion of my chapter on the passive voices of verbs."

Then he said, "I learned Hebrew in Leyden."

"You told me. Why did you do so?"

He said, "Hebrew is the language of revelation. God revealed Himself to Moses in Hebrew upon Mount Sinai, and Jesus revealed Himself to Saul in Hebrew upon the road to Damascus. He said in Hebrew, 'Saul, Saul, why persecutest thou me?' Did you know that the Hebrew verb for persecute is *tirefuni*? And Saul said, 'Who are thou, Lord?' And the Lord said, 'I am Jesus whom thou persecutest.'

"Those few words from God, in Hebrew, converted Paul, the Hebrew-speaking Jew who brought the world to Christ. I sometimes pray in Hebrew. It maketh me to feel closer to God. I prayed in Hebrew after my wife, Dorothy, died. I am anxious to learn your opinion of my book of Hebrew grammar."

I said, "I shall be pleased to provide it when, with God's grace, I return to Plymouth in a year. It is here that, with your permission, I intend to spend the rest of my life."

He said, "I heard as much from Mistress Abigail. You shall be most welcome."

"I thank you, sir, with all my heart."

"And how can that be? For I also heard that you have lost your heart to Mistress Abigail."

"I have, sir."

He laughed and said, "You have a big heart."

Master Brewster said to me, "Above all, remember to sanctify the Sabbath. Mark me! Your colony will stand or fall on whether you keep or profane the Sabbath."

I said, "I will remember, sir."

Henry gave me his dagger in its green velvet scabbard, which I wore hanging from my belt. Edward Winslow gave me a copy of the *Astrological Almanac, The Nature and Disposition of the Moon,* that he had printed in Leyden.

The twenty-third of September was the ninth day of the moon. The Almanac said, "Whatever thing thou wilt do on the ninth day of the moon, shall come to good effect. Get married, go on a journey." Then, one after the other, my friends gave me to put into my knapsack a flint and steel, a burning glass, a needle and thread, an awl, a compass, and a horn cup. Above all, I treasured Abigail's white kerchief, which I wore about my neck. In the days to come, I fancied that it still gave off the sweet aroma of her skin.

PART IV

THE *SWAN*, WITH SIXTY MEMBERS of Weston's company and thirty-three sailors aboard, made land at Wessagusset on the afternoon of Friday, the sixth of September in the year of Christ 1622. Rigdale said to me, "Be of good courage, dear friend. The Lord hath lured us into this dark forest to speak to our hearts."

That night, we lighted fires along the beach. Weston charged ten armed sentinels to watch over the rest of us while we supped on oatmeal porridge and boiled pease and guzzled Aqua Vitae.

One of the drunken sentinels discharged his musket into the sand at his feet. He cried out, "God forgive me, I have murdered a clam. 'Twas an accident. I did it not for any malice."

I wrote Abigail the following:

Sweetheart, I will send you this as soon as I am able. I commend myself unto you for life. And so, kissing your kerchief, I rest yours in true love,

Charles
Wessagusset, the seventh of September

P.S. Weston says the Indians told him that "Wessagusset" means "the place wherein the North River runs."

About midnight, we heard a prolonged, doleful howl from the woods. It was answered by another howl further off. Then the first resounded again, followed by the other. Our sentinels called, "Arm! Arm!" and shot off two muskets. The howling ceased. We concluded it was a company of wolves and returned to the *Swan* for the duration of the night.

The next day, Weston and six men explored the forest near the shore. A quarter of a mile to the south, they discovered a large glade wherein there ran a small brook. Weston decided to establish our settlement in the glade on the brook's right bank. He charged Pratt to oversee building our habitations there, surrounded by a stockade. Pratt walked up and down in the glade, measuring out the ground and making notes in a little leathern bound book.

The next morning, under his direction, the whole company set to work. We first cut down all the trees growing for twenty rods about the glade. The space was cleared to prevent a surprise assault by savages lurking behind the pines. Then we cut and trimmed three hundred and ninety timbers from the young white pines we found growing in a burned-over part of the forest. Each was one foot in diameter and from ten to thirteen foot in length.

It took us a week to finish the work. It took another three days to drag and carry the timber into the glade. We then digged a three-foot-deep trench in the shape of a rectangle that was seventy-four-foot long and forty-five-foot wide in which we buried the butt ends of the sharpened stakes. That took another day. We then erected the sharpened stakes, which were eight foot in height. They comprised our stockade for which we fashioned four gates hung on hinge posts hard by the four corners of the rectangle. We built a big shed, with open sides, in the middle of the stockade in which we stored our victuals and drink from the *Swan*'s hold and all of our trade goods.

Pratt said, "I have decided not to build us a small blockhouse, but a more spacious fortified village within the stockade."

And therein, within the space of another week, we built eight fifteen-by-eighteen timber and clapboard houses with sloping clapboard roofs. Twelve men lodged in each house. The rear walls of the houses were the sharpened stakes of the stockade. The side walls, eight foot in height, were not sharpened because the roof line rested on roof ribs supported atop the wall logs. At their highest point, the sloping roofs were ten foot high. We covered them with earth to prevent them from catching fire. The last thing we did was lay down five logs, each five foot in length and three foot wide, against the walls between the houses. These were to be the platforms from which sentinels could fire upon the savages beyond the walls.

Pratt said, "This is the first fortification I have ever built. The idea came to me of a sudden, whilst I walked about in the sunny glade. I asked myself in my thoughts: how do I provide ample lodging for ninety men, and how could they defend themselves against an Indian assault? Then, praise God, I saw in my mind's eye the fortification standing before you, even unto the roof ribs atop the wall logs."

I said, "You are truly a master carpenter."

Pratt said, "I like to think that Jesus Christ was the same."

The weather turned foul; we had a sore storm of wind and rain lasting a day and a night.

I was chosen to be one of the ten sentinels on guard in the night. I wore my canvas suit. I could not keep my match lit, and therefore my musket could not be discharged in the rain. I carried a hatchet, lest we were attacked by the savages.

The skies cleared on the Sabbath. Rigdale, Pratt, and I spent the day reading Scripture and praying. The other men swilled Aqua Vitae and played at dice and cards. Primero and Gleek were their favorite card games. They played for money. For the first time since arriving in New England, I heard the clink of thruppence, groats, farthings, and shillings.

In the late afternoon, William Butts and Hugh Beere fell out over a game of Primero. Weston tried to restrain them.

Butts yelled at Weston: "All the devils in hell go with you! Would to God that you were underground!"

Weston backed away. The men laughed.

Rigdale said to Weston, "I beseech you, assert your authority."

Weston bade me take a measure of the supplies that remained to us.

Item. 85 bushels of white pease, of which 12 were wormy, left from 120 bushels.

Item. 280 bushels of meal, of which 20 were wormy, left from 480 bushels.

Item. 100 bushels of oatmeal left from 120 bushels, of which 13 were wormy.

Item. No pepper, ginger, sugar, nutmegs, cloves, dates, raisins, damask prunes, rice, saffron, salt left at all.

Item. 1 barrel of pippin vinegar left from 1 barrel of pippin vinegar.

Item. 38 gallons of Aqua Vitae left from 80 gallons of Aqua Vitae.

Item. 48 barrels of beer left from 60 barrels of beer.

Item. 4 and a half tun of cider left from 8 tun of cider.

Weston called a parliament of the whole company. We met about our public business within the east gate. Most of the men were drunk.

Weston addressed us in a loud voice: "We must discipline ourselves and apportion our victuals and drink to an equal degree. Otherwise, we shall descend into chaos, and come winter, we shall starve to death."

The men cursed him. Their mouths were stinking sinks for all the filth of their tongues to fall into. As the drunken company dispersed, one of the sailors cried out, "Let's be merry whilst we are still healthy. Sickness will steal upon us ere we be aware."

Each of us continued to eat and drink as much as he wanted. God forgive us, even Rigdale and I got drunk on a Sabbath. Possessed by the Devil, I lived only for the moment, rejoicing in each time of day. At dawn, the sky changed from black to deep blue to pale grey to white.

The weather was frosty. The leaves were turning on the trees that grew amongst the pines. Those leaves that were freshly fallen upon the ground put me in mind of dragons' scales. I wrote a little verse:

The Turning of the Leaves in New England

In the cold, the leaves turn purple, yellow, and gold.
The trees then shed them, like dragons' scales.
Praise the Lord, ye dragons of the earth,
That shed thy scales before the snow.
Their brightness above will like my flesh below
Change to the brown and grey of soil and clay.

On the day following, I shot a duck. It made an excellent broth, which I gave to Weston, who was stricken with a fever. He ate it as would well have satisfied a man in good health. About an hour after, he was taken sick and vomited. Over-straining himself, he bled at the nose and so continued for the space of an hour. I washed his nose and beard with a linen cloth. He passed four liquid stools. He was stricken with a fever for five more days. His tongue swelled up, and he could not eat. I washed his mouth and scraped his tongue, getting an abundance of corruption out of it. The swelling in his tongue went down, but the rest remained dire.

On the morning of the fifth day, which was a Monday, he said, "Tell me the truth. What do you think of my case?"

I said, "I think your case is desperate. Make your peace with God."

"I am not ready to die. I am but two-and-thirty years of age. My brother is forty. If God wants a Weston, let it be he. Do you hear me, O my God? Take my brother in my stead."

The blood gushed from his nose.

He said, "Where is my brother? Hast thou seen him? Where is he? Hast thou seen him? Where hath he gone?"

He sat up, looked about, and said, "Am I dead?"

"Nay," said I. "Not yet."

"Methinks that I am dead."

"Nay, not yet."

"Are you sure? I swear that I am dead."

Then he let out a long death rattle and died.

We buried him near the southern gate. The sailors called a parliament and elected Captain Green the new governor of our plantation.

Rigdale said to me, "We have exchanged one drunkard for another."

On the day following, eight Massachusetts Indian men from their village to the west came to trade beaver skins for axes, knives, blankets, and hats. Their *sachem* was the self-same Wittuwamat who had greeted Weston. The right side of his face was painted red; the left side was painted black. His long black hair shone with smelly bear grease.

Green said, "Weston is dead. I am now the *sachem* of the Englishmen."

Wittuwamat said, "Let us live together in peace."

His interpreter was Memsowit, who was a comely youth, being in his general carriage very affable and courteous. He told me that he had learned English trading with English fishermen for a year on Cape Cod. He had a great facility for the English tongue. He said that many more of his people had survived the pestilence than Winslow reckoned. "We remain a strong people and great warriors."

A pious English fisherman on Cape Cod had taught Memsowit something of Scripture. He accepted all of the Commandments save the seventh, thinking that there were many inconveniences in it.

He said, "No man should be tied to one woman."

We reasoned about this a good time, but he would not be persuaded. He said, "I have two wives. My second wife is the joy of my life."

Memsowit told me that the Indians loved to wager. They staked their women, clothes, houses, and corn—some even their freedom, the losers reduced to slavery. At Wittuwamat's command, two savages taught some Englishmen their way of gaming. Their game was called "hubbub."

Two savages played against each other. Each had eleven sticks. They squatted facing one another. One held a shallow wooden bowl, eight or ten inches in circumference, on his lap. Five bones colored purple on one side were placed in the bowl. One of the players struck the bowl lightly with his palm, shouting, "Hub, bub, bub, bub, bub!" in a loud voice. The Indians looking on rejoined with hellish cries. The bones bounced and clicked in the bowl. If five of the self-same color bones came up, the player won two sticks from his opponent. If four of the self-same colors came up, the player lost one stick, and his opponent took his turn. If three of the self-same color bones came up, the player lost two sticks. If two of the self-same colors came up, the player likewise lost two sticks. If one came up, the player won two sticks. The game went on until one of the players lost all of his sticks.

Rigdale said, "Only Satan could have invented such an intricate game. These savages are incapable of doing so themselves. Satan is the father of all gaming."

Butts said, "How so?"

I answered thus, "Gaming makes the players believe that the world is governed by chance."

Butts said, "I think it is."

I said, "God governs the world and all the things therein."

"And the Devil?"

"He is subject to God's will in everything. Between the two, chance doth not exist, even unto the bounce of bones in a wooden bowl."

Rigdale said, "What then do you make of Ecclesiastes 9:11? 'Time and chance comes to us all.'"

I said, "I can make nothing of it. Those words are a constant torment to me."

Rigdale said, "To me, too."

Butts laughed.

Butts became proficient at hubbub in the space of the afternoon, whereupon he played against Wittuwamat. Butts wagered his Monmouth cap against the wildcat's skin which Wittuwamat carried over his right arm. Butts won. He wrapped the wildcat's skin about his neck.

Green said, "Give him the cap. Even though you won fairly, give the savage your cap. We do not want to anger him."

Butts said, "I will not!"

Green snatched Butts's cap from his head and gave it to the *sachem*, who put it on. Butts snatched it back. Wittuwamat's nine savages made a great din. He silenced them with a shout: "*Aka!*" ("Stop!") Then he spake to Butts. Memsowit translated his words: "I will remember you."

Late in the afternoon, Green appointed me to trade with Wittuwamat. I gave him seven axes, six knives, and five blankets for fourteen beaver skins, each of which had been worth five shillings when I was last in London. He offered me four skins for my dagger in its green leathern scabbard. I refused.

Hanging from Wittuwamat's girdle was a long leathern bag out of which he filled his pipe with powdered green tobacco. Memsowit told me the savages take tobacco for two causes: first against the rheum, which causes the toothache, and secondly to revive and refresh themselves.

Wittuwamat lighted his pipe and offered me a drink. To be friendly, I drank my first and last mouthful of tobacco smoke, whereupon I coughed and coughed. The savage laughed. I perceived that his fingernails were bitten to the quick, like Reverend Hunt's at Cambridge. My uncle Roger's words returned to me: "The vilest person of the earth is the living image of Almighty God."

We shared our dinner with the Indians, who especially relished eating oatmeal porridge. Weston's men opened a tun of Aqua Vitae; some sailors opened another. Almost everyone got drunk. Night drew on. I watched scores and scores of drunken savages and Englishmen frolic about four huge fires. Butts danced a jig. Wittuwamat hopped on one foot. As his tall, robust men danced with their heads thrown back, they sang together in high voices. One of Weston's men threw two armfuls of brush upon the fire nearest me. The flames flared up. By their light, I spied two naked sailors practicing the abominable vice in the dry, brown grass.

At midnight, when we sent the savages from us, we gave each of them some trifle. Wittuwamat received a pair of stockings. He offered to trade me three skins for my knife, and again I refused. Then he bade us farewell, with a promise that he and his men would soon come again with more skins to truck.

It rained for the next two days. Rigdale and I wore our canvas suits. We slept and ate under our leaky roof. Just before dawn on the second morning, he said to me, "Dear friend, I will die in Wessagusset."

I said, "God forbid!"

Rigdale said, "Such thoughts about death come to me in the night. It came to me upon a spring night that my wife, Ann, would soon die. I said nothing to her but savoured each fleeting moment we had left. I often asked her to sing. She had a sweet voice and sang our babe to sleep. My poor babe! Little Joan. I did not foresee her death.

"My darling Ann died that very summer, on Mid-Summer Eve. Lying abed, she said, 'I have a frightful headache,' and fell asleep in the Lord."

I said, "Would that I had savoured each fleeting moment of my dear Sarah's last days."

———◆———

It snowed on the twenty-fourth of October. It was the earliest day of snow that I could remember anywhere. We built fires in each house between the two rows of sleeping men. The houses filled with smoke. It drifted up through the chinks between the clapboards in the roofs. I wore my cloak over my canvas suit. I still shivered. Rigdale's teeth chattered. He and I trudged through the drifted snow to fetch brush and logs for our fire. Our feet swelled from the cold.

During this time, Rigdale, Pratt, and I again kept the Sabbath. Rigdale could not persuade anyone else to join us. He said to the men, "Take heed! Harken unto me! You will perish if you do not obey the Fourth Commandment to keep the Sabbath holy."

Butts, who was mizzled on Aqua Vitae, replied to him, "Keeping the Sabbath will not keep death at bay. Sooner or later, we will all die. I would rather frolic playing Gleek on the Sabbath than pray it away."

I said, "'Bay' and 'away' and 'pray.' You speak in rhyme, sirrah."

He said, "I will do so again. Let me see. Aqua Vitae makes a poet out of me. If I could read and write, I would drink Aqua Vitae all the day and write poems about playing Gleek. What rhymes with Gleek?"

"Shriek."

"'Shriek!' said Death to me when I lost to him at Gleek. So I shrieked…What comes next? I cannot think. Give me more to drink."

I said, "Another rhyme! That makes four!"

Butts said, "They come to me all on their own."

Rigdale said, "Enough of this childish nonsense! We were talking about the Fourth Commandment."

I said, "I would rather play with words. God forgive me, I sometimes fear that I love the English language more than I love Christ."

Butts said, "Well spoken, sir! Give me to drink again."

I said, "Away, soused herring, pickled in Aqua Vitae!"

On Christmas day, the men feasted and frolicked in a heathenish fashion, only wanting roasted boar to make their celebration complete. Rigdale, Pratt, and I sought the Lord's guidance with a solemn fast.

Rigdale said, "All our victuals will soon be spent. We will starve as punishment for our recklessness."

Pratt said, "How did we do such a thing?"

I said, "'Tis because we are living for the moment, without regard for the future or the after life. That is a grievous sin."

Rigdale and I fetched firewood every afternoon. My wet shoes froze stiff in the snow, and I wrung blood from my stockings when I pulled them off.

On Thursday afternoon, the twenty-third of January, the *sachem* Wittuwamat, his interpreter Memsowit, and twelve other Indians came again to trade beaver skins for our Irish beef. We had none left. I again refused to trade Wittuwamat my dagger in its green leathern scabbard for four beaver skins.

Memsowit told me that his third wife, for whom he had traded a dog, had been very ill.

He said, "My dream cured her cough."

I said, "Your dream? How could your dream cure her cough?"

"I will tell you. One night, I sat up with her. Her coughing kept her awake. I fell asleep. I dreamed that the ground rose near her head, where she lay coughing. I saw that a crow was flying about under the ground and I said, 'Do not hide yourself, brother crow, I see you.' The crow stuck his head out of the ground and opened his beak. He had a snake's forked tongue.

"I said, 'I saw you, brother crow. You were flying about under the ground while my wife coughed.' The crow flew out of the ground, opened his beak again, and stuck out his snake's tongue. Then he died. I woke up. My wife stopped coughing and fell asleep right away. She got completely well. My dream cured her."

I said, "God cured her," and he said, "I believe in what I can see. I see my dreams. I cannot see your God so I do not believe in Him. When I see Him, I will believe in Him, but not until then."

"In what do you believe?"

"I believe in Spirits of the Light and Spirits of the Dark. I also believe in the *manitu*."

"What is the *manitu*?"

"The *manitu* is the spirit that dwells in everything. In stones, in fish, in the stars."

I said, "Have you seen all these spirits?"

"Others have seen them. Have you seen your God?"

"I have faith that by His grace I will see Him after I die, when I will be with Him forever."

He said, "You know not what you are talking about."

Butts challenged Wittuwamat to another game of hubbub. Butts again wagered his Monmouth cap, and Wittuwamat wagered his knife that had the face of a woman carved upon its handle. Wittuwamat lost. Memsowit translated his response: "I will have my revenge."

After the Indians departed, it snowed for three days. The falling snow hid the hills to the south and west. The islands in the bay to the north were blotted out. When it ceased snowing, the water froze in patches. The ebb and flow of the tide lifted the ice high upon the beach, then let it fall in pieces in the inlets and upon the salt marshes. Wolves howled in the forest. Flocks of crows flew in circles above the stockade.

Everyone feasted day and night. I broke my oath to Abigail and drank Aqua Vitae with the rest. God forgive us, Rigdale, Pratt, and I got drunk for the second time on the Sabbath. We were seized with a diabolical reckless-ness induced by our terror of the vast snowy forest and the Indians. We were startled by the breaking boughs, weighed down with snow, that of a sudden fell to earth. Each crack sounded like a musket shot.

The Indians came to us at all hours of the day. They piled their bows and arrows upon blankets without the south gate. We put our muskets aside. They traded their peltry for liquor, axes, and the little round German brass bells they tied to the fringes of their leathern trousers. We heard the bells jangle whenever they walked across the glade in the deep snow toward the south gate.

Captain Green said, "They want us to become accus-tomed to their approach so they can attack us by surprise."

The jangling bells in the stockade made us all anxious. I watched an Indian strip a blue English blanket from one of Green's sailors curled up in the mud. Like my fellow Englishmen, I was too weakened by hunger and too cowed to intervene. Sorely ashamed at feeling so helpless, I looked away. As my countrymen sat scat-tered about steaming pots filled with ground nuts or shellfish, the Indians often stole the victuals. I once saw

Butts protest. An Indian threw a lump of frozen mud in his face. Butts crept away. I was sore ashamed for us all.

Green said to me, "I am a master of a ship and a good one, too. But I do not know how to assert my authority on land." One day ten sentinels in the stockade got drunk and deserted their posts. Green did not punish them.

By the last week in February, we had spent almost all of our victuals. Memsowit told me that the Indians would no longer trade with us for their corn, saying that they had none to spare.

I was hungry all the time. My legs felt weak and were wracked with pains. If I moved too quickly, I became dizzy. My heart pounded in my breast. A mouthful of oatmeal porridge immediately made me feel stronger; my strength from eating it lasted about an hour. Then I was beset with lassitude. Between noon and one of the clock, I could not sit up straight but only bent over.

One morning, two men in my house fell out with each other over a bowl of porridge. Rigdale had just the strength enough to separate them. Rigdale divided the porridge in twain, and the men gobbled up their portions.

Rigdale and I joined the crowd on the beach nearest the stockade searching for shellfish. The clams there, which formerly seemed of infinite store, were most of them already consumed. By God's grace, I found eight of them frozen in the ice and swallowed their sandy flesh on the spot. Rigdale found nine more, three of which he gave to me.

To conserve our strength, we went to bed at sundown. The night was very cold. In spite of our fire, I shivered and lay awake, listening to my stomach rumble. I said, "I would be pleased to eat one raw egg."

Rigdale said, "I love new laid eggs."

I said, "Shall I give you some of this capon?"

"What capon is that?"

"God save me! I fell asleep for a moment and dreamed I was eating a roasted capon."

In the days following, we all lived on ground nuts and acorns we digged up under the snow and the mussels, clams, and a few oysters we digged up on the beach. I twice went a-fowling, but there were no ducks or geese to be seen. I shot a squirrel in a pine tree and roasted it. Rigdale and I supped upon it without salt. It tasted sweet.

Green renewed his efforts to purchase victuals from the Indians. They refused. Green said, "I am determined to take by force what I can get in no other way."

He gave orders to strengthen and perfect the stockade. The frightened men obeyed him.

All the entrances save the south gate were made fast. Ten sentinels, chosen by lot, again stood watch day and night. Before resorting to violence, Green sent a letter with a messenger named Tom Ford five-and-twenty miles through the forest, informing Governor Bradford of the dire straits we were in at Wessagusset and what he proposed to do. Ten days later, the Governor's answer arrived. He wrote,

> *Your course of action is not only in contravention of the laws of God, but is calculated to bring King James's policy to nought, both as respects the enlargement of his dominions and the propagation of the knowledge and law of God, and the glad tidings of salvation among the heathen.*
>
> *Your case is no worse, if so bad, as that of Plymouth, where we have but little corn left and are compelled to sustain life on ground nuts and mussels, all of which you in Wessagusset have in great abundance. Yea, oysters also, which we at Plymouth sorely want.*
>
> *Therefore, your plea of necessity cannot be maintained. If you have recourse to violence, those guilty of like violence will have to take care of yourselves and need look for no*

support from us at Plymouth. Moreover, if you escape the savages, you will not escape the gallows as soon as some special agent of the crown comes over to investigate.

Tom Ford also delivered the following letter from Abigail to me:

My darling Charles,

I know in my heart that my prayers will be answered and that we will be reunited!

Ford told me that you have grown a shaggy beard. Dearest Charles, please shave it off so that, with God's grace, I may once again behold your pitted face and be reminded of my beloved father's countenance.

Ford will give you a pint of corn from me. Consider it a present from me for your coming birthday. May it ease your hunger for a while. We live on a pint of corn a day and are fearful of an Indian attack. Still, I am grateful to God for bringing me to the Plymouth Plantation. He is working His will here in the wilderness and I feel part of it.

Darling Charles, a week ago Tuesday, I spake again with Master Brewster about the state of my soul. I told him that remorse and humiliation beset me because I wished my father to die before I caught his consumption.

Master Brewster said, "Increase your suffering, daughter! Let those three words of Scripture—'Honor thy father'—bore into your soul like Pratt's auger. Abase yourself before God! Humiliate yourself! Suffer remorse until it is well nigh unbearable.

"Then," said he, "of a sudden, the Holy Spirit will rise up within you, and you will truly repent and know that you are predestined to be saved. This revelation can happen to you at any time. It happened to me upon a summer morning in Leyden at my house on Sink Street. What joy!"

Since he spake to me, I have heaped remorse and humiliation on my soul while I await God's forgiveness.

My love to you, Abigail
March 6

I answered Abigail as follows:

Sweetheart,
I rejoice in your news. My own salvation is, God help me, furthest from my thoughts. I am trying only to survive.

Tom Ford will also deliver to you a brief letter I wrote you on the seventh of September. I always wear your handkerchief close to my heart.

Ford will relate to you in detail the dreadful

circumstances that beset us here in Wessagusset. I am always cold and weak from hunger. The snow that hath fallen between the trees makes it difficult to search for ground nuts and roots, while the ice that covers the salt marches makes it almost impossible to dig up shellfish. We too fear an Indian attack.

I love you. I live for the day when, God willing, we will be together again. Thank you for the pint of corn. It is the best birthday gift I have ever received.

Pray for me.

Yours in Christ.
Charles.
March 10

God forgive me, I could not bring myself to share the pint of corn with Rigdale—or anyone else. Hunger traduced my soul. I covertly made the corn into Indian pudding and gobbled it all down after sundown in the glade. God punished me for my selfishness. I vomited up the pudding. The next day, the joints of my arms and legs were swelled, my gums bled, and my whole body shivered and shook. I frequently passed water, and my hands and feet were numb. I prowled the stockade with a feeble gait looking for victuals to steal.

A tall Indian, wrapped in a blue blanket, pushed me aside; the bells tied to his leggings jangled in my ears.

That evening, Hook said to me, "If you want to eat, harken unto me. Come with me on the morrow to the Indian village and work for them. Gather firewood and draw water with their women, and they will pay you with Indian pudding."

I said, "Wherefore? To become their slave?"

He said, "I have been a slave, one way or the other, all my life. The foremost thing is to stay alive. Starving to death is most horrible, almost as horrible to me as drowning. Well, what say you?"

The next morning, at dawn, I joined a score of Englishmen who became slaves of the Massachusetts in their village. Rigdale, Butts, Pratt, and I followed Hook there at first light. It took us three hours to walk two miles to the west through the drifted snow. I was surprised to discover that I was the strongest one of the four. Rigdale leaned upon my arm the whole way.

The Indian women fled with their children into their houses at our approach. The Indians lived in more than a score of circular houses built out of poles. The tops of the poles were bent and bound together with walnut bark forming a round hole through which the smoke of their fires ascended and escaped. The walls of the houses were covered with reed mats. Each house had two doors which were likewise covered with reed mats that could be rolled up and let down.

Memsowit greeted us without his house. He was wearing a mantle made from beaver skins that were sewn together.

I said, "We have come to work for you in exchange for victuals."

He said, "We believe you have come to steal our seed corn that we are saving to plant in the spring once the danger of frost is past. I warn you, do not do so. We will punish you for stealing our seed corn with a severe whipping (*suppondonk*)."

He invited us into his house. Against the walls, on three sides, planks about a foot above the ground were raised upon rails that were borne up upon forks and covered with mats. The planks, laid side by side, were wide enough for four people to sleep upon. We four sat cross-legged upon them.

Memsowit said, "This is a bad winter for us. Our children are hungry. We live on squirrels, acorns, dogs, snakes, and the bark of trees. There are almost no turkeys or deer to be found in the forest. The evil spirits have chased them away.

"After your work is done, I will give each of you a bowl of our seed corn. Grind it into powder, put a little water to it, and eat the meal, which we call *nokake*. It is sweet, toothsome, and hearty."

From whom did he learn "sweet, toothsome, and hearty"? I was again amazed at his command of the English language and hoped that one day his intelligence would be able to grasp the meaning of Holy Scripture and salvation through Christ our Lord.

Cicero wrote that there is no people so barbarous that do not have some religion or other. Tully asked, where is there to be found a race or tribe of men, which without instruction from anybody, doth not hold some sort of innate preconception of the gods? I must conclude against them: the Indians of New England have no religion or gods. They believe only in benign spirits and devils. Perhaps they were incapable of being converted to the true faith.

Wittuwamat entered, wearing a bearhide coat which was dressed and converted into good leather with the black fur next to his body. His hands were in a muff made from brown wildcat fur.

Memsowit translated his words as follows: "If you want to eat today, you will fetch us water and firewood. Our women will show you how."

Rigdale said, "My lord, we are famished and require a bite to eat to give us the strength to do your biding."

Wittuwamat ordered a young woman to serve us each a bowl of hot, unsalted broth. Memsowit explained that it was a liquor made from boiled old deer bones that had first been heated over a fire to drive out the worms and maggots. It immediately assuaged my hunger.

Memsowit said to me, "This woman is my youngest wife."

She was marked across her forehead by the image of a crow that I surmised had been incised into her flesh and dyed with some sort of black ink.

Memsowit said, "Brother crow is the guardian spirit who appeared to me in a dream and saved her life."

Wittuwamat said, "Last night I dreamed that my head fell off. My headless corpse fell into the mud. Then my head spake thus: 'Please bury me in Grandmother Earth where my body already lies. Grandmother Earth shall join us together, so that I can sacrifice tobacco to the *manitu* who squats underground.'

"Now go with our women and gather firewood and draw water from our stream. In return, we shall feed you."

He withdrew his carved pipe from his muff and lighted it. His son, called Tokamahamon, greeted us as we took our leave. He wore a bear claw in each pierced ear and a string of white bone beads about his neck.

Wittuwamat said, "Tokamahamon will become the

sachem of my people when I die. Doth your king have a son?"

I said, "Yes. His name is Charles. With God's grace, he will one day become our sovereign lord."

Memsowit said, "'Sovereign lord.' What doth 'sovereign lord' mean?"

I said, "Sovereign lord means the same as king."

Memsowit said, "'Sovereign lord.' I must remember that."

Wittuwamat said, "Doth your king have a queen (*squa sachem*)?"

I said, "Her Majesty died four years ago."

"Did your king marry again?"

I said, "He did not."

Wittuwamat said, "It is marvelous to me (*wequaiyewmut*) that a king would live without a wife. I have three. My first wife—Tokamahamon's mother—died from the plague. My people died in heaps. Those of us who were left alive fled our houses and let the carcasses lie above ground to rot without burial. Not I! I buried my queen with my own hands. It is our custom (*machitut*) to sew up the corpse in a mat, put it into the earth, and sing the Death Song (*nuppmonk*), which we are forbidden to share with you Englishmen (*Englishmenog*).

"Because I am a *sachem*, my grave shall be filled with

my riches and covered with stones to prevent wild beasts from digging up my corpse."

Then he said, "Tell your sovereign lord that I am his man."

Three women accompanied us to gather firewood. The mantles they wore to cover their nakedness were much longer than the men's. For as the men wore one deerskin, the women wore two, sewed together along the skins' full length. And whereas the men wore one bear-skin for a mantle, the women wore two sewed together. They had as much modesty as civilized people and deserve to be commended for it.

The Indian women smeared their bodies and hair with grease that made them smell very rank, and they were much stronger than we. They each carried almost twice as much firewood on their backs as every Englishman, in addition to strings of fish, baskets of beans, and mats.

They never once paused to rest as we did. I saw famished, exhausted Englishmen carrying firewood and skins filled with water. Then there were those squatting on the icy mud, holding out their hands to the Indians and crying, "Food, for the love of God!" Their blotched skin hung loosely from their bones. Their dull eyes protruded from their gaunt faces. The Indians ignored them.

In the late afternoon, Hook said to me, "Master

Wentworth, I know where they keep some of their seed corn and am waiting for a chance to steal some. Shall I steal some for thee?"

I said, "Yes. Perhaps God will forgive me because I'll share it with some hungry wretch at Wessagusset."

Wittuwamat's house was near a stream that flowed in the center of the village. It was built with poles and planks upon a scaffold, some six foot above the ground. Seven times, during the course of the day, we piled our firewood beneath the entrance. Despite the cold wind, I was drenched with sweat. Wittuwamat invited us up into his house, wherein just before sunset, the women served us each a big bowl of *nokake*. After saying grace, we devoured the victuals. The Indians pressed themselves upon us on the planks and, wrapped in English blankets, sang themselves to sleep. I was light-headed from weariness and hunger. The savages' barbarous singing and the lice and the fleas kept me awake for hours.

In the morning, the Indians served each of us a bowl of roasted squirrel, mixed with parched corn. Observing us to bless our meat before we did eat and afterwards to give thanks to God for the same, Wittuwamat asked, "Does your God appear to you in your dreams?"

I said, "He never has."

He said, "Then how do you know that He exists?"

"We read His words in Scripture, and He speaks to us in our hearts."

"What does He sound like?"

I said, "A still, small voice."

He said, "*Manitu* speaks to us in the thunder." Then he said, "You Englishmen will henceforth address me in English as your 'Sovereign Lord.'"

We labored for our savage sovereign lord from dawn to dusk for another week. I understood what Aristotle meant when he said that a slave is a tool with a voice. Once I saw Butts bow to Wittuwamat. Then Butts said to me, "Because I refused to give this savage my Monmouth cap, he forbids me to labour here for food. Nevermind. I am taking my revenge." He glanced about him, removed his Monmouth cap, and extracted a handful of yellow parched corn from its crown.

"Take it," said he. "'Tis for thee."

"Where did you get it?"

He said, "'Tis seed corn. I stole it."

Rigdale and I followed Butts to a mound of hand-paddled earth on the eastern edge of the village, at the foot of a dead oak tree. Butts looked about to be sure that we were alone and then said, "I spied a savage digging up corn here four days ago and have been stealing a little every day since."

Then he digged in the soft earth until he came to a large reed basket covered with mats. The basket held a hogshead of yellow, red, and blue husked and shelled corn. Rigdale and I stole two handfuls apiece and concealed them in the crowns of our caps, which we replaced upon our heads. Then we re-buried the basket.

I said, "God forgive us for being felons."

Butts said, "A felon, you say? A felon? Fie, sir! I am already a murderer. My mother died on a January night when I was twelve years old, and my drunken father cast me out onto a freezing street in the Borough of Colchester in Essex. I lived upon the victuals that I stole from starving beggar children smaller than me. Once, when I hadn't eaten in three days, I strangled a red-haired girl half my age for a stale crust of bread that she was saving for her supper."

We made our way back to Wessagusset, wherein there was now a score of Indians living in small wattle-and-daub houses in the glade around the stockade. There were no sentinels standing watch at the gates.

We found Captain Green and three sailors tending eight prostrate men stricken with the catarrh. They were all suffering from high fever, chills, running at the nose, and chronic coughs. Green and his sailors were weak from hunger and hadn't changed the sick men's soiled bedclothes in three days.

I asked Captain Green why there were not sentinels in the stockade. He said, "I'm ashamed to say that the men will not take orders from me."

Rigdale and I set about changing the foul bedclothes. Butts went off with Martin Hook to gather shellfish on the muddy beach.

Butts said, "I dare not steal any corn for a while from the Indians. They are on their guard. I'm starved for *nokake*. Look at me! I am all skin and bones!"

Indeed, Butts looked thinner. His cheekbones now protruded from his face.

Rigdale and I concealed our stolen corn in our hats. Green and his three sailors shared their victuals with us: ground nuts, acorns, mussels, and clams. The four men shuffled along with their heads bowed, gasping for breath. Their gums bled, and their eyesight had deteriorated. Green could not see objects farther away than the length of his arms.

Two of his sailors, Andrew Kellway and a boy named Nicholas Pittfold, were stricken by the catarrh. Rigdale and I nursed them for six days. Pittfold's lungs became congested. He sank into a delirium and cried out, "Anon,

anon! I'll come to you by and by." Then he said, "Bid me, farewell, mother."

I said, "Go to sleep, my son, go to sleep."

He brought forth a guttural, gurgling death rattle from deep in his throat and died.

Captain Green told me that, like himself, Pittfold was a member of the Church of England and would be buried according to its rites. Pratt made a coffin. Green ordered a grave dug in the glade without the south gate and conducted the funeral according to the Book of Common Prayer. Held late in the afternoon of the same day, it was attended by two score of our famished company, many of whom were stricken by scurvy and the bloody flux. Some had swelled faces; others had sunken cheeks covered with black stubble. Rigdale and I absented ourselves from the papist service.

Kellway died the next morning at about four of the clock. Six of us had barely enough strength to dig a shallow grave. He was hastily buried without a coffin next to Pittfold in the freezing rain. Green conducted the lengthy service of the Church of England that was attended by five of Kellway's friends. Afterwards, one of them named John Sheave asked me about Puritan funerals, and I explained that we Separatists consider them, like marriages, to be civil, not religious services.

He said, "Do you read the Psalms over the dead?"

I said, "No."

He said, "I caught me a chill today listening to all them Psalms in the rain."

The next day, he was stricken with a bad chest cold and a fever. He lay shivering under three blankets on the earthen floor, where I fed him shellfish soup and boiled acorns. God forgive me, I did not share my corn with him.

He said, "I brought this on myself. God punished me for complaining about the holy Psalms. Can you recite one for me?"

I recited Psalm 90, and he said, "Another."

I recited Psalm 121, and he said, "More."

I recited Psalm 130, Psalm 139, Psalm 23, Psalm 27, and Psalm 106.

He said, "Which one do you like best?"

I said, "Psalm 130."

He said, "Which one is that?"

"'Out of a deep place I have called unto Thee, O Lord.'"

"That's the one that touched my heart."

Shreave gradually recovered and went about the stockade, telling the sick, "Get Master Wentworth to recite Psalm 130 to you. It cured me. It's magic. Master Wentworth is a magician."

Thereafter, day and night, I was beset by the sick begging me to recite Psalm 130 to them. I refused them all, saying, "You want me to make magic. That's a sin."

Those men who were literate read the Psalm aloud to gatherings of the sick. For a few days, the words of Scripture resounded throughout the stockade. Then two of the sick men died, and the recitations ceased.

Hook attended their funerals. Afterwards, he took me aside and removed red and yellow seed corn from his cap, in the amount of two cupfuls, saying, "Do with it as you will." Craving to devour it all myself, I gave it to Rigdale and bade him feed it to the patient that he felt would most benefit from it. He fed a bowl of *nokake* to a gaunt young man named Tristram Burt, who said, "What weather is it abroad?"

Rigdale said, "It is cold and stormy. The rain is mixed with snow."

Burt said, "Behold, my last day on earth! I am no longer hungry. Don't mourn for me when I am dead, for I shall be rejoicing in heaven. Yea, I long for my death. Come quickly, sweet Jesus, and receive my soul."

He fell asleep for a few minutes.

When he awoke, he said, "Don't let me go to sleep again, for I want to know when I die."

Rigdale said, "You are young and strong and shall yet live a long while."

Then Burt said, "I see the lights, sweet Jesus. I see the lights! I commit my spirit into Thy care."

He was the fifth member of our company to die.

Rigdale, Pratt, and I gathered shellfish from the muddy shore at low tide. Pratt and I devoured them all on the beach. Rigdale divided his second catch of the day among the sick in their house. Their number increased daily.

There was now a second house filled with twelve men stricken by scurvy. This was my first close encounter with scurvy. I became familiar with its symptoms: pallor, swelled bleeding gums, and foul-smelling breath. Almost all of the five men sick with scurvy suffered from melancholia. One of them constantly cried out, "God help me, I am damned!"

Rigdale exhorted them all to have faith, but to no avail. He said, "This is the Devil's own disease."

The stricken men could not chew because of their swelled, bloody gums. We fed them shellfish broth. I often stole a savoury spoonful.

The next day, the Indians caught two of our men stealing corn and delivered them to Captain Green for a flogging. They were given twelve lashes each. I could not bear to witness their suffering. But it did not restrain three other starving thieves, who broke into the hidden stores in the Indian village. They were also caught and whipped. Once again, I could not bring myself to watch them suffer.

Late in the afternoon of New Year's Day in the year of Christ 1623, Wittuwamat, Memsowit, and ten Indians arrived at the stockade with Hook, whose hands were bound behind him. Memsowit said to Captain Green, "We caught this thief with a leathern bag filled with stolen red seed corn. Seed corn for next spring's planting! They will grow into next summer's corn that will feed our children. This *askook*—what's the English word? 'Worm!' This worm stole *nokake* from our children."

He showed us Hook's leathern bag filled with husked and shelled red Indian corn and said, "My sovereign lord gives him to you for punishment. What will you do with him?"

Captain Green said, "He will receive twelve lashes."

This time, diabolical curiosity got the better of me, and I watched. Hook was forced to kneel in the mud and embrace a big chopping block about which his wrists were bound together. A tall sailor named John Drake tore the shirt from Hook's back, put a stick between his teeth, and said, "Bite down on this as hard as you can."

Then he gave Hook twelve stripes with a leathern whip that had nine knotted lashes. Hook bit the stick hard. His spittle frothed in the corners of his mouth. He screamed and moaned. Drake was weak from hunger, and after giving the sixth blow, he paused to catch his breath. The wounds across Hook's back were streaming blood.

Drake resumed the whipping. After the ninth stroke, Hook fainted. His chin struck the chopping block, bringing forth more fresh blood. Captain Green raised Hook's head by his hair, Drake threw a bucket of water in Hook's face, and he revived. The gnawed stick dropped from his mouth. Drake replaced it with a longer one. Hook fainted again after the final blow. Drake cut the bonds on Hook's wrists, and Captain Green caught his body under the arms, laid him down in the mud, and bathed his bloody wounds.

Rigdale said to me, "Did you see that seven out of those twelve savages wanted bells on their leggings? Let's truck with 'em. We shall exchange four of our bells with each savage for a goodly portion to eat."

We had left in our possession four-and-fifty brass bells. Rigdale and I traded eight-and-twenty of them with

the seven savages for seven roasted squirrels, of which
Rigdale and I ate one each. The meat was tough to
chew. I sucked the marrow from the little bones. Rigdale
fed Hook some squirrel meat, but he retched it up. Said
he, "I thirst, I thirst."

I fetched him a big bowl of water, and he drank it.

Afterwards, he lay abed upon his stomach and spake
in a hoarse voice. Said he, "I want revenge. Harken unto
me. I found a hidden store of seed corn under a mound
of earth in the southern part of the village. Go and steal a
basketful and share it with me."

Rigdale said, "Is that the mound at the foot of a
dead oak?"

"No. It's the one on the west side of the stream that
flows near Wittuwamat's house. Now let me sleep."

Captain Green divided the five squirrels that were
left among his lusty sailors. I kept the six-and-twenty
remaining bells in my knapsack.

One evening, Pratt said to me, "Alas, my design for
our stockade has turned out to be a trifle of my brain.
'Tis useless without the proper protection afforded by a
disciplined company of defenders."

I said, "What can we do?"

He said, "Discipline ourselves! Act like soldiers!"

The next day, Butts told Rigdale and me that he had

seen Pratt leaving the stockade at dawn, with a pack on his back, and his tool box and a hoe in either hand.

"A hoe?" said I. "Wherefore a hoe?"

Butts said, "Wherefore a hoe? I will now let thee know. I followed him at a distance. He never spied me. He made his way directly to one of the Indian houses a short distance from the stockade and made a show of digging with his hoe in the mud in search of ground nuts. Then, satisfied that no Indian was about, he walked into a thicket and hurried off to the south, in the direction of Plymouth.

"Then I saw three armed savages emerge from a hut and follow Pratt across the glade.

"One of them was carrying a big, carved wooden club."

Rigdale said, "Tom Ford, Bradford's messenger, told me the Plymouth Plantation is but five-and-twenty miles south of here, through the trackless forest over yonder, beyond the meadow. He said that wolves and savage Indians roam amongst the huge trees. He crossed the wild North River. Ford almost drowned therein.

"This time of year there are still deep snow drifts on the north slopes of the hills. The journey took Ford two and one-half days."

I bestirred myself and gazed at the woods to the south. So I was only a five-and-twenty mile march from Abigail, but irrevocably separated from her by a trackless forest, deep snow drifts, savage Indians, and my cowardice.

The clouds gathered as the day wore on, until at length the sun became so obscured that I felt sure that unable to determine his direction, Pratt would lose his way in the forest.

Rigdale said to me, "You have a compass, Charles. Why don't you try to make your way to Plymouth?"

"Because Abigail would take me for a cowardly deserter."

He said, "Let us steal some corn from the Indians!"

"How can we do so?"

"I will think on it."

It rained and snowed for the next two days. Rigdale and I tended the starving and the sick.

Rigdale went at noon each day to fish for eels that were twisted together in the frozen mud. Each night, he returned with six eels. They were fat and sweet. Nevertheless, two more men died with their bellies swelled up from hunger. Toward the end, one of them cried out, "Behold, I am heavy with child. How can that be?"

Rigdale and I joined a score or so of our company and digged up some shellfish with hoes at low tide from the muddy beach. Hook digged alongside us until high tide at about ten of the clock at night. His effort opened one of his wounds that would not close. The fresh blood stained the back of his shirt.

Too many of us digged in one place. Our catch diminished day by day. Just after sunrise one morning, Hook went off to search for shellfish alone. I watched him walk east along the muddy beach as the tide went out. He was walking slowly, with a basket in one hand, leaning on his hoe. The thick mud clung to the soles of his shoes.

A sailor named George Wells found Hook's corpse the next morning. It was stuck fast in the mud on the beach about two miles to the east. He was lying on his back, his head toward the shore. His face was covered by sea weed. I surmised that he had slipped and fallen over backwards and was trapped at low tide in the thick, glutinous mud, wherein, too weak from hunger and his open wound to raise his head or limbs, he was compelled to wait six hours, until noon, for the high tide to come in and drown him.

It took four of us an hour to free his body and wash the mud from it with seawater. His wide-open blue eyes protruded from his face. His bloated hands were red. His fingernails were bloodless. His fingers and lips were a purplish blue in color.

Six of us carried him back to our graveyard, where

he was buried according to the rite of the Church of England. Neither Rigdale nor I attended the service. Our churchyard now contained ten dead men.

I told Rigdale about Hook's terror of drowning.

I said, "Imagine his thoughts, for six hours, as the tide rose slowly about him. He felt the rising sun shining upon the right side of his face. Hour after hour, whilst the tide rose, the sun climbed higher in the sky. He knew the high tide would encompass him about noon. He must have screamed and prayed for help. He felt the rising tide lap at his feet, then his knees, his thighs, his waist, his breast, his neck, the back of his head. The water covered his ears.

"By now, the sun was almost directly above him. The light must have dazzled his eyes. Did he shut them? Or did he gaze upon the sky for one last time? The water covered his mouth and nose. I would think that he held his breath for as long as he could. Then he died the death he had feared the most: he drowned."

Rigdale said, "I hope I would have made a Christian end, praying, 'Though He slay me, yet will I trust in Him.'"

On the morrow, which I reckoned to be the fifteenth day of March, the floor of the forest was covered by fragrant pinkish-white blossoms. Each flower had five petals. They thrived in the moist shade. None of us had ever seen such a flower. At dusk, we were astonished by flying squirrels that glided through the air from tree to tree on outstretched limbs.

Rigdale and I spent the following Sabbath praying and reading aloud from Scripture. Rigdale tried to preach a sermon on Lamentations 4:9: "They that be slain with the sword are better than they that are killed with hunger: for they fade away, as they stricken through for the fruits of the field." But no words on that text from Scripture came to him, and he spake instead of a dinner he enjoyed every Michaelmas at the Company of Joiners on Friars Lane, in London. He said, "To begin with, we had a fat, roasted goose and a savoury roasted veal, then a boiled beef, then a fat woodcock. Afterwards, we were served claret and Canary sack."

Then Rigdale said, "By heaven, the fruit! I forgot the fruit! We were served apples, pears, chestnuts, oranges, grapes, figs, raisins, cherries, and melons. Fruits, if you remember, are very plentiful in England around Michaelmas."

I said, "Let us talk about something else."

Rigdale said, "Let us discuss how to steal corn from the Indians. I reckon that a full knapsack of it will be about a bushel, which will feed four of our people two cupfuls a day for more than a week. Whom will we choose to feed? That's the question. I do not relish the idea of playing God."

I said, "Let us first secure the corn before we worry about dispensing it."

Then I said, "To tell you true, I am a coward. A base coward. I could not bear to be whipped. Hook screamed. I'll howl. Did you not see the froth in the corners of his mouth? Like a mad dog. What of his deep, bloody wounds? One lash laid upon another. I am very sensitive to pain. No, my friend, I could not bear to be whipped. I beg you, steal the seed corn by yourself. Do not share any with me. Keep it all. Let me go hungry. Forgive me for not accompanying thee, and promise not to tell Abigail."

Rigdale said, "Come, weep not! You have my word."

I removed the flint and steel, the burning glass, the needle and thread, the awl, the compass, and the horn cup from the knapsack. Rigdale dropped the six-and-twenty brass bells therein and put it upon his back.

I said, "Butts stole some Indian corn hidden in an earthen mound in the eastern part of the village, under an oak tree. I would search there first."

Rigdale said, "I will."

Then we fell upon our knees and prayed that God would forgive Rigdale for the sin of stealing.

He departed for the Indian village on the morrow before sunrising. An Indian woman and a crippled little Indian maiden emerged from their little house in the glade and watched him walk towards the forest. The girl was about seven years of age. Halting upon her left leg, she scrabbled in the mud for a ground nut or acorn. Just then, an Indian man with a livid scar on his left cheek came up to them and gave the little girl five or six dried shellfish on a long string. She gobbled them up and went back to scrabbling in the mud. She was likely one of the children from whom Rigdale might be presently stealing some of next year's corn.

Rigdale did not return that night. I could not sleep. At about four of the clock in the morning, our stockade was surrounded by thirty or forty savages, armed with bows and arrows. Many of them carried lighted reed torches. I watched them through a knot hole near the post of the south gate. In the flickering firelight, their red, black, and yellow painted faces made them look demonical. Some of them were dancing in a big circle. The brass bells on their leggings jangled together at the same time.

The sounds awakened the rest of the men asleep in the stockade. There were forty-seven of us in all; two were sick abed. We gathered in a noisy bunch in front of the store-house shed. Only about half were armed. Captain Green stood upon a chopping block and tried to address us. The men shouted him down.

Afterwards he said to me, "I am the master of men only at sea. I am, so to speak, at sea on land. At sea, I am a gallant leader of men, but God preserve me, I know not how to fight savages in a dark forest midst these soaring New English trees. Trees, trees, trees! I am weary of trees!"

I said, "You might at least post armed sentinels along the walls of the stockade."

"The men do not obey me, Master Wentworth. They obey only the demands of their empty stomachs. We are undone by hunger."

"Take them in hand, Captain Green. Stand up to 'em! The basest and worst men, trained up in severe discipline and under harsh laws, a hard life, and much labor, prove good members of a community."

He said, "I have come to believe that man is sinful and by nature an enemy of God, a rebel, and a traitor. Only we few enlightened elect are capable of fighting against the sins and corruptions of the mass of humanity."

Of a sudden, the Indians without the stockade fell silent, and I heard Rigdale shout, "Captain Green, pray, open the south gate and allow me and my two captors, Memsowit and Wittuwamat, to enter the stockade. Last night, whilst I was sneaking out of the Indian village, Memsowit caught me with their stolen seed corn in my knapsack. Wittuwamat means to kill me."

Green cried out, "Open the gate."

Memsowit led Rigdale into the stockade by a long leathern thong tied about his wrists. Wittuwamat carried my knapsack. Ten savages followed him into the stockade. Their arrows were strung on their bows. The other savages silently skulked without the south gate. The sun was up and shining on Memsowit's long, greasy black hair.

He said, "This thief stole almost two basketfuls of our seed corn. Whipping him is not punishment enough. His punishment is death. You Englishmen must hang him. Otherwise, my men will kill all of you and burn down your village."

Rigdale said, "I've never seen a hanging. Is it quick?"

Captain Green said to Memsowit, "I must call a parliament of all my people, save those that are sick. They must consult upon this huge complaint and determine whether to hang Mr. Rigdale."

Green called a parliament of us all. We crowded around him standing upon the chopping block. He then addressed

Rigdale, saying, "Zachariah Rigdale, dost thou admit to stealing a large quantity of seed corn from these savages?"

Rigdale said, "I do, sir. Hunger drove me to it. I stole the corn from a buried barn near the *sachem's* house, having been previously informed of its whereabouts. I have not eaten in two days. Friends, please be so kind as to give me something to eat, so that I will have the strength to pray with fervor."

Green bade one of the sailors fetch Rigdale a bowl of shellfish soup. Rigdale drank it in two swallows and said, "Thank you."

Then he got down on his knees and prayed aloud, "Though He slay me, yet will I trust in Him."

Green said, "Master Rigdale committed a felony, and by the laws of England, 'tis to be punished with death by hanging. And this execution must be put for an example and likewise to appease the savages, who have threatened us all with destruction.

"What say you in your defense, Master Rigdale?"

"I plead guilty to stealing the corn. But hanging me will not appease the savages. Instead, seize those who enter the stockade. Wittuwamat is sure to be amongst them. Shut all the gates, and declare to those savages without that if they attack us, we will hang Wittuwamat and put his companions to death. Wittuwamat is a much prized *sachem* amongst the savages. They will exchange him for me. You may be sure of it."

Captain Standish said, "But what happens then? The savages will lay siege to our stockade and burn it down. Pratt made a great error in designing it. The logs of the stockade are the back wall of all the houses therein. They will immediately catch fire, and we will be surrounded by flames and left without a single building in which to seek refuge from the Indian arrows that will rain down upon us."

Someone with a hoarse voice cried out, "Hang the man, and have done with it!"

Rigdale said, "What doth my dear friend Charles Wentworth have to say?"

I said, "I cannot in all good conscience sacrifice the lives of fifty men to save one—even one whom I love. May God forgive me."

Rigdale said, "God will forgive thee, as do I."

"I thank thee for that but will never forgive myself."

Rigdale said, "Tell me this, dear friend. Doth committing a felony mean that I am damned?"

I said, "You are one of the Elect. You are saved. I am sure of it!"

Rigdale said, "I have but two regrets. I regret that I will not be buried in the churchyard at Southwark near my beloved wife and child. And I regret that God did not see fit to give me the words to preach at least one sermon in my life. I should now like very much to preach on Job 13:15, 'Lo though He slay me, yet will I trust in Him.' But I cannot find the words."

Captain Green said, "Let us have a show of hands for all those who would hang Master Rigdale."

I raised my right hand along with all the rest.

Rigdale said to me, "God prosper you and make you happy. Marry Mistress Abigail, and name your son Zachariah after me."

I said, "We will."

He said, "Now hang me and have done with it."

Green said, "So be it. Being here confirmed by an Act of our Parliament, Zachariah Rigdale will now be hanged. May God have mercy on your soul, Master Rigdale. One of you sailors fashion a noose at the end of a long rope and bind Rigdale's hands behind him. Then remove him to one of the oak trees without the stockade and hang him."

In the presence of a noisy crowd of savages and Englishmen, Rigdale was brought to an oak by the edge of the glade, where the dangling end of the long rope was thrown over a low limb some ten foot in height and grasped by five men. One of the men made a hangman's noose and slipped it over Rigdale's head and about his neck. I counted nine coils in the rope.

Captain Green said, "Let us pray."

Rigdale croaked and bellowed, "Revenge me, Charles! Revenge me! Revenge me!"

The five men pulled the rope, hand over hand. The rope grew taut and the noose tightened about Rigdale's neck. He slowly rose until his feet were a yard off the ground. His face turned purple, and his eyes and tongue protruded from his head. He kicked furiously; his left shoe flew off his foot. Of a sudden, without thinking, I pushed my way forward through the crowd, grasped him about the knees, and jerked his body downward with all my strength. I heard his spine crack and was drenched from his bowels that gushed down the back of his thighs. The savages howled in triumph.

———————

I washed my filthy hair and my stinking shirt, breeches, and stockings in the Bay. Then I hung my clothes to dry on a bush and immersed myself in the water up to my neck. It was a fair day. I watched an eagle flying in the eastern sky and listened to the cry of a loon. I saw two wood-ducks swimming near the shore. I spied a crab crawling across the sand. The world teemed with life, but Rigdale was dead. I crushed the crab with a stone.

At length, I stood over Rigdale's fresh grave and resolved that I would avenge his death by killing Wittuwamat. The savages were gone from the stockade and from all the little houses in the glade. Even the crippled little Indian maiden had been taken away. Did that mean that the savages intended to attack us?

It grew dark. I had not eaten all the day. Captain Green shared his meager dinner of shellfish stew with me. I went into my house to recover Rigdale's tool box. It was gone, doubtless stolen by some knave. His clothes were also gone. His Geneva Bible was all that was left of his possessions. I read John 15:13: "Greater love than this hath no man, when any man bestoweth his life for his friends," and cursed my cowardice.

PART V

A T ABOUT FIVE OF THE clock on the following afternoon, whilst searching for ground nuts, I heard a musket shot within the stockade. I ran there through the west gate and saw nine armed men gathered before the shed. The shortest one was clad in a coat of mail and a pikeman's helmet. It was Captain Standish.

I called out his name, and he replied, "Good morrow, Master Wentworth," and I said, "And a good morrow to you, sir, and a good year."

We shook hands. I had forgotten just how short of stature he was. The crest of his helmet reached my chin.

He told me that he and his eight men had just arrived in a shallop, in which they had sailed from Plymouth at dawn.

Said he, "We have learned that Wittuwamat and the Massachusetts have joined in a plot with the Nausets, the Paomets, and the Succonets to annihilate us and burn the Plymouth and Wessagusset plantations. We have come hither to forestall him.

"We also know that the Massachusetts are scattered and do not number more than thirty or forty warriors. My purpose in coming here today is to kill Wittuwamat and as many of his men as we can."

I said, "Let me join you, sir."

I described to him the circumstances of Rigdale's hanging, and he said, "By all means, join us and take your revenge. You shall do God good service."

Said I, "Thank you, Captain Standish. I offer myself as wholly yours."

I greeted Henry Winslow, armed with a musket and his cutlass, along with two other men whom I knew: young Joseph Rogers, whose father, Thomas, died in the general sickness during the winter of 1620, and William White, once a wool carder in Leyden.

Henry said to me, "I have a letter for you from my sister."

Abigail wrote me the following:

Sweetheart,

I have joyful news. Thanks to Master Brewster's spiritual ministrations, I have been born again. By God's grace, I am now among the Elect. Praise the Lord, I have closed with Christ. I live in His love. I have new perceptions and sensations entirely different in their nature from anything I experienced before I was sanctified. An appearance of newness beautifies everything. When you return to the Plymouth Plantation, I shall relate to you how my wondrous regeneration came to pass.

Captain Standish tells me he will presently make war upon the Massachusetts. Dearest, for my sake, do not put thyself in the forefront of the battle so that you will be slain. I pray God to keep you safe from the arrow that flieth by day and the terror that comes upon us in the night.

Yours in Christ,
Love, Abigail

P.S. I enclose a letter to you from your aunt Eliza which arrived here a week ago yesterday on the good ship Furtherance.
The thirtieth of March, 1623

Aunt Eliza's letter read as follows:

My dear nephew Charles,
George Stronge, my attorney, is writing down my words to thee.

I have heavy news. Your uncle Roger is dead. He died two weeks ago at supper by the stroke of God's hand. His mouth sagged on one side. Then his head fell forward and struck the table. I kissed his lips. We had been married three-and-thirty years. The Lord hath not been wont to let me live so long without some affliction or other. Roger's death is a terrible affliction for me, for in it the Lord seemed to withdraw His tender care for me, which He showed by my beloved husband, who loved me dearly even though I am barren.

Roger loved you like a father. Upon my death, he left you twenty pounds in ready money. According to his will, you are also to receive a glover's shop worth five-and-twenty pounds and Hempstead farm, inclusive of buildings, livestock, carts, &c., which is worth two hundred pounds.

However, to claim your inheritance, according to the conditions of the will, you must return to England within two years of the receipt of this letter, reside here at Hempstead for life, and oversee the farm work. Otherwise, your entire fortune goes to my nephew, Tom Foot.

Roger loved you like a son. He awaited a letter from you, which alas never arrived. You promised to send him rhymes from common speech that you gathered in the New World. Ever the fool for words, he collected some for you, viz., "The wine of a flagon, and the love of a whore, at evening is rich, at morning is poor." Thus spake a maimed soldier to Roger at The Sign of the Ram, hard by the House of Correction at Sherborne.

Roger bequeathed six pounds to Tom, who is betrothed to my dutiful maid-servant, Grace Orchard. They work hard, and I have grown very fond of them. Grace has a way with the farm animals. She nursed a sow of mine stricken with the measles back to health. Upon my death, she will receive all the curtains in the house. She sends you her best wishes.

I am now almost totally blind and would like to see your face once more before I die.

Your loving aunt Eliza,
Hempstead Farm
The seventh of December, 1622

I estimated that, if I returned to England, I would inherit property and ready money in the amount of two hundred and twenty-five pounds. Two hundred and twenty-five! Why, I would be as rich as the goldsmith, William Cosh, in Sherborne.

I shed no tears at the news of my uncle's death. I had no desire to pray. I remembered uncle Roger's mysterious words that he had once addressed to me: "In the end the soul comes to meet itself." If that were true, he now knew all the secrets of his sinful soul, and I trembled that the whole of my sinful soul would someday be revealed to me.

But surely uncle Roger was saved. He loved God and God's people dearly. He was fitted for heaven. And his fortune could fit Abigail and me for a gracious life on earth.

Captain Green and five stragglers, with whom he had been searching for ground nuts, entered the stockade.

Standish said to Green, "My men and I boarded the *Swan* and found it abandoned. How durst you do such a thing?"

Green replied, "We have no fear of the Indians, and indeed, we live with them, suffering them to come and go in the stockade with perfect freedom."

Captain Standish said, "Well, they intend to massacre you, unless we can prevent them. Henceforth, I am in command here, and you will all obey my orders on pain of death."

Green said, "I am happy, sir, to relinquish my command to you. God knows, I was not equal to the task."

Standish sent Green and five of his company to bring back the remainder of Green's men, who were out foraging for food. Standish said, "Anyone else who leaves the stockade without my permission will be put to death."

I was relieved to surrender to Standish's will and place my fate in his hands. He allotted each of us a pint of corn a day out of his supplies taken from the little reserve from Plymouth that he had stowed upon the shallop.

Just before sunset, an armed savage came into the stockade to trade four beaver skins for an ax.

Standish said, "I know this rogue. His name means 'White raven' in their heathen tongue. I have traded with him before. But not today. I will have no truck with him today."

The savage had a big nose like Governor Bradford, which he poked everywhere. It was apparent that he was spying upon us.

When he departed, Standish said, "He will undoubtedly report my arrival to Wittuwamat. Good! That should draw the savage here."

The next morning, at about seven of the clock, Wittuwamat lead Memsowit and six other armed savages into the stockade. Every man wore a deer skin mantle. The *sachem* withdrew his knife from its sheath and flourished it before Standish's face. I could not take my eyes away from Wittuwamat's bitten fingernails.

Wittuwamat said as Memsowit translated his words,

"I remember you. We traded together here in the early spring. But now you have come to make war because I have joined my people with the Succonet, the Nauset, and the Paomet. Together we shall kill all of you Englishmen hereabouts and in Plymouth, as well."

Standish said, "We shall see."

Wittuwamat's companion was six foot in height—the tallest Indian I ever saw. He taunted Standish thus: "Beware, little Englishman. My name is Peeksuot. Though I am no *sachem*, I am a man of great strength and courage. Behold my knife! It hath the face of a man carved upon its haft. My knife cannot see, it cannot hear, it cannot speak, but it can eat. It hath eaten the flesh of both Englishmen and Frenchmen (*Frenchmenog*). And anon, it shall eat yours."

Wittuwamat said to Standish, "Gather all your men together and depart from this place within three days or we shall drink your blood."

He and his savages left the stockade. I watched them walk through the forest toward their village. Each carried on his back a leathern quiver filled with arrows.

Standish appointed the ten of us, including himself, to take turns standing watch at the walls for the remainder of the day. We waited in vain for the return of Green, our five messengers, and the twenty-one missing men.

We were armed to the teeth. I took up my piece, six musket balls, two flasks of powder, and a forked gun rest.

Standish asked me, "Have you ever shot a man to death?"

I said, "Never, sir."

He said, "You will find it difficult to kill even a savage. When the time comes, don't think of him as a man. Fancy him as a ravening two-legged beast. Rest your barrel upon your gun rest, take aim, and shoot! Aim at the savage's stomach or breast. Squeeze—do not jerk—the trigger, and you will kill your prey."

I took up my matchlock, primed its breach and pan, and rammed one musket ball, wrapped in a piece of tow, down the muzzle. The one-ounce ball could pierce a savage's breast at a distance of fifty yards. I hoped that was farther than he could shoot an arrow at me.

For the first time, it struck me that the design of the matchlock was diabolically clever. What European gunsmith had thought of the five-foot-long inflammable braided linen match that, when I pressed the trigger, ignited the powder in the pan, which in turn ignited the powder in the breach and propelled the musket ball from the muzzle? I was sure that the ingenious gunsmith had been inspired by the Devil. On the other hand, he had given Christians a weapon far deadlier than that possessed by the heathen savages in New England.

Captain Standish said to me, "Remember! Before you discharge your musket, blow on the burning coal at the end of the match. But take care! A burning match is a constant hazard in the presence of the powder carried upon your person."

"Yes," I said. "I'll remember."

Captain Standish addressed the company. "The undisciplined behavior of Captain Green's men hath undoubtedly inspired the savages with contempt for all Englishmen. They come amongst us, few in number and unafraid. It is likely that the two most dangerous of them—Wittuwamat and Peeksuot—will arrogantly return here on the morrow with a small body of men. Secure all the gates, save the one facing west, to make sure they will use that to enter the stockade. As soon as they are all within, William White will make the west gate fast. My seven other men and Master Wentworth will be concealed with charged muskets within the shed. Let us pray the savages do not smell your burning matches.

"I will welcome them in my shirt-sleeves and unarmed. Then I shall kill Peeksuot. Pray, do not inquire how. I will show him what this runt of an Englishman can do. I will then run the short distance back to the shed as fast as I can, doubtlessly amid a shower of arrows. Pay me no heed. By that time, the eight of you will have emerged from behind the shed and formed two lines, one behind the other, facing the savages. At Stephen Hopkins's command, the first line of four men will shoot, then step back, and the second line of four men, with charged muskets, will take their places. Meanwhile, the four men behind them will charge their muskets, and after the four men standing before them have shot off theirs, the two lines will once more exchange places.

"Obey Hopkins's orders. I have full confidence in him. He is disciplined and a good shot."

Then Standish called out, "Winslow, sharpen your cutlass! I promised Governor Bradford that, with God's help, I will bring Wittuwamat's head back to Plymouth and display it atop the blockhouse."

Henry said, "I sharpened my cutlass this morning."

For the remainder of the afternoon, we rehearsed our parts in the morrow's battle, but without discharging our muskets for fear the noise would alert the savages to our purpose. Trusting in Providence and wanting to display my courage, like Caesar in his red cloak, I chose to be the last man on the right hand in the first line, one of the positions which was most exposed to the Indian arrows.

Again and again as we rehearsed, I stepped back and forth, carrying my musket, my gun rest, my bullet bag, and two powder flasks. It seemed to me that I was dancing an English war dance.

Standish removed his dented helmet, his coat of mail, and his rapier. He and William White ran five times from the west gate to the shed. They ran the forty-foot distance not in a straight line, but hither and yon, as if they were dodging falling arrows.

Standish did not say how he intended to kill Peeksuot. Why did he not first kill Wittuwamat? Was Standish vain? Did he intend to kill Peeksuot to revenge himself upon the savage for publicly taunting him about his short stature? I gazed upon Standish's bearded face. It was the countenance of a reliable, seasoned soldier. Perhaps I was wrong, and he planned to kill Peeksuot first for sound military reasons. I did not have the courage to inquire.

We secured all the gates, save the one facing west. That evening, after we had supped on *nokake*, Standish said, "Let us make our peace with God, as some of us may die on the morrow."

He then led us in prayer and read aloud from the ninety-first Psalm. When he recited the fifth verse, "Thou shalt not be afraid for the terror by night, nor for the arrow that flieth by day," I was reminded of Abigail's letter, in which she had paraphrased the same verse from Scripture.

I took the coincidence as a bad omen. Of a sudden, I was terrified of being killed by a flying arrow.

The next morning, being Monday, the fourteenth of April, was a fair, spring day. We cleansed and charged our muskets. Eight of us concealed ourselves in the crowded shed. Hopkins and I each digged a peephole in the wall that faced west. We watched Wittuwamat and Peeksuot, accompanied by six other armed savages, come into the stockade, wherein they were greeted by Captain Standish in his shirt-sleeves. I saw William White surreptitiously make the west gate fast. None of the savages observed him. They were gathered about Captain Standish.

Behind me, Hopkins said in a loud voice, "Light your matches."

We all ignited both ends of our matches with firebrands. The smoke was stifling. Everyone save Hopkins and myself fled without, behind the shed.

Behold the providential care of God! The wind was from the west. It blew the smell of our burning matches away from the savages.

I peered again with watery eyes through the hole and saw Captain Standish snatch Peeksuot's knife from its scabbard, leap upon him, and stab the savage in his left breast. Peeksuot slowly sank to his knees and fell over upon his back, where he lay still.

Hopkins yelled, "Quick! Each man to his appointed place."

We did as we were bidden. The savages let their arrows fly. Yet, by the especial Providence of God, none of them hit us. I saw an arrow flying at me, and I stooped down; it flew over my head and likewise missed the man behind me.

Standing up straight again, I replaced the barrel of my musket on my gun rest and took aim at the left breast of a savage, who at that very moment reached over his right shoulder with his left hand for an arrow from the quiver upon his back. Without waiting for the order to shoot, I squeezed the trigger. My musket went off. My eyes burned from the sulphurous smoke blown back in my face; a man on my left hand called for a firebrand to ignite his match. Then I spied the savage I had shot. Directed by the provident hand of the most high God, my ball had shattered his left elbow and severed his forearm, which lay upon the ground at his feet in a growing puddle of blood.

I heard three more of our pieces go off. Two more savages fell. The dreadful cry of another was after this manner: "*Hadree, hadree, succomee, succomee!*" Memsowit cried out in English: "We have come to drink your blood!"

I exchanged places with the man behind me, whose

name I did not know. I watched him shoot Wittuwamat in the bowels. Robbed of my revenge, I howled.

Standish shot off his musket. His ball struck a savage in his mouth, scattering his teeth all about. The three savages who were left alive neither tried to flee, nor asked for quarter. I shot at Memsowit but missed. He let fly an arrow that flew over all our heads. Then blood spurted from a wound in the right thigh of the savage near him, who fell upon his back.

We then quickly overpowered Memsowit and the unwounded savage and bound their hands behind them.

We took up thirty arrows from the ground. Some were tipped with brass, others with deer horns or eagles' claws. By the especial Providence of God, none of them either wounded or killed any of us, though many came close. We thanked God for our deliverance. Then Standish shot the unwounded savage in his forehead, and we hanged Memsowit from the same oak upon which Rigdale had died. Memsowit spake not a word. I watched him slowly strangle.

We examined the corpses of the eleven savages. They had all emptied their bowels and stank of excrement. I stared at the face of the one I had slain. He was the savage with a big nose who had lately spied upon us. The ground all about him was red from his blood. A bone protruded from his shattered left elbow. His severed forearm lay near his left thigh. A black-and-yellow-striped wasp alighted upon his right palm.

I said, "Death, there is thy sting," and Henry laughed.

Standish found Wittuwamat's corpse, swarming with fat black flies. His belly was caked with blood from his wound. His left eye was shut, and his mouth was wide open.

Standish said to Henry, "Cut off his head."

I said, "Allow me, sir."

Henry gave me his cutlass. I knelt down, hacked through Wittuwamat's throat and spine, and cut off his head. There was but little blood; his stomach wound had bled him dry.

Henry took the cutlass from my trembling hand and said, "How dost thou, Charles?"

I said, "To tell thee true, I am of such a cowardly nature that I was terrified during the entire battle."

He said, "To tell thee true, so was I."

I said, "Now I am sick at heart."

Henry said, "How so?"

I said, "I know not. I delighted in killing and beheading those savages. But now I am sad. And you?"

He said, "Not a whit. Why, I feel merry! I only regret that I did not kill Wittuwamat."

I said, "I too. He wanted your dagger and its green

leathern scabbard. I shall always treasure them as mementos of our friendship."

Said he, "And of our victory today over fear, when we two cowards stood our ground and faced death down."

By that time, we were surrounded by more than a score of Green's men, who had returned to the stockade.

William Butts grasped Wittuwamat's head by its long, greasy hair, held it up, and spat in its gaping mouth.

Standish wrapped the head in a length of soiled white linen. To prevent it from being devoured by vermin, ravens, and wolves, he hung it in my knapsack from a rafter within Captain Green's empty house, midst a multitude of flies. Then Standish donned his coat of mail and dented helmet and ordered the nine of us in his company to cleanse and charge our pieces and march through the woods to Wittuwamat's village.

Behind us, as we marched west, a flock of ravens circled above the stockade. We lit our matches. There was no wind amongst the trees. The smoke from the matches swirled about our heads. It was hard going; each of us carried two flasks of powder, a bullet bag, a musket, and a five-foot-long gun stick. Standish showed us how to carry our gun sticks in our musket barrels.

We found five women in the village. All the men, save two, had fled. One of them was Wittuwamat's son, Tokamahamon, whom I recognized by his bone necklace and his ears pierced with bear claws. He was stricken with a bad cough.

Standish said, "You shall do well to be bled. 'Tis a sure cure for an obstinate cough. I will bleed thee."

He lay down his lighted musket and gun stick upon the ground. Then he withdrew his rapier from its scabbard and stabbed Tokamahamon through the right side of his neck, under his ear. When Standish pulled out his blade, blood spurted all over his face and dented helmet. The women wailed.

The other savage was little more than a boy. Standish picked up his piece and shot the boy through his right eye. His face burst apart. The women wailed again. The youngest was Memsowit's widow, marked across her forehead by the black image of a crow.

Standish washed himself in the village stream. He permitted the women to drink their fill and then released them. But they remained in the village, wherein they heaped handfuls of earth upon their dead.

It was about five of the clock in the afternoon when we returned to the stockade. The eyes of all the corpses had been pecked out by ravens, which were now tearing gobbets of flesh from the bodies. I watched two birds with bloodstained beaks squabble over an ear.

Standish discharged his musket in the air. The ravens all rose, cawed at the musket's report, and once again circled above the stockade.

Standish said, "On the morrow, Captain Green's men will cast away these corpses in the forest before they swell, break wind, and breed maggots. Meanwhile, I and my small company will hunt down and kill all the savages we can find."

We were beset all the night in our house by buzzing flies. A sailor named Gillingham slept on the floor beside me. A fly stung me upon the back of my neck. The sting swelled into the circumference of a shilling.

Gillingham said, "I am sorry I missed the battle with the savages. I can tell you tales of sea-fights and name all the chief pirates, but alas, I have never slain a man on land. Tell me, sir, what's it like?"

I could not reply. I closed my eyes. A fly crawled into my left nostril, and I stopped my right nostril with my thumb and blew hard out of the other. The expelled fly flew away. Then I fell asleep and dreamed that a maggot, bred from my decaying brain, wriggled out of my nose.

———•◦•———

The next morning, I marched through the woods to the west with Standish and eight other men. We had gone less than a mile when we spied about ten savages making their way east through the trees in the direction of Wessagusset. Both parties caught sight of each other at the same time and hurried to secure the advantage of a nearby rise. We got there first, thrust our gun rests in the ground, placed our musket barrels upon them, and blew upon our matches. The savages, protected by the trees, let fly their arrows at us. We then shot at them. No one on either side was hit.

The savages fled and hid themselves in an adjacent swamp that stank of rotting meat and sour milk.

Standish said, "That swamp must be where Green and his men cast away the corpses."

I said, "How so, sir?"

Standish said, "The stench, sir, the peculiar stench."

We charged our muskets; neither our taunts nor our challenges could induce the savages to show themselves. I cried out, "*Hadree, hadree, succomee, succomee!*" ("We have come to drink your blood.")

There was no reply. Standish ordered five of us to shoot into the long grass, the shrubs, and the undergrowth of the swamp, whilst the other four stood watch. The roar of our muskets stilled the croaking frogs in the swamp. The savages remained silent. I was relieved that they would not come out and fight.

The frogs resumed croaking. The five of us cleansed and charged our muskets. Then we all returned to the stockade, wherein I spake with Gillingham.

He said to me, "Why look you so sad?"

"I am beset by perpetual guilt and melancholy."

"Tell me what it is that troubles thee, and I shall try to help thee by comfort or counsel."

I said, "I braked my dearest friend's neck while he was being hanged to spare him from being slowly strangled to death. I spared him an agonizing dying but brought perpetual guilt and melancholy upon myself."

Gillingham said, "Pray for forgiveness."

That evening, trying to pray, I found in my heart that I could not serve God.

I trembled and sweated. My heart beat faster. My entire body was first hot and then cold. It was hard to breathe. The answer came to me. I was damned. God had damned my immortal soul before He had created the heaven and the earth.

At dawn, I left the stockade with my charged musket on my shoulder and walked about a mile into the woods. I had but one thought: I must kill myself. I walked discoursing with this thought for the better part of an hour. At length, I chose the lesser of two evils, which was to kill myself rather than live and sin against God.

I removed my right shoe and right stocking and set my matches alight. Then I stood atop a big stone and set the musket's butt upon the ground. I put the muzzle under my chin with the intention of pressing the trigger with the big toe of my right foot. I thought of Abigail. Many things about her came into my head; one was my memory of the full moon shining upon her uplifted face on the *Swan*'s quarterdeck. Her face had a bluish tinge in the moonlight. What would she think of me if I killed myself?

I stepped down from the rock, donned my stocking and shoe, and much lost in my soul, I walked with my musket back to the stockade.

Standish addressed us in the stockade. He said that Weston's people could return to England or remain in Wessagusset, if they so desired. The crowd refused the latter choice with a tumultuous uproar. Then Standish said, "Let me proffer Governor Bradford's invitation to return with me to the Plymouth Plantation, where for the rest of your lives, you will live, work, and pray with the rest of the Elect."

No one in the crowd showed any interest in returning to the Plymouth Plantation.

I alone called out, "I am with thee, Captain Standish."

He replied, "You are most welcome, sir."

Standish then proposed that Weston's men sail on the *Swan* to the coast of Maine, buy victuals from the fishing boats at the fishing stations there, and then sail back to England.

The crowd cheered.

When it quieted, Butts called out, "A word, I beseech you, sir. What if there are no fishing boats on the coast? From whence would we get the victuals to sail back home?"

Standish said, "Why, from the savages. On the morrow, we shall return once more to their village and steal all their seed corn."

I cheered with the rest.

Captain Green said, "With God's grace, in three or four days, we shall set sail for London—for home. Home, lads! The city of London! Castles, towers and gates, parks and taverns, swans on the Thames. Swans with their tails above water and their long necks below, diving to catch tasty little gudgeons. My good wife, Alice, buys gudgeons from a fishmonger on Lime Street and serves 'em before the mutton at Sunday dinner. Hurrah for tasty little English gudgeons! Hurrah for England!"

Some in the crowd cheered; others grumbled at the prospect of crossing the sea.

Captain Green said, "'Tis well for you to groan. Let us now pray together that during our voyage God tempers the ruthless tempests of the deep."

I could not bring myself to beg forgiveness for killing the savage with the big nose. I prayed to be able to pray again.

———————————

The next day, we sacked the deserted Indian village. We stole some five-and-thirty bushels of seed corn, along with five beaver skins, tobacco pipes carved from stone, clay pots with thin walls and round bottoms, and various and sundry ornaments, viz., bone beads, shell and stone pendants, and bundles of eagle feathers, &c., all of which were to be sold in England. I found two brass bells. Had they belonged to Rigdale? I shook them. Their jangling called up no memories of my friend. I remembered without remorse the crippled little Indian maiden who would go hungry next winter because we Englishmen had stolen her people's seed corn.

Standish set ten men to stand watch all the following five nights and days at the stockade's fence lest the savages we fought at the swamp attack us. They never showed themselves.

I moped about. I lived on the verge of tears but never fell to weeping. I ached all over. I was unable to sleep, save for an hour or so toward dawn. I wandered about the stockade, then lay abed for two days. I could not keep my victuals down. I was tortured with divers affrights, viz., I was scared that I would starve to death.

On the morning of the third day, Green lovingly fed me a bowl of *nokake*, one spoonful at a time. I held it down. He said he was taking forty beaver skins back to England, which were worth five shillings each in London.

Said I, "A pox on money! Rigdale once said to me that the Lord lured us into this wilderness to speak to our hearts. Alas, mine hath gone deaf."

Later in the morning, Standish brought me my knapsack with Wittuwamat's head therein. It buzzed with fat, black flies and stank of rotting meat.

Standish said, "God give you a good morrow, Master Wentworth."

"And to you, sir," I replied.

"God make you happy."

"I wish the very same to you, sir."

Standish said, "I have chosen you to carry this traitor's head back to Plymouth and accompany me when I present it to Governor Bradford."

I said, "'Tis an honor, sir."

He unwrapped the head. It was covered by fat, white, wriggling maggots. They wriggled on the eyeballs, the lashes, and eyebrows, and in the long, thick strands of greasy hairs dangling from the scalp.

Standish said, "With God's help, we shall deliver Wittuwamat's head to the Governor tomorrow night.

"Is this your first glimpse of maggots eating putrid human flesh? Aye, I can see it is. Scripture tells us that flesh is as grass. What nonsense! 'Tis food for carrion beetles and maggots.

"We shall set sail for Plymouth in the shallop on the morrow at dawn. With God's help, we will arrive there before sunset."

For the remainder of the day, as I wandered about the stockade, I carried the knapsack dangling from the staff upon my shoulder. I was followed by a cloud of stinging black flies.

Standing over Rigdale's grave, I said, "Thou art well out of it, dear friend. All our days are sorrow, and our travail grief. Our hearts also taketh not rest in the night."

After sunset, I bid farewell to Captain Green and thanked him for all his kindness to me. We embraced.

He said, "I warrant that you and Abigail will soon be betrothed."

I said, "I am unworthy of her love."

He said, "Let her decide."

I said, "I will, and she will say, 'How miserably you have changed! You are not worthy of my love.'"

Then Butts came up to us and said, "Good sirs, we have been here eight months. I was to be paid three pounds a year in ready money. How much must Weston pay me?"

Captain Green said, "Two pounds. God only knows if ready money can be made in this wilderness. Weston believes that profit and religion will someday dance here together."

Butts said to me, "Your knapsack, sir, is much beset by flies. Therefore, that must be Wittuwamat's head therein, Master Wentworth. There's a good gentleman. Allow me to gaze upon it."

Said I, "Get you hence!"

Henry hung the knapsack from the rafter by the door. He said, "And how goes it with you, friend?"

Said I, "I am attended in the dark by terror and grief."

Said he, "I will stay by you all the night."

But he fell asleep by eleven of the clock and snored. The flies buzzed about the knapsack. I sat up in bed and said aloud, "I am mad, yea, Bedlam mad."

At first light, I shaved off my beard. Standish said, "You look much younger, Charles. You have shaved years from your face. Your ragged beard gave you the look of a minor prophet."

William White said, "I see that you had the smallpox. My youngest sister, Nell, was stricken with it at ten years of age. It blinded her. Her chief joy is hearing. She says, 'Song birds sound not so sweet to me as the children's laughter I sometimes hear beyond the fence whilst sitting in our little vegetable garden.'"

We set sail in the shallop at about six of the clock in the morning. The wind being fair from the northwest, we rowed out of the Bay and raised the mainsail. When the wind rose, we hoisted the staysail.

Of the eleven men aboard, I was the only one who knew nothing of sailing upon the sea in an open, six-and-twenty-foot boat. The sea was passably calm, but I was still queasy. I sat on the bench after the mast, with my knapsack between my legs, and my bundle of clothes, &c., upon my lap.

Everyone knew my knapsack contained Wittuwamat's head and that I had hacked it from his corpse with Henry's cutlass. He passed his sword from hand to hand. Its blood-stained blade was much admired. The men questioned me and George Soule about the killing of Wittuwamat.

Soule said, "I will tell my story in Plymouth to Governor Bradford, who shall surely reward me for shooting Wittuwamat in the bowels. Wentworth here beheaded the corpse."

I said, "I will not speak of it."

The flies had followed the knapsack out to sea. They buzzed between my legs. I waved some away and was stung twice more, on the back of each hand.

William White was at the tiller. He steered us south, following the shore. I caught a glimpse of the *Swan* under full sail. She was about two leagues away, beyond the bay, to the northeast. My little verse came back to me:

Charles and Abigail
Set sail.
And Charles loved Abigail.
One night,
By the bluish light
Of the full moon,
He said, "I love thee Abigail.
But what doth it avail me?"

We made land at Plymouth about four of the clock. I gazed with apathy at the broad sand bank, directly before the town, the small island on the north side of the Bay, the town itself upon the slope of the hill that stretched east toward the shore. Then I saw upon the hill a large square house with a flat roof, mounted with six pieces of artillery. It was the new blockhouse. Wittuwamat's putrefying head would doubtless be displayed atop its flagstaff. Before the governor's large, new clapboard house, on the cross street, was a square stockade in which four more artillery pieces were mounted, so as to command the surrounding country.

Governor Bradford, six musketeers, and many divers others greeted us before his house, which was just below the blockhouse. I spied Abigail amidst the crowd.

George Soule said to the Governor, "Sir, allow me to tell you how I shot Wittuwamat in the bowels."

The Governor said, "Perhaps later, sirrah, perhaps later."

With Bradford was an Indian youth named Mosq (which means a bear). Captain Standish told me that Mosq was ever of a courteous and loving disposition toward us. He was a Succonet; his *sachem* being Obtakiest, who planned to attack the Plymouth Plantation. Mosq had come to Plymouth two weeks before and had confessed to Captain Standish in broken English that the Massachusetts intended to kill all of us at Wessagusset. He said that he had come to the Captain without fear, saying that his good conscience and love towards Englishmen had emboldened him to do so.

Standish said, "I then resolved to massacre the Massachusetts."

He reached into my knapsack and held up Wittuwamat's head by its long, greasy hair. I saw Abigail cover her eyes.

The Governor cried out, "Well done, Captain Standish!"

Mosq looked mournfully upon the head.

Standish asked Mosq, "Did that not belong to Wittuwamat?"

Mosq answered, "Yea."

The crowd cheered. Governor Bradford then spake to one of the musketeers, who took the head from Standish and the bloodstained length of linen from me. Then he climbed the hill and entered the blockhouse by its biggest door. The blockhouse was built of thick-sawn planks, stayed with oaken beams. The crowd cheered again when the musketeer emerged from a trap door upon the flat roof. Standing upon a block of wood, he took down the standard of St. George and fixed the bloodstained length of linen in its place. It caught the wind. The crowd cheered once more. The musketeer stuck Wittuwamat's head atop the flagstaff. Then he descended through the open trap door. Abigail gazed at the putrid head and the bloody banner.

Five ravens dropped upon the roof and, with their thick, sharp beaks and claws, fought each other for possession of Wittuwamat's decaying flesh. Two of them pecked at the maggots therein. Another ripped a length of skin from Wittuwamat's forehead. The fading sunlight turned the ravens' plumage purple. Then the largest raven of the flock flapped his wings and cawed and chased the other birds away from the roof. He stood upon the crown of the head and preened his feathers with his black beak.

I made my way through the throng to Abigail.

When she saw me, she burst into tears. Then she said, "Charles! These are tears of joy. This is the first time in my life I have wept for joy. Now that I think on it, weeping for joy is very strange. What a pity that we cannot kiss in public. Wait! I have it!"

She kissed the tip of her forefinger and with it caressed my lips that were sorely sunburnt from sailing on the shallop.

I flinched at the pain, but then said, "Never mind. The pain from your caress gives me pleasure."

Abigail said, "Dearest Charles, forgive me. In your absence, I kept your face in my mind the whole time.

But I forgot that your left eye is slightly smaller than your right. Allow me to make amends for my forgetfulness."

She again kissed the tip of her forefinger but, this time, caressed my left eyelid with it.

I said, "I am unworthy of your love."

"Why?"

I said, "Because I am damned."

"How do you know?"

Said I, "I enjoyed killing an Indian in a battle and beheading the corpse of another. I was an accomplice to Rigdale's death. We all were. Wittuwamat gave us the choice: hang Rigdale or be slain."

"Who is Wittuwamat?"

"The *sachem* of the Massachusetts. He bit his fingernails."

"Was it he you killed?"

"No. I beheaded his corpse."

"Is that his rotting head on the flagstaff?"

"Yes."

"Horrible," she said. "'Tis horrible, but I cannot look away from it. Why is that? I did not think that you were capable of beheading a corpse. You have returned to me a different man. There is now a toughness within thee. But I love thee still. Nay, even more than before!"

"I am not mine own man anymore. I have been

entirely given over to melancholy. All my days are sorrow. I take not rest in the night."

Said she, "You must confide in Master Brewster. He helped regenerate me."

Said I, "How so?"

Said she, "Through prayer and suffering. He bade me immerse myself every night for two months in these words of the Fifth Commandment: 'Honor thy father.' Afterwards my guilt and remorse for wishing my beloved father dead kept me awake for hours. Sometimes, to relieve my anguish, I summoned up your comely, pitted face. Yes, your pitted face is comely to me. But it painfully reminded me of my beloved father's countenance. Thus, every night, my thoughts went round and round.

"Then about five of the clock on the cold afternoon of Friday, the twenty-fifth of November, whilst wiping my snotty nose upon the back of my hand, I was overcome with delight at the loveliness of God. My delight in it was entirely different from anything I had ever experienced. Even my love for you, Charles! I was immediately delivered from guilt and remorse. I became a new person. Do I look different than before?"

Said I, "Your curls are longer. You are altogether more beautiful in my eyes."

She said, "You cannot see the changes wrought in my

soul by the Spirit of God. With God's grace I hope in time to show them to you."

Then Standish sought me out and brought me and Abigail back with him to his house, wherein we supped upon a roasted goose.

He said to Abigail, "Master Wentworth here proved himself a brave soldier. You should be proud of him."

I said, "I reveled in each blow that I gave Wittuwamat's neck with the cutlass. I rejoiced in shooting off the arm of another savage, who bled to death. God forgive me, I have never enjoyed myself more. My satanical pleasure in such things hath blotted out any hope for me of everlasting joy in heaven. I know now that my inborn cruelty destines me to burn in hell."

Standish said, "Your delusion that you are damned because you rejoiced in your first battle is common to many godly soldiers. We veterans call such bloodlust 'wearing the red veil.' It will pass."

Said I, "I think not."

Abigail said, "I agree. You must most painfully be reborn in Christ and become an entirely new man. Master Brewster can help thee."

I said, "I think not."

Abigail said to me, "Do you still have my white kerchief?"

"'Tis tattered from all my sweaty kisses."

She said, "Then take my blue one and wear it about your neck."

As I tied its ends together under my chin, I thought of the hangman's noose that had strangled Rigdale. I remembered that it is called a "collar" in England.

Master Brewster lived in a new, large house on the corner of the Street and the Highway, across from Governor Bradford. I resumed lodging with the Brewster family. Every morning, I went to work for Master Brewster, pulling weeds in his six acres of corn, which lay on the south side of the brook to the baywards. The adjacent single acre to the west had been recently granted to Stephen Deane, one of the lusty young men who had arrived at Plymouth on the *Fortune.*

Deane said, "I come from Southwark, where I was a gunsmith and a worker in metals."

Said I, "Southwark, you say? My best friend's wife and daughter are buried in St. Olave's churchyard."

Said he, "'Tis where my parents lie! St. Olave was where I was baptized and took communion. Well, well. I must talk with your friend. Pray tell me his name."

Said I, "Zachariah Rigdale. But alas, he hath been dead these last ten days."

Said he, "Is he not the man who was hanged by his fellow Englishmen at Wessagusset?"

"The same," said I.

"How could his fellow Englishmen do such a thing?"

"Cowardice." said I. "The *sachem* of the savages named Wittuwamat gave us a choice. Either hang Rigdale or be slain. We hanged him."

"Never mind! Remember what Scripture says, ''Tis every man for himself.'"

Said I, "Where is that writ in Scripture?"

Said he, "If it is not, it should be!"

Said I, "Wittuwamat was truly diabolical. Only a devilish mind would have thought to make us all accomplices to his crime. Just think what a subtle, evil idea that was!"

Said he, "All them savages are evil. They worship the devil."

Governor Bradford told me that Stephen Deane was one of the leaders of the men who, four months before, had implored him to allow them to work for themselves, rather than the company of Merchant Adventurers. They would continue to divide all the assets equally, and each man would pay to the Plantation a yearly tax of Indian corn. The Governor consulted with his assistant, Isaac Allerton, and Master Brewster. They agreed to allow each man to work for himself and pay a tax to the Plantation's common store of two bushels of corn a year. Taxes could not be paid in ready money. Every man was assigned a plot of land, the extent depending upon the size of the man's family. The land could not be inherited.

The Governor said to me, "The young men that were most able and fit for labor and service did complain that they should spend their time and strength to work for other men's wives and children without any recompense. Permitting each man to work for himself makes all hands very industrious. Much more corn was planted this spring than ever."

Brewster said, "Alas, my dream of creating an apostolic community of equals in New England was not to be. I should have known. We are all fallen. Even the Elect amongst us are fallen. We look only to enrich ourselves. You have seen my big house. My fellow Saints built it for me and my family. I accepted it without demur. I who once dreamed of rebuilding an antique Christian commonwealth in New Plymouth."

Said I, "Abigail tells me that she hath been regenerated."

"Praise God, so she has," Brewster said. "She tells me that you want to be saved, as well."

I said, "I have no hope of it, for I am damned. God

will not forgive my sins. I sinned against my father and my best friend."

"Do you pray for forgiveness?"

"My best friend once said that his soul was a dry land. So it is with me. My soul is a dry land, wherein no prayer can take root."

Said he, "That, sir, is a mediocre metaphor. Now get you hence, and return to me only when you want to learn to pray for forgiveness from the God of Israel in plain English."

Henry Sampson, the musketeer who stuck Wittuwamat's head atop the flagstaff, returned my knapsack. He had washed the canvas clean of maggots and carrion beetles in the bay. I turned the knapsack inside out and hung it in the sunshine on the gate of Master Brewster's vegetable garden.

Sampson said, "Tell me about cutting off Wittuwamat's head. Was there much blood?"

Said I, "I will save my breath for my broth."

Within the last three or four days, Wittuwamat's head had become a fleshless skull. The ravens had eaten almost all the skin upon it. There was a patch beneath the jawbone, and three or more round its crown, from which his long strands of hair dangled. The biggest raven often perched atop the crown, preening his lustrous feathers. I saw him pluck a thick strand of hair from the crown and fly off with it streaming from his black beak. Our bloodstained banner hung limply from the flagstaff.

That afternoon, Phineas Pratt and Mosq visited Brewster's house, wherein we supped on fat, sweet, smoked eels.

I said to Pratt, "I never expected to see thee alive again."

Bradford said, "Master Pratt hath found himself a new occupation. He hath become a scout. He bravely made his way here all alone through the woods from Wessagusset without a compass, armed only with a dagger. May he borrow your compass? He and Mosq are going scouting for me on Cape Cod, among the people of Nauset, Paomet, the Succonet, and the Manomet to discover if they still plan to attack us, despite our massacre of the Massachusetts."

Said I, "I will gladly lend my compass to Pratt. But let him relate to me the circumstances of his escape from Wessagusset."

Pratt said, "I fled Wessagusset out of cowardice. I deserted the stockade, fearing that I would be killed there by the savages. I said in my thoughts, 'I made a grave mistake.' My design was lacking. I should have built a blockhouse, in addition to my impaled fortification. The blockhouse should have stood in place of the hut. It would have provided us with additional protection, a fort in which to retreat in case the savages broke into the stockade. I said in my thoughts, 'I overreached myself.' Truth is, I am only a simple carpenter.

"As soon as I reached the woods at the edge of the glade, I spied three savages, armed with bows and arrows, following me at a distance of about two hundred yards. One of them was also carrying a dagger on a leathern thong about his neck. I ran southward, till about three of the clock. I heard a great howling of wolves and ran on. My mouth was dry from fear. I came to a river. The water was deep and cold, with many rocks. I passed through the icy water with much ado.

"My thirst was quenched. I was still faint for want of food, weary from running, and afraid to make a fire because the savages were doubtless still pursuing me. Then I came to a deep dell, with much wood fallen into it. I said in my thoughts, 'This is God's Providence that I may here make a fire.' I did so, and its heat began drying my clothes. The stars began to appear. I saw Ursa Major and the polestar. The following day, at about three of the clock, the sun broke through the clouds, and I resumed running south.

"At length, I lay face down to rest behind a big granite stone. Of a sudden, I was no longer afraid of savages, wolves, or getting lost in the woods. Nor was I frightened of being frightened. For a moment or two, I calmly gazed down at my body from a great height. I saw my steel dagger grasped in my right hand. I said in my thoughts, 'If I live, what a story I will have to tell.'

"I rose to my feet. Running down a hill, I saw a group of Englishmen. I sat down on a fallen tree, then rose to salute them.

"One of them said, 'I am glad and full of wonder to see you alive, Mister Pratt.'

"I said, 'Let me eat some parched corn.'

"The long and the short of it was that Governor Bradford called me to him, bade me welcome, and after I related what had happened to me, asked me to become a scout with Mosq. I agreed without hesitation. My little amble through the woods made a new man of me."

Said I, "Here. Take my compass as a gift."

Said he, "Thank you. I have a favor to ask of thee."

"Speak!"

"If I do not come back alive, tell my story."

"I promise," said I.

He and Mosq left the next morning at dawn for Cape Cod, the habitation of the Nauset, the Paomet, the Succonet, and the Manomet. Pratt was armed with a musket and a dagger. Mosq also carried a steel dagger, and a bow and a quiver filled with arrows. His face was painted black, with a wide red streak on each cheek.

———•◦•———

I supped that evening with Abigail in the Winslow house. Afterwards, she and I walked east on the Street, between the new thatched huts. I said, "The letter you sent me from my aunt Eliza informed me that my dear uncle Roger is dead and hath, when my aunt dies, bequeathed to me his farm near Winterbourne. It is worth two hundred pounds. Ay, you heard me! Two hundred pounds! Why, I shall be one of the richest land owners in the parish of Harrow Hill!

"Aunt Eliza is three-and-seventy years of age and blind in one eye. God preserve her, but she will not live many more years. Now harken to me! According to the conditions of the will, I must return to England and oversee my farm.

"Marry me and you shall be the mistress of one hundred and twenty acres of rich pasture land, a broad stream, two ponds, an apple orchard, and divers and sundry sheep, cattle, and swine tended by a shepherd and a cowman. You shall have a serving maid, whose name is Grace Foot. Her husband, Tom, is our bailiff of husbandry. You and I shall abide together in a seven-room farmhouse, impaneled with red clay. The walls within are hanged with painted cloths. The house hath two storeys. On the first floor, there are three living rooms at one end, and a kitchen, buttery, and dairy at the other.

"Did I mention the rose garden near our bedroom window? The blooming roses seem to be afire, even in the rain.

"Dearest Abigail, I have been thinking about all this for some time. I know we had plans to marry and live in Plymouth. But I have come to a different decision. I cannot remain in Plymouth because of my damnable pride. I am not one of the Elect. Abigail, as I love thee, let me tell you true. God forgive me, I am envious of thy regeneration. I cannot help it. I envy your delight in the loveliness of God."

Then I said, "Pride and envy. There's a devil loose in me."

Abigail said, "I love roses. We shall one day grow them in Plymouth and warm our souls over their fires. Dear Charles, I will never return to England. I love living like a godly Christian woman in Plymouth. I cannot again submit my soul to the papist Church of England. I will not live amongst people who play at cards and bowl on the holy Sabbath. I beg you: remain here with me. Let us marry and raise our children in what is surely the only godly commonwealth on earth, wherein we live to do the most good to others. For, as one saith, 'He whose living is but for himself, it is time he were dead.'

"What say you? O, Charles! Do not envy my delight in the loveliness of God. Consult with Master Brewster. He will tell you how you too can be regenerated. That is, if you are predestined to be saved. Be brave and discover your soul's final destiny, be it heaven or hell."

Said I, "O, Abigail, till this very moment I had not thought how brave you were to discover thy soul's eternal destiny! I have never loved thee more! I shall consult anon with Master Brewster and prove myself worthy of your love for me."

I spake with Brewster the next morning whilst we were weeding his cornfield.

He always worked side by side with his four laborers in the hot sun.

He said, "God hath been good to me. I reckon my six acres will, for the first time, bear at least two hundred bushels of corn."

I said, "Tell me, sir. What should I do? I caused my beloved father's death and did nothing to protest the hanging of my best friend. My heart is well nigh consumed with guilt."

Said he, "Scripture says, 'For if you do not forgive, your Father which is in heaven will not pardon your trespasses.'"

Said I, "Whom shall I forgive?"

Said he, "I cannot say. You must search your soul. Trust in God. He may lead thee into a new place wherein you have never been. God is great and we know not His ways. He takes from us all that we have, but if we possess our souls in patience, we may pass through the valley of the shadow and come out in sunlight again."

Late that afternoon, I said to Abigail, "Wittuwamat and myself! My soul tells me that to find peace, I must forgive Wittuwamat and myself. Myself! Who ever heard of such a thing? How can I forgive myself?"

In the evening, Governor Bradford called me to him. Said he, "I should like you to give me your opinion of my Hebrew grammar, which I have but recently completed. What a singular language! As you know, parts of the body that come in pairs—like eyes and hands—are masculine. Whereas a single feature, like the nose, hath a feminine ending."

Said I, "I am a great sinner, sir, and am no longer worthy of studying the holy tongue in which God spake unto the prophets and Jesus prayed in the temple."

Said he, "Tush! You are too hard on yourself."

"Not hard enough," said I. "Not hard enough."

Pratt and Mosq returned on Friday, the twenty-ninth of August. The meeting house was crowded for the next day's Sabbath services. Everyone in the Plantation, save the very sick and those who kept watch, stayed to listen to Pratt's address after the morning service.

He said, "Mosq and I learned that Captain Standish's sudden and unexpected execution of the Massachusetts hath so terrified and amazed the other Indians all throughout Cape Cod that they forsook their houses and ran to and fro like men distracted, living in swamps and other desert places, wherein in the last month, they brought manifold diseases upon themselves. I said in my thoughts, 'God forgive us.' Many innocent women and children—babes in arms—are amongst the dead. Many more, hiding in swamps and remote islands, shall starve to death as they are unable to plant their crops."

I said, "Tell me more of their children."

"They are already starving. I saw eight or ten of them with swelled bellies and arms and legs as thin as twigs. They had not the strength to weep or cry aloud. Mosq and I gave the mother of twins half of the parched corn we carried with us."

Said I, "Did you perchance see a crippled little Indian maiden, about seven years of age?"

Pratt said, "Nay."

Mosq said, "Nay."

Then Pratt said, "The Indians call us '*wotawquenange*.' Cutthroats."

———

Now behold an act of Providence! The next afternoon, the jawbone fell off Wittuwamat's skull.

Master Brewster said, "Let us bury the loathsome things and have done with them."

I said, "I will do it."

Brewster said, "Then do so! But leave our bloody banner where it is. Let it remind us of our sins."

Governor Bradford said, "Let it be a warning to our enemies and a reminder to us of our victory in Wessagusset." Then he said, "The word in Hebrew for 'skull' is '*gulgolet*.' Hence, Golgotha, which means 'the place of the skull' in Aramaic. I learned a little Aramaic from the old rabbi in Leyden who taught me Hebrew. He studied the Talmud in Aramaic. The Talmud is a holy book to the Jews. As I recall, it teaches that Jesus was a magician who brought a dead sparrow back to life when he was a child."

Then he said to me, "Do not bury the accursed skull and its jawbone. Cast them away in the woods like the bones of an animal. Leave our bloody banner where it is as a warning to the savages that may visit us to trade."

I climbed to the roof of the blockhouse with my knapsack and placed the jawbone and the rest of the skull within it. The bloodstained banner reminded me of the Indian whom I had slain, and I vomited. I carried my knapsack half a mile south on the Highway. There I vomited again.

I digged a deep hole beneath an oak tree with my dagger and buried my knapsack therein.

I said, "Wittuwamat, I will give your skull the burial worthy of a *sachem*."

Next, I placed my dagger, in its green leathern scabbard, atop the knapsack and said, "Wittuwamat, this is the dagger you coveted. I give it to you now as the treasure due to a *sachem's* buried bones."

I covered up the knapsack and the dagger in its green leathern scabbard with handfuls of earth and three flat stones. Then I said, "Now, as you did for your wife, I shall sing thee a death song."

I sang the old song that Mary Puckering sang to me in my childhood:

O death, rock me asleep,

Bring me to quiet rest.

Toll on thou passing bell,

Let thy sound

My death tell,

For I must die,

There is no remedy,

For now I die.

Then I said, "Wittuwamat, I forgive you."

I vomited bitter choler. My whole body was in a tremor. Then I said, "Hear me, O my God! Is it permissible to forgive myself in Thy name?"

Of a sudden, my heart beat very quick. There arose in me such a sense of God taking care of those who put their trust in Him that I wept for joy. I felt no guilt for what I had done to my father and Rigdale. My heart beat faster. I wept again and laughed.

I cried out, "What rapture! My rapture will kill me."

I was not afraid. My rapture increased. I was utterly full of the love and grace of God. My heart seemed about to burst. Then I heard the Holy Spirit speak within me in a still, small voice, saying, "Forgive thyself in My name."

I groaned like a man in pain, though I was in no pain at all. I said, "Lord, I forgive myself in Thy name."

For a few moments, I felt the greatest joy that was ever my lot to know. I shouted and praised Him who loved me and had washed away my sins.

Then I walked quickly back to Plymouth. I could not stop praising the Lord. I raised one foot, and it seemed to say, "Glory!" Then I lifted the other, and it seemed to say "Amen!" They kept up like that all the time I hurried along.

I found Abigail washing dishes in her house. I sang,

Hey down-a down, down-derry,
Among the leaves so green, o!
In love we are, in love we'll stay,
Among the leaves so green, o!

Said she, "Sweetheart! Why so merry? Where hath your melancholy gone?"

I spake a little verse to her extempore:

Joy hath revived
In the tomb of my soul,
Which, like a womb,
Was quickened by
A word from God:
"Forgive!"

So I forgave my enemy

And myself,

And was reborn.

I then said to Abigail, "Praise God, who predestined the rebirth of my soul."

Thus God preserved and kept me all the days of my youth. At times I lost His special presence, yet He returned to me in mercy again.

On the twentieth day of January, in the year of Christ 1625, the godly Saints of the Plymouth Colony elected me to their Fellowship of the Gospel after I made to them the entire aforesaid public confession of my sins and declared my public regeneration. Thereafter, on the following Monday, being the twenty-seventh day of the month, Abigail Winslow and I were wed.

Don't miss Hugh Nissenson's *The Days of Awe*,
also available from Sourcebooks Landmark.

Artie Rubin couldn't keep his mind on Odin. His thoughts buzzed around the corpses of the two Arab kids in Nablus. At eleven, he called Johanna at her office. He read her the headline on the front page of the *Times* that was eating at him: "Israeli Raid Kills 8 at Hamas Office; 2 Are Young Boys; Palestinians Call for Revenge; Violence on Both Sides Shows No Sign of Letup."

Artie said, "The boys were brothers, five and six. One was found on top of the other."

"I saw the article. Their poor parents. Leslie and Chris are having dinner with us tonight. I made a reservation at Shun Lee for 8:30."

"Any bleeding this morning?"

"Yes. I spoke to Dr. Gunning. He's convinced it's just hemorrhoids. I hope he's right. But we'll soon know for sure. I've never had a colonoscopy, so he insisted I schedule one for next Monday at ten. "

"Finally! You'll be woozy from the anesthetic. I'll pick you up."

Leslie said to Johanna, "Send Daddy my love."

Johanna said good-bye to Artie. Leslie clicked on their five bellwether stocks: Citigroup 50.34, Intel 30.30, Cisco 65.79, Microsoft 66.71, Johnson & Johnson 54.25. No significant change this week; no significant change since late spring.

Leslie said, "Chris and I are going shopping after lunch. He needs a summer jacket. I'm thinking dark brown. To go with his tan pants."

Artie drank a Bass ale. It went right to his head. He squeezed out five sentences: "The god Odin appears among us as a warrior in his mid-fifties with one blue eye; his reddish-brown beard is turning gray. Instead of a helmet, he wears a blue broad-brimmed hat and carries a magic spear called Gungnir. Men hanged from trees are sacrificed to him."

Don't start with Odin. Begin at the beginning.

Artie wrote, "In the beginning was fire and ice."

He sketched Odin in pencil. The bearded, one-eyed god stood in the open doorway of a broken-down log hut with a spear in his right hand. He wore a Yankees cap. The cap and the beard made Odin look like a one-eyed Jew.

Artie tore up the sketch.

Aug. 1, 2001. Wed. Noon. *This morning began* Norse Myths Retold & Illustrated—*my 20th book on mythology in 41 yrs. My main source is 13th century* Prose Edda of Snorri Sturluson, *trans. by Jean Young, Univ. of Cal. Press 1996. Will illustrate in style of Viking carvings; source,* Viking Art *by Charles Sullivan, Harry Abrams, 1995.*

I often wondered why I put off tackling the Norse gods. Now, at 67, I know. The Norse gods die. Much thoughts of death these days.

Though we don't mention it, the blood in Johanna's stool over the last three weeks reminds us of Johnny Havistraw, my former editor at Harper's, *who died of colon cancer in July.*

At a quarter to three, Artie walked Muggs, the Rubins' four-year-old English sheepdog, up West End. He kept on the shady west side of the street. A sparrow chirped among the leaves of the big plane tree planted near the curb at the far corner of 80th Street; it chirped louder than the traffic. Artie couldn't spot it among the leaves.

Muggs, who had never learned to heel, tried crossing 81st Street against the light. Artie yanked him to a halt.

Artie and Johanna were crazy about sheepdogs. Muggs was their fourth in thirty-one years. Johanna gave him to Artie for his sixty-third birthday. He said to the four-month-old pup, "We'll grow old together."

Over spare ribs at Shun Lee, Leslie said, "I'm three months pregnant."

Artie would cherish the moment made of his daughter's words, the big dish of ribs, and a Chinese waiter serving a crispy Peking duck to the couple at the table to his left.

He and Johanna said, "Congratulations!" and Leslie and Chris each answered, "Thank you."

Artie said, "This calls for another drink. Waiter!" Johanna gave him a look. "Never mind, waiter."

Johanna said, "Oh, darling, we're so happy. Your guest room is perfect for a nursery. Take a long maternity leave. Not to worry about the office. I'll manage things."

My God, I'm going to be a grandfather. I want a grandson. Wait a sec! What's all the excitement? I'll be almost eighty when he's ten.

Leslie: "Chris and I went for an ultrasound this

afternoon. Look at these pictures. The baby's about four inches long. Its heart is beating. This graph shows the movement. The baby's face is developing. Here it is in profile. See the nose? The smudge near the mouth is a hand. The mouth's open."

Artie reached for more sweet sauce. "When will we know the sex?"

"I have an appointment for another ultrasound the second week in September. We might know then. It depends on what position the baby's in—whether we can see between the legs."

"It's a girl," said Johanna. "Mark my words."

The waiter served steaming cloths on a plate. Artie wiped his greasy hands, lost in the loud conversation at the table on his left between a guy about thirty and a pretty redhead: "Don't you dare call me cheap."

"I take it back."

"You're sore we have to split the check."

"Forget it. Let's eat."

"I won't forget it."

"You're upset about the market."

Tonight was Johanna's turn to walk Muggs. Not a breath of air. Muggs panted. Johanna walked him around the block under the yellow street lamps. He crapped on the corner of Riverside and 81st Street. Johanna thought, I've got blood in my stool like Johnny Havistraw. She picked up Muggs's shit with a plastic bag from Zabar's and dumped the load in the steel mesh garbage can on the corner. She was reminded of tossing Leslie's smelly Pampers down the incinerator. My baby's carrying a baby. Let them live and be well. She said aloud, "That's a wish, not a prayer."

She'd quit Hebrew school in New Rochelle when she was going on thirteen. All of a sudden, it hit her then that nobody was listening to her prayers and thoughts. There's no God. What a relief. He couldn't read her mind about blond Tommy Rand who sat next to her in math.

A motorcycle backfire spooked Muggs on West End; Johanna held him short. I haven't thought about Tommy Rand in fifty years. There's no God. Artie feels the same. He goes to shul only because it connects him to his dad. Dead and gone twenty-three years. That pious old Jew still has his hooks in Artie. More than ever since he turned sixty-five. He's feeling his age.

Artie had high blood pressure. Before going to bed, he took his daily dose of 5 mg. Norvasc, 4 mg. Cardura, and 10 mg. Altace that kept his pressure normal: 120/80. The drugs made him impotent.

Artie and Johanna lay under a sheet and a light cotton blanket in the chilled air.

Johanna said, "A grandchild! I'm so happy."

"Me too. I hope it's a boy."

"I couldn't care less—so long as it's healthy."

The air conditioner whirred behind her voice.

Artie said, "If it is a boy, I'm gonna ask Leslie and Chris to have a bris."

"I wonder if Chris is circumcised."

Artie would have been happier if Leslie had married a Jew. At least Chris had money. He worked for his father, who owned and managed fifteen garden apartment complexes in southern Westchester.

Muggs sighed; he was asleep on the faded blue carpet at the foot of the bed.

Artie said, "Sweetheart, let's celebrate."

"Let's."

Artie went into the bathroom and popped 50 mg. of Viagra. It would take twenty minutes or so to work. He unbuttoned his pajama top and looked down at his big pot belly covered with grey hair and mottled by three big brown moles. He looked in the mirror at his sagging hairy tits. I'm part woman. He examined the reflection of his high, bald forehead, bulbous nose, and wrinkled, wattled neck. Two parallel wattles hid his Adam's apple.

Long hairs grew out of his ears. I look more and more like Dad.

Artie slipped back into bed in his pajama tops. Johanna was wearing one of his T-shirts; it reached her thighs. She dozed off. Artie shut his eyes. Think sexy thoughts! He played with his limp cock while searching his memory for images of Johanna when she was young. He came up with her naked at twenty-two sitting on a camp bed in a sublet on East 92nd Street. She was putting up her long auburn hair. She spread open a hairpin with her top front teeth.

ACKNOWLEDGMENTS

I could not have written *The Pilgrim* without the extraordinary assistance of Terry Hearing, Donald Hutslar, and John Kemp, who are both friends and scholars. I am deeply grateful for their expertise and their encouragement.

I am also indebted to the following for their help: Diana Beste, Jill Claster, Frank Peters, Rabbi Jules Harlow, Nava Harlow, Dr. Jeffrey Fisher, Richard Pendleton, Peter East, David and Clarissa Pryce-Jones, Jill Minchin, Sir Wilson of Dinton, Sarah Bendall, the late John Mosedale, Richard Marek, Mario Materassi, Alan Berger, Christopher Lehmann-Haupt, and Natalie Robins.

Thanks also to my agents, Richard Morris and Lynn Nesbit, my editor, Peter Lynch, and his colleagues at Sourcebooks: Anne Hartman, Heather Moore, Diane Dannenfeldt, and Pat Esposito.

ABOUT THE AUTHOR

Hugh Nissenson is the author of nine books. His previous novel, *The Tree of Life*, was a finalist for the National Book Award and the Pen/Faulkner Award in 1985. He lives in New York City.